Geoffrey Chaucer

Poetical Works of Geoffrey Chaucer

Vol. VI

Geoffrey Chaucer

Poetical Works of Geoffrey Chaucer
Vol. VI

ISBN/EAN: 9783337124366

Printed in Europe, USA, Canada, Australia, Japan

Cover: Foto ©Andreas Hilbeck / pixelio.de

More available books at **www.hansebooks.com**

THE POETICAL WORKS OF GEOFFREY CHAUCER

WITH MEMOIR BY SIR HARRIS NICOLAS

VOL VI

LONDON

BELL AND DALDY FLEET STREET

1866

CONTENTS.

VOL. VI.

THE ROMAUNT OF THE ROSE.

ANY men sayen that in swevenynges,
Ther nys but fables and lesynges ;
But men may some swevene sene,
Whiche hardely that false ne bene,
But afterwarde ben apparaunt.
This maye I drawe to warraunt,
An authour that highte Macrobes,
That halte nat dremes false ne lees,
But undoth us the avysyoun,
That whylom mette kyng Cipioun.   10
    And who-so sayth, or weneth it be
A jape, or elles nycetie
To wene that dremes after falle,
Lette who-so lyst a foole me calle.
For this trowe I, and saye for me,
That dremes signifiaunce be
Of good and harme to many wightes,
That dremen in her sleep a-nyghtes
Ful many thynges covertly,
That failen after al openly.   20
    Within my twenty yere of age,
Whan that love taketh his corage
Of yonge folk, I wente soon
To bed, as I was wont to doon,

And fast I slept; and in slepyng,
Me mette suche a swevenyng,
That lykede me wonderous wele ;
But in that sweven is never a dele
That it nys afterwarde befalle,
Ryght as this dreme wol tel us alle.   30
   Now this dreme wol I ryme aryghte,
To make your hertes gaye and lyghte ;
For Love it prayeth, and also
Commaundeth me that it be so.
   And yf there any aske me,
Whether that it be he or she,
How this boke which is here
Shal hatte, that I rede you here ;
It is the Romaunce of the Rose,
In which alle the art of love I close.   40
   The mater fayre is of to make ;
God graunt me in gre that she it take
For whom that it begonnen is !
And that is she that hath, ywys,
So mochel pris ; and therto she
So worthy is biloved to be,
That she wel ought of pris and ryght
Be cleped Rose of every wight.
   That it was May me thoughte tho,
It is .v. yere or more ago ;   50
That it was May, thus dremede me,
In tyme of love and jolité,
That al thing gynneth waxen gay,
For ther is neither busk nor hay
In May, that it nyl shrouded bene,
And it with newe leves wrene.
These wodes eek recoveren grene,

That drie in wynter ben to sene;
And the erth wexith proude withalle,
For swote dewes that on it falle; 60
And the pore estat forgette,
In which that wynter had it sette.
And than bycometh the ground so proude,
That it wole have a newe shroude,
And makith so queynt his robe and faire,
That it had hewes an hundred payre,
Of gras and flouris, ynde and pers,
And many hewes ful dyvers:
That is the robe I mene, iwis,
Through which the ground to preisen is. 70
 *The briddes, that hav*en lefte her song,
While thei *han suffr*ide cold so stroug
In wedres gryl and derk to sigh*te*,
Ben in May for the sonne brigh*te*,
So glade, that they shewe in syngyng,
That in her hertis is sich lykyng,
That they mote syngen and be light.
Than doth the nyghtyngale hir myght,
To make noyse, and syngen blythe.
Than is blisful many sithe, 80
The chelaundre, and the papyngay.
Than younge folk entenden ay,
For to ben gay and amorous,
The tyme is than so faverous.
 Hard is the hert that loveth nought
In May, whan al this mirth is wrought;
Whan he may on these braunches here
The smale briddes syngen clere
Her blesful swete song pitous,
And in this sesoun delytous: 90

Whan love affraieth all*e* thing.
  Me thought a nyght, in my sleping,
Right in my bed ful redily,
That it was by the morowe *erly*,
And up I roos, and gan me cloth*e*;
Anoon I wisshe myn hondis both*e*;
A sylvre nedle forth Y droughe,
Out of an aguler queynt ynoughe,
And gan this nedle threde anon,
For out of toun me list to gon,   100
The song of briddes for to here
That in thise buskes syngen clere,
And in *the* swete seson that *leve* is;
With a threde bastyng my slevis,
Alone I wente in my plaiyng,
The smale foules song harknyng,
They peyned hem ful many peyre,
To synge on bowes blosmed feyre,
Joly and gay, ful of gladnesse,
Toward a ryver gan I me dresse,   110
That I herd renne fast*e* by;
For fairer plaiyng non saugh I
Than playen me by that ryvere,
For from an hille that stood ther nere,
Cam doun the streme ful stif and bold,
Cleer was the water, and as cold
As any welle is, sooth to seyn,
And somdele lasse it was than Seyn,
But it was strayghter, wel-away!
And never saugh I er that day,   120
The watir that so wel lyked*e* me;
And wondir glad was I to se
That lusty place, and that ryvere;

And with that watir that ran so clere
My face I wysshe.   Tho saugh I welle,
The botme paved everydelle
With gravel, ful of stones shene.
The medewe softe, swote, and grene,
Beet right *up* on the watir syde.
Ful clere was than the morow tyde, 130
And ful attempre, out of drede.
Tho gan I walke thorough the mede,
 Dounward ay in my pleiyng,
The ryver syde costeiyng.
 And whan I had a while goon,
I saugh a gardyn right anoon,
Ful long and brood, and everydelle
Enclosed was, and walled welle,
With high*e* walles enbatailled,
Portraied without, and wel entailled 140
With many riche portraitures;
And bothe the ymages and the peyntures
Gan I biholde bysyly.
And I wole telle you redyly,
Of thilk ymages the semblaunce,
As fer as I have in remembraunce.
 Amyd saugh I a Hate stonde,
That for hir wrathe, yre, and onde,
Semede to ben an *mov*eresse,
An angry wight, a chideresse. 150
And ful of gyle, and felle corage,
By semblaunt was that ilke ymage.
And she was no thyng wel arraied,
But lyk a wode womman afraied,
Frounced foule was hir visage,
And grennyng for dispitous rage,

Hir nose snorted up for tene.
Ful hidous was she for to sene,
Ful foule and rusty was she this.
Hir heed *y*writhen was, y-wis, 160
Ful grymly with a greet towayle.
 An ymage of another entayle,
A lyft half, was hir by;
Hir name above hir heed saugh I,
And she was called Felony.
 Another ymage, that Vilany
Clepid was, saugh I and fonde
Upon the wal on hir right honde.
Vilany was lyk somdelle
That other ymage; and, trustith wel, 170
She semede a wikked creature.
By countenaunce in portrayture,
 She semede be ful dispitous,
And eek ful proude and outragious.
Wel coude he peynte I undirtake,
That sich ymage coude make.
Ful foule and cherlysshe semede she,
And eek vylayneus for to be,
And litel coude of norture,
To worshipe any creature. 180
 And next was peynted Coveitise,
That eggith folk in many gise,
To take and yeve right nought ageyne,
And gret tresouris up to leyne.
And that is that for usure
Leneth to many a creature,
The lasse for the more wynnyng,
So coveitise is her brennyng.
And that is that penyes fele,

That techith for to robbe and stele 190
These theves, and these smale harlotes;
And that is routh, for by her throtes,
Ful many oon hangith at the laste.
She makith folk compasse and caste
To taken other folkis thyng,
Thorough robberie, or myscoveiting.
And that is she that makith trechoures.
And she makith false pleadoures,
That with hir termes and hir domes,
Doon maydens, children, and eek gromes, 200
Her heritage to forgo.
Ful croked were hir hondis two,
For coveitise is evere wode,
To gripen other folkis gode.
Coveityse for hir wynnyng,
Ful leef hath other mennes thing.
   Another ymage set saugh I
Next coveitise faste by,
And she was clepid Avarice.
Ful foule in peyntyng was that vice; 210
Ful sade and caytif was she eek,
And also grene as ony leek.
So yvel hewed was hir colour,
Hir semede to have lyved in langour.
She was lyk thyng for hungre deed,
That ladde hir lyf oonly by breed
Kneden with eisel strong and egre.
And therto she was lene and megre,
And she was clad ful porely,
Al in an old torn courtepy, 220
As she were al with doggis torne;
And bothe bihynde and eke biforne

Clouted was she beggarly.
A mantyl henge hir faste by,
Upon a perche, weike and smalle,
A burnet cote henge therwith alle,
Furred with no menyvere,
But with a furre rough of here,
Of lambe skynnes hevy and blake ;
It was ful old I undirtake,   230
For Avarice to clothe hir welle,
Ne hastith hir never a delle ;
For certeynly it were hir loth
To weren ofte that ilk cloth ;
And if it were forwered, she
Wolde have ful gret necessité
Of clothyng, er she bought hir newe,
Al were it bad of wolle and hewe.
This Avarice hilde in hir hande
A purs, that henge by a bande ;   240
And that she hidde and bonde so strong,
Men must abyde wondir long.
Out of that purs er ther come ought,
For that ne cometh not in hir thought ;
It was not certein hir entente,
That fro that purs a peny wente.

    And by that ymage nygh ynougn,
Was peynted Envye, that never lough,
Nor never wel in hir herte farede
But if she outher saugh or herede   250
Som gret myschaunce, or gret disese.
No thyng may so moch hir plese
As myschef and mysaventure ;
Or whan she seeth discomfiture
Upon ony worthy man falle,

Than likith hir wel with-alle.
She is ful glade in hir corage,
If she se any grete lynage
Be brought to nought in shynful wise.
And if a man in honour rise   260
Or by his witte, or by his prowesse,
Of that hath she gret hevynesse,
For, trustith wel, she goth nygh wode,
Whan any chaunge happith gode.
Envie is of such crueltee,
That feith ne trouthe holdith she
To freend ne felawe, bad or good.
Ne she hath kynne noon of hir blood,
That she nys ful her onemye.
She nolde, I dar seyn hardelye,   270
Hir owne fadir farede welle.
And sore abieth she everydelle
Hir malice, and hir male-talent:
For she is in so gret turment
And hath such, whan folk doth good,
That nygh she meltith for pure wood.
Hir herte kervyth and so brekith
That God tho puple wel a-wrekith.
Envie, i-wis, shal nevere lette
Som blame upon the folk to sette.   280
I trowe that if Envie, i-wis,
Knewe the beste man that is,
On this side or biyonde the see,
Yit somwhat lakken hym wolde she.
And if he were so hende and wis,
That she ne myght al abate his pris,
Yit wolde she blame his worthynesse,
Or by hir wordis make it lesse.

I saugh Envie in that peyntyng,
Hadde a wondirful lokyng ; 290
For she ne lokide but a-wrie,
Or overthart, alle baggyngly.
And she hadde *a foul* usage ;
She myghte loke in no visage
Of man or womman forth right pleyn,
But shette hir eien for disdeyn ;
So for envie brennede she
Whan she myght any man *yse*
That fairer, or worthier were, or wise,
Or elles stode in folkis pryse. 300
    Sorowe was peynted next Envie
Upon that walle of masonrye.
But wel was seyn in hir colour
That she hadde lyved in langour ;
Hir semede to have the jaunyce.
Nought half so pale was Avarice.
Nor no thyng lyk of lenesse ;
For sorowe, thought, and gret distresse,
That she hadde suffred day and nyght,
Made hir ful yolare, and no thyng bright, 310
Ful fade, pale, and megre also.
Was never wight yit half so wo
As that hir semede for to be,
Nor so fulfilled of ire as she.
I trowe that no wight myght hir please
Nor do that thyng that myght hir ease,
Nor she ne wolde hir sorowe slake,
Nor comfort noon unto hir take.
So depe was hir wo bigonnen,
And eek hir hert in angre ronnen, 320
A sorowful thyng wel semede she.

Nor she hadde no thyng slowe be
For to foreracchen al hir face,
And for to rent in many place
Hir clothis, and for-to tere hir swire,
As she that was fulfilled of ire ;
And al to-torn lay eek hir here
Aboute hir shuldris, here and there,
As she that hadde it al to-rent
For angre and for maltalent. 330
And eek I telle you certeynly
Hough that she wepe ful tendirly.
[In worlde nys wyght so harde of hert*e*
That had*de* sene hir sorowes smerte,
That nolde have had of her pytye,
So wo-begonne a thyng was she.
She al to-dasht her-selfe for woo,
And smote togyder her hondes two.
To sorowe was she ful ententyfe,
That woful rechelesse caytyfe ; 340
Her rought*e* lytel of playing,
Or of clyppynge or kyssynge ;
For who-so sorowful is in herte
Hym luste not to playe ne sterte,
Ne for to dauncen, ne to synge,
Ne may his herte in tempre brynge
To make joye on even or morowe,
For joye is contrarie unto sorowe.
    Elde was paynted after this,
That shorter was a fote, iwys, 350
Than she was wont in her yonghede.
Unneth her-selfe she myght*e* fede ;
So feble and eke so olde was she
That faded was al her beauté.

Ful salowe was waxen her coloure,
Her heed for hore was whyte as floure.
Iwys, great qualme ne were it none,
Ne synne, although her lyfe were gone.
Al woxen was her body unwelde
And drye and dwyned al for elde.   360
A foule forwelked thynge was she
That whylom rounde and soft had*de* be.
Her eeres shoken fast withall*e*,
As from her heed they wolde fall*e*.
Her face frounced and forpyned,
And both her hondes lorne for-dwined.
So olde she was that she ne went*e*
A fote, but it were by potent*e*.
The tyme, that passeth nyght and daye,
And restelesse travayleth aye,   370
And steleth from us so privcly,
That to us semeth sykerly
That it in one poynt dwelleth ever,
And certes it ne resteth never,
But goth so fast, and passeth aye,
That there nys man that thynke may
What tyme that nowe present is:
(Asketh at these clerkes this,
For men thynke it redily
Thre tymes ben *y*passed by)]   380
The tyme, that may not sojourne,
But goth, and may never retourne,
As watir that doun renneth ay,
But never drope retourne may;
Ther may no thing as tyme endure,
Metalle, nor erthely creature,
For alle thing it frette and shalle:

The tyme eke, that chaungith alle,
And alle doth waxe, and fostred be,
And alle thing distroieth he: 390
The tyme, that eldith our auncessours
And eldith kynges and emperours,
And that us alle shal overcomen
Er that deth us shal have nomen:
The tyme, that hath al in welde
To elden folk, had maad hir Elde
So ynly, that to my witing
She myghte helpe hir-silf no thing,
But turned ageyn unto childhede;
She hadde no thing hir-silf to lede   400
Ne witte ne pithe in hir holde
More than a child of two yeer olde.
But natheles I trowe that she
Was faire sumtyme, and fresh to se,
Whan she was in hir rightful age:
But she was past al that passage
And was a doted thing bicomen.
A furred cope on hadde she nomen;
Wel hadde she clad hir-silf and warme,
For colde myght elles don hir harme.   410
These olde folk have alwey colde,
Her kynde is sich, whan they ben olde.
    Another thing was don there write,
That semede lyk an ipocrite,
And it was clepid Poope-holy.
That ilk is she that pryvely
Ne spareth never a wikked dede,
Whan men of hir taken noon hede,
And maketh hir outward precious,
With pale visage and pitous,   420

And semeth a semely creature;
But ther nys no mysaventure,
That she ne thenkith in hir corage.
Ful lyk to hir was that ymage,
That makid was lyk hir semblaunce.
She was ful symple of countenaunce,
And she was clothed and eke shod,
As she were for the love of God
Yolden to relygioun,
Sich semede hir devocioun.   430
A sauter helde she fast in honde,
And bisily she gan to fonde
To make many a feynt praiere,
To God, and to his scyntis dere.
Ne she was gay, ne fresh, ne jolyf,
But semede to be ful ententyf
To gode werkis, and to faire;
And therto she had on an haire.
Ne certis she was fatt no thing
But semede wery for fasting,   440
Of colour pale and deed was she.
From hir the gate ay werned be
Of Paradys, that blisful place;
For sich folk maketh lene her grace,
As Crist seith in his Evangile,
To gete prys in toun a while;
And for a litel glorie reigne,
They lesen God and *al* his reigne.
    And alderlast of everychon,
Was peynted Povert al aloon,   450
That not a peny hadde in wolde,
Alle-though she hir clothis solde,
And though she shulde an-honged be,

For nakid as a worme was she.
And if the wedir stormy were,
For colde she shulde have deyd there.
She nadde on but a streit olde sak,
And many a cloute on it ther stak;
This was hir cote, and hir mantelle,
No more was there never a delle 460
To clothe hir with; I undirtake,
Grete leyser had*de* she to quake.
And she was putt, that I of talke,
Fer fro these other, up in an halke;
There lurked and there coure*de* she,
For pover thing where so it be,
Is shamefast, and dispised ay.
Acursed may wel be that day,
That povere man conceyved is;
For, God wote, al to selde, iwys, 470
Is ony povere man wel fedde,
Or wel araied or *y*-cledde,
Or wel-biloved, in sich wise,
In honour that he may arise.
 Alle these thingis welle avised,
As I have you er this devysed,
With gold and asure over alle,
Depeynted newe upon the walle.
Square was the walle, and high sumdelle;
Enclosed, and *y*-barred welle, 480
In stede of hegge, was that gardyne;
Come nevere shepherde therynne.
Into that gardyn, wel *y*-wrought,
Who-so that me coude have brought,
By laddris or elles by degré,
It wolde wel have liked me.

For sich solace, sich ioie, and play,
I trowe that nevere man ne say,
As was in that place delytous.
The gardeyn was not daungerous   490
To herberwe briddes many oon.
So riche a yeer was never noon
Of briddes songe, and braunches grene.
Therynne were briddes mo I wene,
Than ben in alle the rewme of Fraunce.
Ful blisful was the accordaunce,
Of swete and pitous songe thei made,
For alle this world it owghte glade.
  And I my-silf so mery ferde,
Whan I her blisful songes herde,   500
That for an hundreth pounde wolde I,
If that the passage opunly
Hadde be unto me fre,
That I nolde entren for-to se
Thassemble (God kepe it fro care!)
Of briddis, whiche therynne ware,
That songen thorugh her mery throtes,
Daunws of love, and mery notes.
  Whan I thus herde foules synge,
I felle fast in a weymentyng,   510
By which art, or by what engyne,
I myghte come into that gardyne;
But way I couthe fynde noon,
Into that gardyne for to goon.
Ne nought wist I if that ther were
Eyther hole or place where,
By which I myghte have entré,
Ne ther was noon to teche me,
For I was al aloone i-wys,

For wo and angwishis of this.   520
Til atte last bithought I me,
That by no weye ne myght it be,
That ther nas laddre or wey to passe,
Or hole, into so faire a place.
Tho gan I go a fulle grete pas,
Envyronyng evene in compas,
The closing of the square walle,
Tyl that I fonde a wiket smalle
So shett, that I ne myght in gon,
And other entré was ther noon.   530
  Uppon this dore I gan to smyte
That was *so* fetys, and so lite,
For other weye coude I not seke.
Ful long I shof, and knokkide eke,
And stood ful long and of herknyng
If that I herde ony wight comyng;
Til thil*ke* dore of that entré
A mayden curteys openyde me.
Hir heer was as yelowe of hewe
As ony basyn scoured newe.   540
Hir flesh tendre as is a chike,
With bent browis, smothe and slyke;
And by mesure large were
The openyng of hir yen clere.
Hir nose of good proporcioun,
Hir yen grey, as is a faucoun,
With swete breth and wel savoured.
Hir face white and wel coloured,
With litel mouth, and rounde to see;
A clove chynne eke hadde she.   550
Hir nekke was of good fasoun
In lengthe and gretnesse by resoun,

Withoute bleyne, scabbe, or royne.
Fro Jerusalem unto Burgoyne
Ther nys a fairer nekke, iwys,
To fele how smothe and softe it is.
Hir throte also white of hewe,
As snawe on braunche snawed newe.
Of body ful wel wrought was she;
Men nedede not in no cuntré   560
A fairer body for to seke.
And of fyn orfrays hadde she eke
A chapelet; so semly oon
Ne werede never mayde upon.
And faire above that chapelet
A rose gerland hadde she sett.
She hadde a gay mirrour,
And with a riche gold tresour
Hir heed was tressed queyntely;
Hir sleves sewid fetously.   570
And for to kepe hir hondis faire
Of gloves white she had a paire.
And she hadde on a cote of grene
Of cloth of Gaunt; withouten wene,
Wel semyde by hir apparayle
She was not wont to gret travayle.
For whan she kempte was fetisly
And wel arayed and richely,
Thanne hadde she don al hir journé;
For merye and wel bigoon was she.   580
She hadde a lusty lyf in May,
She hadde no thought, by nyght ne day
Of no thyng, but if it were oonly
To graythe hir wel and uncouthly.
  Whan that this dore hadde opened me

This may, semely for to see,
I thanked hir as I best myght*e*,
And axide hir how that she hight*e*,
And what she was, I axide eke.
And she to me was nought unmeke,   590
Ne of hir answer daungerous,
But faire answeride, and seide thus :—
' Lo, sir, my name is Ydelnesse;
So clepe men me, more and lesse.
Ful myghty and ful riche am I,
And that of oon thyng, namely,
For I entende to no thyng
But to my joye, and my pleyng,
And for to kembe and tresse me.
Aqueynted am I and pryvé   600
With Myrthe, lord of this gardyne,
That fro the lande of Alexandryne
Made the trees hidre be fette,
That in this gardyne ben *y*-sette.
And whan the trees were woxen on hight,
This walle, that stant heere in thi sight,
Dide Myrthe enclosen al aboute ;
And these ymages al withoute
He dide hem bothe entaile and peynte,
That neithir ben jolyf ne queynte,   610
But they ben ful of sorowe and woo,
As thou hast seen a while agoo.
  ' And ofte tyme hym to solace
Sir Myrthe cometh into this place,
And eke with hym cometh his meynee,
That lyven in lust and jolité.
And now is Myrthe therynne to here
The briddis how they syngen clere,

The mavys and the nyghtyngale,
And other joly briddis smale.   620
And thus he walketh to solace
Hym and his folk; for swetter place
To pleyen ynne he may not fynde,
Al-though he sought oon in tyl Ynde.
Tho alther faireste folk to see
That in this world may founde be
Hathe Mirthe with hym in his route,
That folowen hym always aboute.'
    Whan Ydelnesse tolde had al this,
And I hadde herkned wel, ywys,   630
Thanne seide I to dame Ydelnesse,
'Now also wisly God me blesse,
Sith Myrthe, that is so faire and fre,
Is in this yerde with his meyné,
Fro thilk assemblé, if I may,
Shal no man werne me to-day,
That I this nyght ne mote it see.
For wel wene I there with hym be
A faire and joly companye
Fulfilled of alle curtesie.'   640
And forth withoute wordis mo
In at the wiket went I tho,
That Ydelnesse hadde opened me,
Into that gardyne faire to see.
    And whan I was *ther*-inne, iwys,
Myn herte was ful glad of this.
For wel wende I ful sikerly
Have ben in Paradys erthly;
So faire it was, that trusteth wel,
It semede a place espirituel.
For certys, as at my devys,

Ther is no place in Paradys
So good inne for to dwelle or be,
As in that gardyne, thoughte me.
For there was many a bridde syngyng,
Thorough-oute the yerde al thringyng.
In many places were nyghtyngales,
Alpes, fynches, and wodewales,
That in her swete song deliten
In thilke places as they habiten.   660
Thero myghte men see many flokkes
Of turtles and laverokkes.
Chalaundres fele sawe I there,
That wery nygh forsongen were.
And thrustles, terins, and mavys,
That songen for to wynne hem prys,
And eke to sormounte in her songe
That other briddes hem amonge,
By note made faire servyse.
These briddes, that I you devise,   670
They songe her songe as faire and wele,
As angels don espirituel.
And, trusteth wel, that I hem herd
Ful lustily, and wel I ferde;
For never yitt sich melodye
Was herd of man that myghte dye.
Sich swete song was hem amonge,
That me thought it no briddis songe,
But it was wondir lyk to be
Song of meremaydens of the see;   680
That, for her syngyng is so clere,
Though we mermaydens clepe hem here
In English, as is oure usaunce,
Men clepe hem screyns in Fraunce.

Ententif weren for to synge
These briddis, that nought unkunnyng
Were of her craft, and apprentys,
For of song sotil and wys.
And certis, whan I herde her songe,
And sawe the grene place amonge,   690
In herte I wexe so wondir gay,
That I was never erst, er that day,
So jolyf, nor so wel bigoo,
Ne merye in herte, as I was thoo.
And than wist I, and sawe ful welle,
That Ydelnesse me servede welle,
That me putte in sich jolité.
 Hir freend wel ought I for to be,
Sith she the dore of that gardyne,
Hadde opened, and me leten inne.   700
      From hennes-forth, hou that I wroughte
I shal you tellen, as me thoughte.
First wherof Myrthe servede there,
And eke what folk there with hym were,
Withoute fable I wol discryve.
And of that gardyne eke as blyve
I wole you tellen aftir this.
The faire fasoun alle, ywys,
That wel y-wrought was for the nones,
I may not telle you alle at ones;   710
But as I may and can, I shalle
By ordre tellen you it alle.
      Ful faire servise and eke ful swete
These briddis maden as they sete.
Layes of love, ful wel sownyng
They songen in their yarkonyng ;
Summe high, and summe eke lowe songe

Upon the braunches grene spronge.
The swetnesse of her melodye
Made al myn herte in reverye.   720
And whan that I hadde herde I trowe
These briddis syngyng on a rowe,
Than myght I not withholde me
That I ne wente inne for to see
Sir Myrthe ; for my desiryng
Was hym to seen, over alle thyng,
His countenaunce and his manere :
That sight was *tho* to me ful dere.
Tho wente I forth on my right honde
Doun by a lytel path I fonde   730
Of mentes fulle, and fenelle grene ;
And faste by, withoute wene,
Sir Myrthe I fonde ; and right anoon
Unto sir Myrthe gan I goon,
There as he was hym to solace.
And with hym in that lusty place,
So faire folk and so fresh had he,
That whan I sawe, I wondrede me
Fro whenne siche folk myghte come,
So faire they weren alle and some ;   740
For they were lyk, as to my sight*e*,
To angels, that ben fethered bright*e*.
This folk, of which I telle you soo,
Upon a karole wenten thoo.
A lady karolede hem, that hyght*e*
Gladnesse, blisfulle, and the light*e*,
Wel coude she synge and lustyly,
Noon half so wel and semely ;
And couthe make in song sich refreynynge,
It sat hir wondir wel to synge.   750

Hir voice ful clere was and ful swete.
She was nought rude ne unmete,
But couthe ynow of sich doyng
As longeth unto karolyng :
For she was wont in every place
To syngen first, folk to solace,
For syngyng moost she gaf hir to ;
No craft had*de* she so leef to do.
   Tho myghtist thou karoles sene,
And fol*ke* daunce and mery bene,   760
And made many a faire tournyng
Upon the grene gras springyng.
There myghtist thou see these flowtours,
Mynstrales, and eke jogelours,
That wel to synge dide her peyne.
Somme songe songes of Loreyne ;
For in Loreyn her notes bee
Fulle swetter than in this contré.
There was many a tymbester,
And saillouris, that I dar wel swere   770
Couthe her craft ful parfitly.
The tymbres up ful sotilly
They caste*n*, and hente fulle ofte
Upon a fynger faire and softe,
That they failide never mo.
Ful fetys damysel*es* two,
Ryght yonge, and fulle of semelyhede,
In kirtles, and noon other wede,
And faire tressed every tresse,
Hadde Myrthe doon, for his noblesse,   780
Amydde the karole for to daunce ;
But herof lieth no remembraunce,
Hou that they dauncede queyntely.

That oon wolde come alle pryvyly
Agayn that other; and whan they were
To-gidre almost, they threwe yfere
Her mouthis so, that thorough her play
It semed as they kiste alway;
To dauncen welle koude they the gise;
What shulde I more to you devyse? 790
Ne bode I never thennes go,
Whiles that I sawe hem daunce so.
Upon the karolle wonder faste,
I gan biholde; til atte laste
A lady gan me for to espie,
And she was cleped Curtesie,
The worshipfulle, the debonaire;
I pray to God evere falle hir faire!
Ful curteisly she callede me,
'What do ye there, beau sir?' quod she, 800
'Come, and if it lyke yow
To dauncen, dauncith with us now.
And I withoute tariyng
Wente into the karolyng.
I was abasshed never a delle,
But it to me likede right welle,
That Curtesie me clepede so,
And bad me on the daunce go.
For if I hadde durst, certeyn
I wolde have karoled right fayn, 810
As man that was to daunce right blithe.
Thanne gan I loken ofte sithe
The shape, the bodies, and the cheres,
The countenaunce and the maneres
Of alle the folk that dauncede there,
And I shal telle what they were.

Ful faire was Myrthe, ful longe and high,
A fairer man I nevere sigh.
As rounde as appille was his face,
Ful rody and white in every place.   820
Fetys he was and wel beseye,
With metely mouth and yen greye ;
His nose by mesure wrought ful right ;
Crispe was his heer, and eek ful bright.
Hise shuldris of a large brede,
And smalish in the girdilstede.
He semede lyke a portreiture,
So noble he was of his stature,
So faire, so joly, and so fetys,
With lymes wrought at poynt devys,   830
Delyver, smert, and of grete myght ;
Ne sawe thou nevere man so lyght.
Of berde unnethe hadde he no thyng,
For it was in the firste spryng.
Ful yonge he was, and mery of thought,
And in samette, with briddis wrought,
And with gold beten ful fetysly,
His body was clad ful richely.
Wrought was his robe in straunge gise,
And al to-slytered for queyntise   840
In many a place, lowe and hie.
And shode he was with grete maistrie,
With shoon decoped, and with laas,
By druery, and by solas.
His leef a rosyn chapelet
Hadde made, and on his heed it set.
    And wite ye who was his leef ?
Dame Gladnesse there was hym so leef,
That syngith so wel with glad courage,

That from she was xij. yeer of age, 850
She of hir love graunt hym made.
Sir Mirthe hir by the fynger hadde
Daunsyng, and she hym also ;
Grete love was atwixe hem two.
Bothe were they faire and bright of hewe ;
She semede lyke a rose newe
Of colour, and hir flesh so tendre,
That with a brere smale and slendre
Men myght it cleve, I dar wel sey*n*e.
Hir forheed frounceles al pley*n*e, 860
Bent were hir browis two,
Hir yen greye, and glad also,
That laugheden ay in hir semblaunt,
First or the mouth, by covenaunt.
I wot not what of hir nose I shal descryve ;
So faire hath no womman alyve.
Hir heer was yelowe, and clere shynyng,
I wot no lady so likyng.
Of Orfrays fresh was hir gerland,
I, which seyen have a thousand, 870
Saugh never, ywys, no gerlond yitt,
So wel *y*-wrought of silk as it.
And in an overgilt samet
Cladde she was, by grete delit,
Of which hir leef a robe werede,
The myrier she in hir herte ferede.
    And next hir wente, in hir other side,
The God of Love, that can devyde
Love, and as hym likith it be.
But he can cherles daunten, he, 880
And maken folkis pride fallen.
And he can wel these lordis thrallen,

And ladyes putt at lowe degre,
Whan he may hem to proude see.
    This God of Love of his fasoun
Was lyke no knave, ne quystroun;
His beauté gretly was to preyse.
But of his robe to devise
I drede encombred for to be.
For nought *y*-clad in silk was he,   890
But alle in floures and in flourettes,
Ipainted alle with amorettes;
And with losynges and scochouns,
With briddes, lybardes, and lyouns,
And other beestis wrought ful welle.
His garnement was everydelle
Portreied and wrought with floures,
By dyvers medlyng of coloures.
Floures there were of many gise
I-sett by compas in assise;   900
Ther lakkide no flour to my dome,
Ne nought so mych as flour of brome,
Ne violete, ne eke pervynke,
Ne flour noon, that man can on thynke,
And many a rose leef ful longe,
Was entermelled ther amonge:
And also on his heed was sette
Of roses reed a chapelett.
But nyghtyngales a fulle grete route,
That flyen over his heed aboute,   910
The leeves felden as they flyen,
And he was alle with briddes wryen;
With popynjay, with nyghtyngale,
With chalaundre, and with wodewale,
With fynche, with lark, and with archaungelle.

He semede as he were an aungelle,
That doun were comen fro hevene clere.
  Love hadde with hym a bachelere,
That he made alleweyes with hym be,
Swete-lokyng cleped was he. 920
This bacheler stode biholdyng
The daunce, and in his honde holdyng
Turke bowes two, fulle wel devysed had he.
That oon of hem was of a tree
That bereth a fruyt of savour wykke ;
Ful crokid was that foule stikke,
And knotty here and there also,
And blak as bery, or ony slo.
That other bowe was of a plant
Withoute wem, I dar warant, 930
Ful evene, and by proporcioun
Treitys and long, of ful good fasoun.
And it was peynted wel and twythen,
And over al diapred and writen
With ladyes and with bacheleris,
Fulle lyghtsom and glad of cheris.
These bowes two helde Swete-lokyng,
That semede lyk no gadelyng.
And ten brode arowis hilde he there,
Of which v. in his right hond were. 940
But they were shaven wel and dight,
Nokked and fethered right ;
And alle they were with gold bygoon,
And stronge poynted everychoon,
And sharpe for to kerven welle.
But iren was ther noon ne stelle,
For al was golde, men myght it see,
Outake the fetheres and the tree.

The swiftest of these arowis fyve
Out of a bowe for to dryve, 950
And best fethered for to flee,
And fairest eke, was clepid Beauté.
That other arowe that hurteth lasse
Was clepid (as I trowe) Symplesse.
The thridde cleped was Fraunchise,
That fethred was in noble wise
With valour and with curtesye.
The fourthe was cleped Compaignye,
That hevy for to shoten ys;
But who-so shetith right, ywys, 960
May therwith doon grete harme and wo.
The fifte of these, and laste also,
Faire-semblaunt men that arowe calle,
The leeste grevous of hem alle.
Yit can it make a ful grete wounde,
But he may hope his soris sounde,
That hurt is with that arowe, ywys;
His wo the bette bistowed is.
For he may sonner have gladnesse,
Hir langour oughte be the lesse. 970
 Five arowis were of other gise,
That ben ful foule to devyse;
For shaft and ende, soth for to telle,
Were also blak as fende in helle.
 The first of hem is called Pride;
That other arowe next hym biside,
It was ycleped Vylanye;
That arowe was as with felonye
Envenymed, and with spitous blame.
The thridde of hem was cleped Shame. 980
The fourthe, Wanhope cleped is,

The fifte, the Newe-thought, ywys.
  These arowis that I speke of heere,
Were alle fyve on oon maneere,
And alle were they resemblable.
To hem was wel sittyng and able,
The foule croked bowe hidous,
That knotty was, and al roynous.
That bowe semede wel to shete
These arowis fyve, that ben unmete   990
And contrarye to that other fyve.
But though I telle not as blyve
Of her power, ne of her myght,
Herafter shal I tellen right
The soothe, and eke signyfiaunce,
As fer as I have remembraunce :
Alle shal be seid, I undirtake,
Er of this book an ende I make.
  Now come I to my tale ageyn.
But aldirfirst, I wole you seyn   1000
The fasoun and the countenaunces
Of alle the folk that on the daunce is.
The God of Love, jolyf and lyght,
Ladde on his honde a lady bright,
Of high prys, and of grete degré.
This lady called was Beauté,
And an arowe, of which I tolde.
Ful wel thewed was she holde,
Ne she was derk ne broun, but bright,
And clere as the mone-lyght,   1010
Ageyn whom alle the sterres semen
 But smale candels, as we demen.
Hir flesh was tendre as dewe of flour,
Hir chere was symple as byrde in bour ;

As whyte as lylye or rose in rys,
Hir face gentyl and tretys.
Fetys she was, and smale to se,
No wyntred browis had*de* she,
Ne popped hir, for it nedede nought
To wyndre hir, or to peynte hir ought. 1020
Hir tresses yelowe, and longe straughten,
Unto hir helys doun they raughten:
Hir nose, hir mouth, and eyhe and cheke
Wel wrought, and alle the remenaunt eke.
A ful grete savour and a swote,
Me thought*e* in myn herte rote,
As helpe me God, whan I remembre,
Of the fasoun of every membre!
In world is noon so faire a wight;
For yonge she was, and hewed bright 1030
Sore plesaunt, and fetys with alle,
Gente, and in hir myddille smalle.
Biside Beauté yede Richesse,
And high*te* 'Lady' of gret noblesse,
And gret of prys in every place.
But who so durste to hir trespace,
Or til hir folk, in werk or dede,
He were fulle hardy, out of drede,
For bothe she helpe and hyndre may.
And that is nought of yisterday 1040
That riche folk have fulle gret myght
To helpe, and eke to greve a wyght.
The beste and the grettest of valour
Diden Rychesse ful gret honour,
And besy were hir to serve,
For that they wolde hir love deserve.
They cleped hir 'Lady,' grete and smalle;

This wide world hir dredith alle.
This world is alle in hir daungere.
Hir court hath many a losengere, 1050
And many a traytour envyous,
That ben ful besy and curyous
For to dispreisen, and to blame
That best deserven love and name.
Bifore the folk hem to bigilen,
These losengeris hem preyse and smylen,
And thus the world with word anoynten;
But aftirward they prile and poynten,
The folk right to the bare boon,
Bihynde her bak whan they ben goon, 1060
And foule abate the folkis prys,
Ful many a worthy man, ywys,
An hundrid, have *they* do to dye.
These losengers thorough flaterye,
Have maad folk ful straunge be,
There hem oughte be pryvé.
Wel yvel mote they thryve and thee,
And yvel a-chyved mote they be
These losengers ful of envye!
No good man loveth her companye. 1070
Richesse a robe of purpur on hadde,
Ne trowe not that I lye or madde;
For in this world is noon hir lyche,
Ne by a thousand deelle so riche,
Ne noon so faire; for it ful welle
With orfrays leyd was everydeelle,
And portraied in the ribanynges
Of dukes storyes, and of kynges.
And with a bend of gold tasseled,
And knoppis fyne of gold enameled, 1080

Aboute hir nekke of gentyl entayle
Was shete the riche chevesaile,
In which ther was fulle gret plenté
Of stones clere and bright to see.
Rychesse a girdelle hadde upon,
The bokele of it was of a stoon,
Of vertu gret, and mochel of myght
For who so bare the stoon so bright,
Of venym durst hym no thing doute,
While he the stoon hadde hym aboute.   1090
That stoon was gretly for to love,
 And tyl a riche man byhove
Worth alle the gold in Rome and Frise.
The mourdaunt, wrought in noble wise,
Was of a stoon fulle precious,
That was so fyne and vertuous,
That hole a man it koude make
Of palasie, and tothe ake.
And yit the stoon hadde such a grace,
That he was siker in every place   1100
Alle thilke day not blynde to bene,
That fastyng myghte that stoon seene.
The barres were of gold ful fyne,
Upon a tyssu of satyne,
Fulle hevy, gret, and no thyng lyght,
In everiche was a besaunt wight.
Upon the tresses of Richesse
Was sette a cercle for noblesse
Of brend gold, that fulle lyghte shoon ;
So faire trowe I was never noon.   1110
But she were kunnyng for the nonys,
That koude devyse alle the stonys
That in that cercle shewen clere ;

It is a wondir thing to here.
For no man koude preyse or gesse
Of hem that valewe or richesse.
Rubyes there were, saphires, *jagounces*,
And emeraudes, more than two ounces.
But alle byfore ful sotilly
A fyn charboncle sette saugh I.   1120
The stoon so clere was and so bright,
That, also soone as it was nyght,
Men myght*e* seen to go for nede
A myle or two, in lengthe and brede.
Sich lyght *tho* sprang oute of the stone,
That Richesse wondir bright*e* shone
Bothe hir heed, and alle hir face,
And eke aboute hir al the place.
    Dame Richesse on hir honde gan lede
A yong man fulle of *semelyhede*,   1130
That she best loved of ony thing;
His lust was mych in housholding.
In clothyng was he ful fetys,
And loved*e* to have welle hors of prys.
He wende to have reproved be
Of theft or moordre, if that he
Hadde in his stable ony hakeney.
And therfore he desired ay
To be aqueynted with Richesse;
For alle his purpos, as I gesse,   1140
Was for to make gret dispense,
Withoute wernyng *or* diffense.
And Richesse myght it wel sustene,
And hir dispence welle mayntene,
And hym alwey sich plenté sende,
Of gold and silver forto dispende

Withoute lakke or daunger,
As it were poured in a garner.
   And after on the daunce wente
Largesse, that settith al hir entente   1150
For to be honourable and free;
Of Alexandres kyn was she.
Hir moste joye was, ywys,
Whan that she yaf, and seide, ' Have this.'
Not Avarice, the foule caytyf,
Was half to gripe so ententyf,
As Largesse is to yeve and spende.
And God ynough alwey hir sende,
So that the more she yaf awey,
The more, ywys, she hadde alwey.   1160
Gret loos hath Largesse, and gret pris;
For bothe *wyse* folk and unwys
Were hooly to hir baundon brought,
So wel with yiftes hath she wrought.
And if she hadde an enemy,
I trowe that she coude tristely
Make hym fulle soone hir freend to be,
So large of yift, and free was she;
Therfore she stode in love and grace
Of riche and pover in every place.   1170
   A fulle gret fool is he, ywys,
That bothe riche and nygart is.
A lord may have no maner vice,
That greveth more than avarice.
For nygart never with strengthe of honde
May wynne gret lordship or londe.
For freendis alle to fewe hath he
To doon his wille perfourmed be.
And who-so wole have freendis heere,

He may not holde his tresour deere. 1180
For by ensample I telle this,
Right as an adamaund, iwys,
Can drawen to hym sotylly
The yren, that is leid therby,
So drawith folkes hertis, ywis,
Silver and gold that yeven is.
   Largesse hadde on a robe fresh
Of riche purpur sarlynysh.
Wel fourmed was hir face and cleere,
And opened hadde she hir colere; 1190
For she right there hadde in present
Unto a lady maad present
Of a gold broche, ful wel *y*-wrought.
And certys it myssatte hir nought;
For thorough hir smokke wrought with silk,
The flesh was seen as white as mylk.
   Largesse, that worthy was and wys,
Hilde by the honde a knyght of prys,
Was sibbe to Artour of Britaigne.
And that was he that bare the ensaigne 1200
Of worship, and the gounfaucoun.
And yit he is of sich renoun,
That men of hym seye faire thynges
Byfore barouns, erles, and kynges.
This knyght was comen alle newely
Fro tourneiyng faste by;
There hadde he don gret chyvalrie
Thorough his vertu and his maistrie,
And for the love of his lemman
He caste doun many a doughty man. 1210
   And next hym dauncede dame Fraunchise,
Arayed in fulle noble gyse.

She was not broune ne dunne of hewe,
But white as snowe falle newe.
Hir nose was wrought at poynt devys,
For it was gentyl and tretys;
With eyen gladde, and browes bente;
Hir here doun to hir helis wente.
And she was symple as dowve of tree,
Ful debonaire of herte was she.　　　　1220
She durst_e_ never seyn ne do,
But that that hir longed_e_ to.
And if a man were in distresse,
And for hir love in hevynesse,
Hir herte wolde have fulle gret pité,
She was so amiable and free.
For were a man for hir bistadde,
She wolde ben right sore adradde,
That she dide over gret outrage,
But she hym holpe his harme to aswage;　　1230
Hir thought it elles a vylanye.
And she hadde on a sukkenye,
That not of hempe ne heerdis was;
So fair was noon in alle Arras.
Lord, it was ridled fetysly!
Ther nas a poynt, trew_e_ly,
Tha_t_ it nas in his right assise.
Fulle wel _y_-clothed was Fraunchise,
For ther is no cloth sittith bet
On damyselle, than doth roket.　　　　1240
A womman wel more fetys is
In roket than in cote, ywis.
The whyte roket rydled faire,
Bitokeneth, that fulle debonaire
And swete was she that it bere.

Bi hir daunced a bachelere;
I can not telle you what he hight*e*,
But faire he was, and of good hight*e*
Alle hadde he be, I sey no more,
The lordis sone of Wyndesore. 1250
And next that daunced*e* Curtesye,
That preised was of lowe and hye,
For neither proude ne foole was she.
She for to daunce called*e* me,
(I pray God yeve hir right good grace!)
Whanne I come first into the place.
She was not nyce, ne outrageous,
But wys and ware, and vertuous,
Of faire speche, and of faire answere;
Was never wight mysseid of hire; 1260
She *ne* bar rancour to no wight.
Clere broune she was, and therto bright
Of face, of body *avenaunt*,
I wot no lady so plesaunt,
She *were* worthy for to bene
An emperesse or crowned quene.
And by hir wente a knyght dauncyng
That worthy was and wel spekyng,
And ful wel koude he don honour.
The knyght was faire and styf in stour, 1270
And in armure a semely man,
And wel-biloved of his lemman.
Faire Idilnesse thanne saugh I,
That alwey was me faste by.
Of hir have I, withoute fayle,
Told yow the shap and apparayle;
For (as I seide) loo, that was she
That dide to me so gret bounté,

That she the gate of the gardyn
Undide, and lete me passen in,   1280
And after daunced as I gesse.
And she fulfilled of lustynesse,
That nas not yit xij yeer of age,
With herte wylde, and thought volage.
Nyce she was, but she ne mente
Noon harme ne slight in hir entente,
But oonly lust and jolyté.
For yonge folk wole, witen ye,
Have lytel thought but on her play.
Hir lemman was biside alway,   1290
In sich a gise that he hir kyste
At alle tymes that hym lyste,
That alle the daunce myght it see ;
They make no force of pryveté.
For who spake of hem yvel or welle,
They were ashamed never adelle,
But men myghte seen hem kisse there,
As it two yonge dowves were.
For yong was thilke bachelere,
Of beauté wot I noon his pere ;   1300
And he was right of sich an age,
As youthe is leef, and sich corage.
    The lusty folk that dauncede there,
And also other that with hem were
That weren alle of her meyné
Ful hende folk, and wys, and free,
And folk of faire port truely,
There were alle comunly.
    Whanne I hadde seen the countenaunces
Of hem that ladden thus these daunces,   1310
Thanne hadde I wille to gon and see

The gardyne that so lyked*e* me,
And loken on these faire loreyes,
On pyntrees, cedres, and oliveris.
The daunces thanne eended were ;
For many of hem that daunced*e* there,
Were with her loves went awey
Undir the trees to have her pley.
　A, Lord ! they lyved*e* lustyly !
A gret fool were he sikirly,			1320
That nolde, his thankes, such lyf lede !
For this dar I seyn oute of drede,
That who-so myght*e* so wel fare,
For better lyf durst hym not care,
For ther nys so good paradys,
As to have a love at his devys.
　Oute of that place wente I thoo,
And in that gardyn gan I goo,
Pleyyng a-longe fulle meryly.
The God of Love fulle hastely			1330
Unto hym Swete-lokyng clepte,
No lenger wolde he that she kepte
His bowe of gold, that shoon so bright.
He hadde hym bent anoon ryght ;
And he fulle soone sette an ende, ．
And at a braid he gan it bende,
And toke hym of his arowes fyve,
Fulle sharp and redy forto dryve.
Now God that sittith in magesté
Fro deedly woundes he kepe me !			1340
If so be that he hadde me shette,
For if I with his arowe mette,
It hadde me greved sore, iwys.
But I, that no thyng wist of this,

Wente up and doun fulle many a wey,
And he me folwede fast alwey;
But no-where wold I reste me,
Tille I hadde in alle the gardyn be.
  The gardyn was by mesuryng
Right evene and square in compassing;   1350
It as long was as it was large.
Of fruyt hadde every tree his charge,
But it were any hidous tree
Of which ther were two or three.
There were, and that wote I fulle welle,
Of pome-garnettys a fulle gret delle;
That is a fruyt fulle welle to lyke,
Namely to folk whanne they ben sike.
And trees there were of gret foisoun,
That baren notes in her sesoun,   1360
Such as men notemygges calle,
That swote of savour ben with-alle.
 And almandres gret plenté,
Fyges, and many a date tree
There wexen, if men hadde nede,
Thorough the gardyn in length and brede.
Ther was eke wexyng many a spice,
As clowe-gelofre, and lycorice,
Gyngevre, and greyn de Parys,
Canelle, and setewale of prys,   1370
And many a spice delitable,
To eten whan men rise fro table.
And many homly trees ther were,
That peches, coynes, and apples beere,
Medlers, plowmes, perys, chesteyns,
Cherys, of which many oon fayne is,
Notes, aleys, and bolas,

That forto seen it was solas;
With many high lorey and pyn,
Was renged clene alle that gardyn;   1380
With cipres, and with olyvers,
Of which that nygh no plenté heere is.
There were elmes grete and stronge,
Maples, asshe, oke, aspe, planes longe,
Fyne ew, popler, and lyndes faire,
And othere trees fulle many a payre.
What shulde I telle you more of it?
There were so many trees yet,
That I shulde all encombred be,
Er I had*de* rekened every tree.   1390
    These trees were sette, that I devyse,
One from another in assyse
Five fadome or syxe, I trowe so,
But they were hye and great also:
And for to kepe oute well the sonne,
The croppes were so thycke yronne,
And every braunche in other knytte,
And full of grene leves sytte,
That sonne myght*e* there noon dyscende,
Lest the tender grasses shende.   1400
There myght*e* men does and roes yse,
And of squyrels ful gret plenté,
From bowe to bowe alwaye lepynge.
Connies there were also playenge,
That comyn out of her clapers
Of sondry colours and maners,
And maden many a tourneynge
Upon the freshe grasso spryngynge.
    In places sawe I welles there,
In whych there no frogges wero,   1410

And fayre in shadowe was every well*e*;
But I ne can the nombre tell*e*
Of stremys smal*e*, that by devyse
Myrthe had*de* done come through condyse,
Of whych the water in rennynge
Gan make a noyse full lykynge.
Aboute the brynkes of these welles,
And by the stremes over al elles
Sprange up the grasse, as thycke yset
And softe as any velvet,   1420
On whych men myght hys lemman ley*e*,
As on a fetherbed to pley*e*,
For the erthe was ful softe and swete.
Through moysture of the welle wete
Spronge up the sote grene gras,
As fayre, as thycke, as myster was.
But moche amended it the place,
That therth was of suche a grace
That it of floures hath plenté,
That both in somer and wynter be.   1430
There sprange the vyolet al newe,
And fresshe pervynke ryche of hewe,
And floures yelow*e*, white, and rede;
Suche plenté grewe there never in mede.
Ful gaye was al the grounde, and queynt,
And poudred, as men had it peynt,
With many a freshe and sondrye floure,
That casten up ful good savoure.
I wol not longe holde you in fable
Of al this garden delectable.   1440
I mote my tonge stynten nede,
For I ne maye withouten drede
Naught tellen you the beauté all*e*,

Ne halfe the bounté therewythalle.
  I went on ryght hande and on lefte
Aboute the place; it was not left,
Tyl I had al the garden bene
In the esters that men myghte sene.
  And thus whyle I wente in my playe,
The God of Love me folowed aye.   1450
Ryght as an hunter can abyde
The beest, tyl he seeth hys tyde
To shoten, at goodnesse, to the dere,
When that hym nedeth go no nere.
  And so befyl I restede me
Besydes a wel under a tree,
Whych tree in Fraunce men cal a pyne.
But, syth the tyme of kynge Pepyne,
Ne grewe there tree in mannes syght
So fayre, ne so wel woxe in hyght;   1460
In al that yarde so hygh was none.
And spryngynge in a marble stone
Hadde nature set, the soth to telle,
Under that pyne tree a welle.
And on the border al withoute
Was wryten on the stone aboute,
Letteres smale, that sayden thus,
' Here starfe the fayre Narcisus.'
  Narcisus was a bachelere,
That Love hadde caught in hys daungere, 1470
And in hys nette gan hym so strayne,
And dyd hym so to wepe and playne,
That nede hym muste hys lyfe forgo,
For a fayre lady that hyght Echo,
Hym loved over any creature,
And gan for hym suche payne endure,

That on a tyme she hym tolde,
That yf he her *y*-loven nolde,
That her behovede nedes dye,
There laye none other remedye.　　　1480
But nathelesse, for hys beauté
So fyers and daungerous was he,]
That he nolde graunte hir askyng,
For wepyng, ne for faire praiyng.
And whanne she herd hym werne soo,
She hadde in herte so gret woo,
And took it in so gret dispite,
That she, withoute more respite,
Was deed anoon.　But er she dide,
Fulle pitously to God she preide,　　　1490
That proude hertid Narcisus,
That was in love so daungerous,
Myght on a day ben hampred so
For love, and ben so hoot for woo,
That never he myght to joye atteygne ;
And that he shulde feele in every veyne
What sorowe trewe lovers maken,
That ben so velaynesly forsaken.
This prayer was but resonable,
　Therfore God helde it forme and stable : 1500
For Narcisus shortly to telle,
By aventure come to that welle
To resten hym in that shadowing
A day, whanne he come fro huntyng.
This Narcisus hadde suffred paynes
For rennyng alday in the playnes,
And was for thurst in grete distresse
Of heet, and of his werynesse,
That hadde his breth almost bynomen.

Whanne he was to that we*lle* comen,   1510
That shadowid was with braunches grene,
He thoughte of thilke water shene
To drynke and fresshe hym wel withalle;
And doun on knees he gan to falle,
And forth his heed and necke he straught
To drynken of that welle a draught.
And in the water anoon was seen
His nose, his mouth, his yen sheen,
And he therof was alle abasshed;
His owne shadowe was hym bytrasshed. 1520
For welle wende he the forme see
Of a child of gret beauté.
Welle kouthe Love hym wreke thoo
Of daunger and of pride also,
That Narcisus somtyme hym beere.
He quytte hym welle his guerdoun there;
For he musede so in the welle,
That, shortly alle the sothe to telle,
He lovede his owne shadowe soo,
That atte laste he starf for woo.   1530
For whanne he saugh that he his wille
Myght in no maner wey fulfille;
And that he was so faste caught
That he hym kouthe comforte nought,
He loste his witte right in that place,
And diede withynne a lytel space.
And thus his warisoun he took
For the lady that he forsook.
    Ladyes, I preye ensample takith,
Ye that ageyns youre love mistakith: 1540
For if her deth be yow to wite,
God kan ful welle youre while quyte.

Whanne that this lettre of which I telle,
Hadde taught me that it was the welle
Of Narcisus in his beauté,
I gan anoon withdrawe me,
Whanne it felle in my remembraunce,
That hym bitidde such myschaunce.
But at the laste thanne thought I,
That scathles, fulle sykerly,   1550
I myght unto the welle goo.
Wherof shulde I abaisshen soo?
Unto the welle than wente I me,
And doun I loutede for to see
The clere water in the stoon,
And eke the gravelle, which that shoon
Down in the botme, as silver fyn,
For of the welle, this is the fyn,
In world is noon so clere of hewe.
The water is evere fresh and newe   1560
That welmeth up with wawis bright*e*
The mountance of two fynger hight*e*.
Aboute it is gras spryngyng,
For moiste so thikke and wel likyng,
That it ne may in wynter dye,
No more than may the see be drye.
Downe atte the botme sette sawe I
Two cristalle stonys craftely
In thilke fresh and faire welle.
But o thing sothly dar I telle,   1570
That ye wole holde a gret mervayle
Whanne it is tolde, withouten fayle.
For whanne the sonne, clere in sight*e*,
Cast in that welle his bemys bright*e*,
And that the heete descendid is,

Thanne taketh the cristalle stoon ywis,
Agayn the sonne an hundrid hewis,
Blewe, yelowe, and rede, that fresh and newe is.
Yitt hath the merveilous cristalle
Such strengthe, that the place overalle,   1580
Bothe foule and tree, and leves grene,
And alle the yerde in it is scene.
And for to don you to undirstonde,
To make ensample wole I fonde;
Ryght as a myrrour openly
Shewith alle thing that stondith therby,
As welle the colour as the figure,
Withouten ony coverture;
Right so the cristalle stoon shynyng,
Withouten ony disseyvyng,   1590
The entrees of the yerde accusith
To hym that in the water musith.
For evere in which half that ye be,
Ye may welle half the gardyne se.
And if he turne, he may right welle
Sene the remenaunt everydelle.
For ther is noon so litil thyng
So hidde ne closid with shittyng,
That it ne is sene, as though it were
Peyntid in the cristalle there.   1600
This is the mirrour perilous,
In which the proude Narcisus
Sawe alle his face faire and bright,
That made hym swithe to ligge upright.
For who-so loketh in that mirrour,
Ther may no thyng ben his socour
That he ne shalle there sene some thyng
That shal hym lede into laughyng.

Fulle many worthy man hath it
Y-blent; for folk of grettist wit   1610
Ben soone caught heere and awayted;
Withouten respite ben they baited.
Heere comth to folk of newe rage,
Heere chaungith many wight corage;
Heere lith no rede ne witte therto;
For Venus sone, daun Cupido,
Hath sowne there of love the seed,
That help ne lith there noon, ne rede,
So cerclith it the welle aboute.
His gynnes hath he sett withoute   1620
Ryght for to cacche in his panters
These damoysels and bachelers.
Love wille noon other bridde cacche,
Though he sette oither nette or lacche.
And for the seed that heere was sowen,
This welle is clepid, as welle is knowen,
The Welle of Love, of verray right,
Of which ther hath ful many a wight
Spoke in bookis dyversely.
But they shulle never so verily   1630
Descripcioun of the welle heere,
Ne eke the sothe of this matere,
As ye shulle, whanne I have undo
The craft that hir bilongith too.
    Alle way me likede for to dwelle.
To sene the cristalle in the welle,
That shewide me fulle openly
A thousand thinges faste by.
But I may say, in sory houre
Stode I to loken on to poure.   1640
For sithen I sore sighede,

That mirrour hath me now entriked.
But hadde I first knowen in my wit
The vertues and strengthes of it,
I nolde not have mused there;
Me had*de* bette bene ellis where,
For in the snare I felle anoon,
That hath bitrisshed many oon.
    In thilk*e* mirrour sawe I tho,
Among a thousand thinges mo,   1650
A roser chargid fulle of rosis,
That with an hegge aboute enclosid is.
Tho had I sich lust and envie,
That for Parys ne for Pavie,
Nolde I have left to goon att see
There grettist hepe of roses be.
Whanne I was with this rage hent,
That caught hath many a man and shent,
Toward the roser gan I go.
And whanne I was not fer therfro,   1660
The savour of the roses swote
Me smote right to the herte rote,
As I hadde alle enbawmed *be*.
And if I ne hadde endouted me
To have ben hatid or assailed,
Me thankis, wole I not have failed
To pulle a rose of alle that route
To bere*n* in myn honde aboute,
And smellen to it where I wente;
But ever I dredde me to repente,   1670
And leste it grevede or forthought*e*
The lord that thilk*e* gardyn wrought*e*.
Of roses ther were grete wone,
So faire woxe never in Rone.

Of knoppes clos, some sawe I there,
And some wel beter woxen were.
And some ther ben of other moysoun,
That drowe nygh to her sesoun,
And spedde hem faste for to sprede ;
I love welle sich roses rede ;   1680
For brode roses, and open also,
Ben passed in a day or two ;
But knoppes wille freshe be
Two dayes atte leest, or thre.
The knoppes gretly likede me,
For fairer may ther no man se.
Who-so myghte have oon of alle,
It ought hym ben fulle lief withalle.
Might I *oon* gerlond of hem geten,
For no richesse I wolde it leten.   1690
 Among the knoppes I chese oon
So faire, that of the remenaunt noon
Ne preise I half so welle as it,
Whanne I avise it in my wit.
For it so welle was enlomyned
With colour reed, as welle ifyned
As nature couthe it make faire.
And it hath leves wel foure paire,
That Kynde hath sett thorough his knowyng
Aboute the rede roses spryngyng.   1700
The stalke was as rish right,
And theron stode the knoppe upright,
That it ne bowide upon no side.
The swote smelle spronge so wide,
That it dide alle the place aboute.
Whanne I hadde smelled the savour swote,
No wille hadde I fro thens yit goo,

But somdelle neer it wente I thoo
To take it; but myn hond for drede
Ne dorste I to the rose bede,   1710
For thesteles sharpe of many maners,
Netles, thornes, and hokede breres;
For my*chel* they distourble*d*e me,
For sore I dradde to harmed be.
 The god of love, with bowe bent,
That alle day sette hadde his talent
To pursuen and to spien me,
Was stondyng by a fige tree.
And whanne he sawe hou that I
Hadde chosen so ententifly   1720
The botheum more unto my paie,
Than ony other that I say,
He toke an arowe fulle sharply whette,
And in his bowe whanne it was sette,
He streight up to his ere drough
The stronge bowe, that was so tough,
And shette att me so wondir smert*e*,
That thorough myn ye unto myn her*te*
The takel smote, and depe it wente.
And therwith alle such colde me hente, 1730
That under clothes warme and softe,
Sithen that day I have chevered ofte.
 Whanne I was hurt thus in *a* stounde,
I felle doun platte unto the grounde.
Myn herte failed and feynted ay,
And long*e* tyme a-swoone I lay.
But whanne I come out of swonyng,
And hadde witt, and my felyng,
I was alle maate, and wende fulle welle
Of bloode have loren a fulle gret delle. 1740

But certes the arowe that in me stode,
Of me ne drewe no drope of blode,
For-why I founde my wounde alle drie.
Thanne toke I with myn hondis tweie
The arowe, and ful fast out it plight*e*,
And in the pullyng sore I sight*e*.
So at the last the shaft of tree
I drough out, with the fethers thre.
But *yit* the hokede heed, y-wis,
The which*e* Beauté callid is,   1750
Gan so depe in myn herte passe,
That I it myght*e* nought arace;
But in myn herte still*e* it stode,
Al bledde I not a drope of blode.
I was bothe anguyssous and trouble.
For the peril*e* that I sawe double,
I nyste what to seye or to do,
Ne gete a leche my woundis to;
For neithir thurgh gras*se* ne rote,
Ne hadde I hope of helpe ne bote.   1760
But to the bothum evermo
Myn herte drewe; for alle my wo,
My thought was in noon other thing.
For hadde it ben in my kepyng,
It wolde have brought my lyf agayn.
For certis evenly, I dar wel seyn,
The sight oonly, and the savour,
Alegged*e* mych of my langour.
    Thanne gan I for to drawe me
Toward the bothom faire to se,   1770
And Love hadde gete hym in his throwe
Another arowe into his bowe,
And for to shete gan hym dresse;

The arowis name was Symplesse.
And whanne that love gan nyghe me nere,
He drowe it up, withouten were,
And shette at me with alle his myght,
So that this arowe anoon right
Thourgh-out*en* eigh, as it was founde,
Into myn herte hath maad a wounde.   1780
Thanne I anoon dide al my crafte
For to drawen out*e* the shafte,
And therwith alle I sighede ofte.
But in myn herte the heed was lefte,
Which ay encreside my desire
Unto the bothom drawe nere ;
And evermo that me was woo
The more desir hadde I to goo
Unto the roser, where that grewe
The freysshe bothum so bright of hewe.   1790
Betir me were to have leten be,
But it bihovede nedes me
To done right as myn herte badde.
For evere the body must be ladde
Aftir the herte ; in wele and woo,
Of force togidre they must goo.
But never this archer wolde feyne
To shete at me with alle his peyne,
And for to make me to hym mete.

    The thridde arowe he gan to shete,   1800
Whanne best his tyme he myght espie,
The which was named Curtesie,
Into myn herte he dide avale.
A-swoone I felle, bothe deed and pale ;
Long tyme I lay, and stired*e* nought,
Tille I abraide out on my thought.

And faste thanne I avysede me
To drawe oute the shafte of tree;
But evere the heed was left bihynde
For ought I couthe pulle or wynde.   1810
So sore it stikith whanne I was hit,
That by no craft I myght flit it;
But anguyssous and fulle of thought
I lefte; sich woo my wounde ay wrought,
That somonede me al-way to goo
Toward the rose, that plesede me soo;
But I ne durste in no manere
Bi-cause the archer was so nere.
For evermore gladly, as I rede,
Brent child of fier hath mych drede.   1820
And, certis, yit for al my peyne,
Though that I sigh, yit arwis reyne,
And grounde quarels sharpe of steelle,
Ne for no payne that I myghte feelle,
Yit myght I not my-silf witholde
The faire roser to biholde;
For Love me yaf sich hardement
For to fulfille his comaundement.
Upon my fete I rose up thanne
Feble, as a forwoundid man;   1830
And forth to gon *my* myght I sette,
And for the archer nolde I lette.
Toward the roser fast I drowe;
But thornes sharpe mo than ynowe
Ther were, and also thisteles thikke,
And breres brymme for to prikke,
That I ne myghte gete grace
The rowe thornes for to passe
To sene the roses fresshe of hewe.

I must abide, though it me rewe, 1840
The hegge aboute so thikke was,
That closide the roses in compas.
   But o thing lykede me right welle ;
I was so nygh, I myghte fele
Of the bothom the swote odour,
And also se the fresshe colour ;
And that right gretly likede me,
That I so neer it myghte se.
Sich joie anoon therof hadde I,
That I forgate my maladie. 1850
To sene I hadde siche delit,
Of sorwe and angre I was al quyte,
And of my woundes that I hadde thore ;
For no thing liken me myghte more,
Than dwellen by the roser ay,
And thennes never to passe away.
   But whanne a while I hadde be thare,
The god of love, which al to-share
Myn herte with his arwis kene,
Castith hym to yeve me woundis grene. 1860
He shette at me fulle hastily
An arwe named Company,
The whiche takelle is fulle able
To make these ladies merciable.
Thanne I anoon gan chaungen hewe
For grevaunce of my wounde newe,
That I agayn felle in swonyng,
And sighede sore in compleynyng.
Soore I compleynede that my sore
On me gan greven more and more. 1870
I hadde noon hope of allegeaunce ;
So nygh I drowe to desperaunce,

I rought of dethe, ne of lyfe,
Wheder that love wolde me dryfe.
Yf me a martir wolde he make,
I myght his power nought forsake.
And while for anger thus I woke,
The God of Love an arowe toke ;
Ful sharpe it was and pugnaunt,
And it was callid Faire-semblaunt,   1880
The which in no wise wole consente,
That ony lover hym repente,
To serve his love with herte and alle,
For ony perille that may bifalle.
But though this arwe was kene grounde,
As ony rasour that is founde,
To kutte and kerven at the poynt,
The God of Love it hadde anoynt
With a precious oynement,
Somdelle to yeve a-leggement   1890
Upon the woundes that he hadde
Thurgh the body in my herte made,
To helpe her sores, and to cure,
And that they may the bette endure.
But yit this arwe, withoute more,
Made in myn herte a large sore,
That in fulle grete peyne I abode.
But ay the oynement wente abrode ;
Thourgh-oute my woundes large and wide,
It spredde aboute in every side ;   1900
Thorough whos vertu and whos myght,
Myn herte joyfulle was and light.
I hadde ben deed and al to-shent
But for the precious oynement.
The shaft I drowe out of the arwe,

Rokyng for wo right wondir narwe ;
But the heed, which made me smerte,
Lefte bihynde in myn herte
With other foure, I dar wel say*e*,   1910
That never wole be take away*e*,
But the oynement halpe me wele.
And yit sich sorwe dide I fele,
That al*le* day I chaunged hewe,
Of my woundes fresshe and newe,
As men myght*e* se in my visage.
The arwis were so fulle of rage,
So variaunt of diversitee,
That men in everiche myght*e* se
Bothe gret anoy and eke swetnesse,
And joie *y*-meynt with bittirnesse.   1920
Now were they esy, now were they wode,
In h*e*m I felte bothe harme and goode.
Now sore without aleggement,
Now soft*en*yng with oynement ;
It softnede heere, & prikkith there,
Thus ese and anger to-gidre were.
The God of Love delyverly
Come lepande to me hastily,
And seide to me in gret rape,
‘ Yelde thee, for thou may not escape !   1930
May no defence availe thee heere ;
Ther*f*ore I rede make no daungere.
If thou wolt yelde thee hast*e*ly,
Thou shalt rather have mercy.
He is a foole in sikernesse,
That with daunger or stoutenesse
Rebellith there that he shulde plese ;
In sich folye is litel ese.

Be meke, where thou must nedis bowe;
To stryve ageyn is nought thi prowe.   1940
Come at oones, and have y-doo,
For I wole that it be soo.
Thanne yelde thee heere debonairly.'
And I answeride ful hombly,
' Gladly, sir ; at youre biddyng
I wole me yelde in al*le* thyng.
To youre servyse I wole me take ;
For God defende that I shulde make
Ageyn youre biddyng resistence ;
I wole not don so grete offence,   1950
For if I dide, it were no skile.
Ye may do with me what ye wile,
Save or spille, and also sloo ;
Fro you in no wise may I goo.
My lyf, my deth, is in youre honde,
I may not laste out of youre bonde.
Pleyn at youre lyst I yelde me,
Hopyng in herte, that sumtyme ye
Comfort and ese shulle me sende ;
Or ellis shortly, this is the eende,   1960
Withouten helthe I mote ay dure,
But if ye take me to youre cure.
Comfort or helthe how shuld I have,
Sith ye me hurt, but ye me save ?
The helthe of love mut be founde,
Where as they token firste her wounde.
And if ye lyst of me to make
Youre prisoner, I wole it take
Of herte and wille fully at gree.
Hoolly and pleyn Y yelde me,   1970
Withoute feynyng or feyntise,

To be governed by youre emprise.
Of you I here so myche pris,
I wole ben hool at youre devis
For to fulfille youre lykyng,
And *to* repente for no thyng,
Hopyng to have yit in some tide
Mercy, of that *that* I abide.'
And with that covenaunt yelde I me,
Anoon down knelyng upon my kne,   1980
Proferyng for to kisse his feete;
But for no thyng he wolde lete,
And seide, ' I love thee bothe and preise.
Sen that thyn aunswar doth me ease,
For thou answeride so curteisly.
For now I wote wel uttirly,
That thou art gentylle by thi speche.
For though a man fer wolde seche,
He shulde not fynden, in certeyn,
No sich answer of no vileyn;   1990
For sich a word ne myghte nought
Issue out of a vilayns thought.
Thou shalt not lesen of thi speche,
For thy helpyng wole I eche,
And eke encresen that I may.
But first I wole that thou obaye,
Fully for thyn avauntage,
Anoon to do me heere homage.
And sith kisse thou shalt my mouthe,
Which to no vilayn was never couthe   2000
For to aproche it, ne for to touche;
For sauff of cherlis I ne vouche
That they shulle never neigh it nere.
For curteis, and of faire manere,

Welle taught, and fulle of gentilnesse
He mus*e* ben, that shal me kysse,
And also of fulle of high fraunchise,
That shal atteyne to that emprise.

And first of o thing warne I thee,
That peyne and gret adversité 2010
He mote endure, and eke travaile,
That shal me serve, withoute faile.
But ther ageyns thee to comforte,
And with thi servise to desporte,
Thou mayst fulle glad and joyfulle be
So good a maister to have as me,
And lord of so highe renoun.
I bere of Love the gonfenoun,
Of curtesie the banere;
For I am of the silf manere, 2020
Gentil, curteys, meke and fre;
That who ever ententyf be
Me to honoure, doute, and serve,
And also that he hym observe
Fro trespasse and fro vilanye,
And hym governe in curtesie,
With wille and with entencioun;
For whanne he first in my prisoun
Is caught, thanne must he uttirly,
Fro thense-forth fulle bisily, 2030
Caste hym gentylle for to bee,
If he desire helpe of me.'

Anoon withoute more delay,
Withouten daunger or affray,
I bicome *tho* his man anoon,
And gave hym thankes many a oon,
And knelide doun with hondis joynt,

And made it in my port fulle queynt;
The joye wente to myn herte rote.
Whanne I hadde kissed his mouth so swote,
I hadde sich myrthe and sich likyng,   2041
It curede me of langwisshing.
He askide of me thanne hostages:—
' I have,' he seide, ' taken fele homages
Of oon and other, where I have bene
Disteyned ofte, withouten wene.
These felouns fulle of falsité,
Have many sithes biguyled me,
And thorough her falshede her lust achieved,
Wherof I repente and am agreved.   2050
And I hem gete in my daungere,
Her falshede shulle they bie fulle dere.
But for I love thee, I seie thee pleyn,
I wole of thee be more certeyn;
For thee so sore I wole now bynde,
That thou away ne shalt not wynde,
For to denyen the covenaunt,
Or don that is not avenaunt.
That thou were fals it were gret reuthe,
Sith thou semest so fulle of treuthe.'   2060
' Sire, if thee lyst to undirstande,
I merveile the askyng this demande.
For why or wherfore shulde ye
Ostages or borwis aske of me,
Or ony other sikirnesse,·
Sithen ye wote in sothfastnesse,
That ye have me susprised so,
And hole myn herte, taken me fro,
That it wole do for me no thing,
But if it be at youre biddyng?   2070

Myn herte is youres, and myn right nought
As it bihoveth, in dede and thought,
Redy in alle to worche youre wille,
Whether so turne to good or ille.
So sore it lustith you to plese,
No man therof may you desese.
Ye have theron sette sich justice,
That it is werreid in many wise.
And if ye doute it nolde obeye,
Ye may therof do make a keye, 2080
And holde it with you for ostage.'
' Now certis this is noon outrage,'
Quod Love, ' and fully I acorde ;
For of the body he is fulle lord,
That hath the herte in his tresour ;
Outrage it were to asken more.'
 Thanne of his awmener he drough,
A litelle keye fetys ynowgh,
Which was of gold polisshed clere
And seide to me, ' with this keye heere 2090
Thyn herte to me now wole I shette ;
For alle my jowelle loke and knette,
I bynde undir this litel keye,
That no wight may carie aweye ;
This keye is fulle of gret poesté.'
With which anoon he touchide me,
Undir the side fulle softely,
That he myn herte sodeynly,
Without anoye hadde spered,
That yit right nought it hath me dered. 2100
Whanne he hadde don his wille al oute,
And I hadde putte hym out of doute,
' Sire,' I seide, ' I have right gret wille,

Youre lust and plesaunce to fulfille.
Loke ye my servise take atte gree,
By thilke feith ye owe to me.
I seye nought for recreaundise,
For I nought doute of youre servise.
But the servaunt traveileth in vayne,
That for to serven doth his payne   2110
Unto that lord, which in no wise,
Kan hym no thank for his servyse.
Love seide, ' Dismaie thee nought,
Syn thou for sokour hast me sought,
In thank thi servise wole I take,
And high of degre I wole thee make,
If wikkidnesse ne hyndre thee;
But (as I hope) it shal nought be.
To worshipe no wight by aventure
May come, but if he peyne endure.   2120
Abide and suffre thy distresse,
That hurtith now; it shal be lesse,
I wote my silf what may thee save,
What medicyne thou woldist have.
And if thi trouthe to me thou kepe,
I shal unto thyn helpyng eke,
To cure thy woundes and make hem clene,
Where-so they be olde or grene;
Thou shalt be holpen at wordis fewe.
For certeynly thou shalt wolle shewe,   2130
Where that thou servest with good wille,
For to compleysshen and fulfille
My comaundementis day and nyght,
Whiche I to lovers yeve of right.'
    ' A, sire, for Goddis love,' seide I,
' Er ye passe hens, ententyfly

Youre comaundementis to me ye say,
And I shalle kepe hem if I may,
For hem to kepen is alle my thought.
And if so be I wote hem nought,   2140
Thanne may I unwityngly.
Wherfore I pray you enterely,
With alle myn herte, me to lere,
That I trespasse in no manere.'
    The god of love thanne chargide me
Anoon, as ye shalle here and see,
Worde by worde, by right emprise,
So as the Romance shalle devise.
    The maister lesith his tyme to lere,
Whanne that the disciple wole not here.   2150
It is but veyn on hym to swynke,
That on his lernyng wole not thenke.
Who-so luste love, late hym entende,
For now the Romance bigynneth to amende.
Now is good to here in fay,
If ony be that can it say,
And poynte it as the resoun is
Y-set; for other gate, ywys,
It shalle nought welle in alle thyng
Be brought to good undirstondyng.   2160
For a reder that poyntith ille,
A good sentence may ofte spille.
The book is good at the eendyng,
Y-maad of newe and lusty thyng;
For who-so wole the eendyng here,
The crafte of love he shalle mowe lere,
If that ye wole so long abide,
Tyl I this Romance may unhide
And undo the signifiance

Of this dreme into Romance. 2170
The sothfastnesse that now is hidde,
Withoute coverture shalle be kidde.
Whanne I undon have this dremyng,
Wherynne no word is of lesyng.
  'Velanye, atte the bigynnyng,
I wole,' sayde Love 'over alle thyng
Thou leve, if thou *ne* wolt be
Fals, and trespasse ageynes me.
I curse and blame generaly
Alle hem that loven vilanye ; 2180
For vilanye makith vilayn
And by his dedis a cherle is seyn.
Thise vilayns arn withouten pitee,
Frendship, love, and alle bounté.
I nyl resseyve unto my servise
Hem that ben vilayns of emprise.
  ' But undirstonde in thyn entent,
That this not myn entendement,
To clepe no wight in noo ages
Oonly gentille for his lynages. 2190
But who-so is vertuous,
And in his port nought outrageous,
Whanne sich oon thou seest thee biforn,
Though he be not gentille born,
Thou maist welle seyn, this is in soth,
That he is gentil, by-cause he doth
As longeth to a gentilman ;
Of hem noon other deme I can.
For certeynly, withouten drede,
A cherle is demed by his dede, 2200
Of hie or lowe, as ye may see,
Or of what kynrede that he bee.

Ne say nought for noon yvel wille
Thyng that is *for* to holden stille ;
It is no worshipe to mysseye.
Thou maist ensample take of Keye,
That was somtyme for mysseiyng,
Hated bothe of olde and yong.
As fer as Gaweyn the worthy,
Was preised for his curtesie,   2210
Kay was hated, for he was felle,
Of word dispitous and cruelle.
Wherfore be wise and aqueyntable,
Goodly of word, and resonable
Bothe to lesse and eke to more.
And whanne thou comest there men are,
Loke that thou have in custome ay,
First to salue hym if thou may :
And if it falle, that of hem somme
Salue thee first, be not *thou* domme,   2220
But quyte hym curteisly anoon
Without abidyng, er they goon.
   ' For no thyng eke thy tunge applye
To speke wordis of rebaudrye.
To vilayne speche in no degré
Late never thi lippe unbounden be.
For I nought holde hym, in good feith,
Curteys, that foule wordis seith.
And alle wymmen serve and preise,
And to thy power her honour reise.   2230
And if that ony myssaiere
Dispise wymmen, that thou maist here,
Blame hym, and bidde hym holde hym stille.
And *set* thy myght and alle thy wille
Wymmen and ladies for to please,

And to do thyng that may hem ese,
That they over speke good of thee,
For so thou maist best preised be.
  ' Loke fro pride thou kepe thee wele;
For thou maist bothe perceyve and fele, 2240
That pride is bothe foly and synne;
And he that pride hath hym withynne,
Ne may his herte in no wise
Meken ne souplen to servyse.
For pride is founde, in every part,
Contrarie unto Loves art.
And he that loveth trewely,
Shulde hym contene jolily,
Withoute pride in sondry wise,
And hym disgysen in queyntise. 2250
For queynte array, withoute drede,
Is no thyng proude, who takith hede;
For fresh array, as men may see,
Withoute pride may ofte be.
Mayntene thy-silf aftir thi rent,
Of robe and eke of garnement;
For many sithe faire clothyng
A man amendith in mych thyng.
And loke alwey that they be shape,
(What garnement that thou shalt make) 2260
Of hym that kan best do,
With alle that perteyneth therto.
Poyntis and sleves be welle sittande,
Right and streght on the hande.
Of shone and bootes, newe and faire,
Loke at the leest thou have a paire;
And that they sitte so fetisly,
That these ruyde may uttirly

Merveyle, sith that they sitte so pleyn,
How they come on or off ageyn.   2270
Were streite gloves, with awmere
Of silk.   And alwey with good chere
Thou yeve, if thou have richesse ;
And if thou have nought, spende the lesse.
Alwey be mery, if thou may,
But waste not thi good alway.
Have hatte of floures as fresh as May,
Chapelett of roses of Wissonday ;
For sich array ne costneth but lite.
Thyn hondis wasshe, thy teeth make white,
And lete no filthe upon thee bee.   2281
Thy nailes blak, if thou maist see,
Voide it awey delyverly,
And kembe thyn heed right jolily.
Farce not thi visage in no wise,
For that of love is not themprise ;
For love doth haten, as I fynde,
A beauté that cometh not of Kynde.
Alwey in herte I rede thee,
Glad and mery for to be,   2290
And be as joyfulle as thou can ;
Love hath no joye of sorowful man.
That yvelle is fulle of curtesie,
That knowith in his maladie ;
For ever of love the sijknesse
Is meynde with swete and bitternesse.
The sore of love is merveilous ;
For now the lover *is* joyous,
Now can he pleyne, now can he grone,
Now can he syngen, now maken mone.   2300
To day he pleyneth for hevynesse,

To morowe he pleyneth for jolynesse.
The lyf of love is fulle contrarie,
Which stounde-mele can ofte varie.
But if thou canst mirthis make,
That men in gre wole gladly take,
Do it goodly, I comaunde thee;
For men shulde, where-so-evere they be,
Do thing that hem *most* sittyng is,
For therof cometh good loos and pris.   2310
Whereof that thou be vertuous,
Ne be not straunge ne daungerous.
For if that thou good ridere bo,
Prike gladly that men may se.
In armes also if thou konne,
Pursue to thou a name hast wonne.
And if thi voice be faire and clere,
Thou shalt maken grete daungere.
Whanne to synge they goodly preye,
It is thi worship for tobeye.   2320
Also to you it longith ay,
To harpe and gitterne, daunce and play,
For if he can wel foote and daunce,
It may hym greetly do avaunce.
Among eke, for thy lady sake,
Songes and complayntes that thou make;
For that wole meven in hir herte,
Whanne they reden of thy smerte.
Loke that no man for scarce thee holde,
For that may greve thee many-folde.   2330
Resoun wole that a lover be
In his yiftes more large and fre,
Than cherles that ben not of lovyng.
For who therof can ony thyng,

He shal be leef ay for to yeve,
In londes lore who-so wolde leve;
For he that thorough a sodeyn sight,
Or for a kyssyng, anoon right
Yaff hoole his herte in wille and thought,
And to hym-silf kepith right nought,   2340
Aftir this swiffte, it is good resoun,
He yeve his good in a-boundoun.
  'Now wole I shortly heere reherce,
Of that I have seid in verce,
Al thilke sentence by and by,
In wordis fewe compendiously,
That thou the better mayst on hem thenke,
Whether so it be thou wake or wynke;
For *that* the wordis litel greve,
A man to kepe, whanne it is breve.   2350
  'Who-so with Love wole goon or ride
He mote be curteis, and voide of pride,
Mery and fulle of jolité,
And of largesse a-losed be.
  'Firste I joyne thee that heere in penaunce,
That evere withoute repentaunce,
Thou sette thy thought in thy lovyng
To laste withoute repentyng;
And thenke upon thi myrthis swete,
That shalle folowe aftir whan ye mete.   2360
  'And for thou trewe to love shalt be,
I wole and comaunde thee,
That in oo place thou sette, alle hoole,
Thyn herte, withoute halfen doole,
Fro trecherie and sikernesse;
For I lovede nevere doublenesse.
To many his herte that wole departe,

Everiche shal have but litel parte.
But of hym drede I me right nought,
That in oo place settith his thought.   2370
Therfore in oo place it sitte,
And lat it nevere thannys flitte.
For if thou yevest it in lenyng,
I holde it but a wrecchid thyng.
Therfore yeve it hoole and quyte,
And thou shalt have the more merite.
If it be lent than aftir soone,
The bounté and the thank is doone ;
But, in love, fre yeven thing
Requyrith a gret guerdonyng.   2380
Yeve it in yift al quyte fully,
And make thi yift debonairly ;
For men that yift holde more dere
That yeven *is* with gladsome chere.
That yift nought to preisen is
That man yeveth maugre his.
Whanne thou hast yeven thyn herte, as I
Have seid thee heere openly,
Thanne aventures shulle thee falle,
Which harde and hevy ben with-alle.   2390
For ofte whan thou bithenkist thee
Of thy lovyng, where-so thou be,
Fro folk thou must departe in hie,
That noon perceyve thi maladie,
[But hyde thyne harme thou must alone,
And go forth sole, and make thy mone.
Thou shalt no whyle be in o state,
But whylom colde and whylom hate ;
Nowe reed as rose, now yelowe and fade.
Such sorowe I trowe thou never hade.   2400

Cotidien, ne quarteyne,
It is nat so ful of peyne.
For often tymes it shal fall*e*
In love, amonge thy paynes all*e*,
That thou thy selfe al holy,
Foryeten shalt so utterly,
That many tymes thou shalt be
Styl as an ymage of tree,
Dome as a stoon, without steryng
Of fote or hande, wythout*e* spekyng.   2410
Than sone after al*le* thy payne,
To memorye shalt thou come agayne,
As man abashed wonder sore,
And after syghen more and more.
For wytte thou wele, withouten wene,
In such estate ful ofte have bene
That have the yvel of love assayde,
Wherthrough thou art so dismayde.
  ' After, a thought shal take the so,
That thy love is to ferre the fro :   2420
Thou shalt saye, ' God ! what maye thys be,
That I ne may my lady se ?
Myne hert alone is to her go,
And I abyde al sole in wo,
Departed from myn owne thought,
And with myne eyen se ryght nought.
Alas, myne eyen sene I ne may,
My careful hert*e* to convay !
Myne hertes gyde, but they be,
I prayse nothyng what ever they se.   2430
Shule they abyde than ? nay ;
But gonne and visiten without*e* delay
That myne herte desyreth so.

For certaynly, but yf they go,
A foole my selfe I may wel holde,
Whan I ne se what myne herte wolde.
Wherfore I wol gone her to sene,
Or eased shal I never bene,
But I have som tokenyng.'
Then gost thou forth withoute dwelling,   2440
But oft thou faylest of thy desyre,
Er thou mayst come her any nere,]
And wastest in vayn thi passage.
Thanne fallest thou in a newe rage ;
For want of sight thou gynnest morne,
And homewarde pensyf thou dost retorne.
In gret myscheef thanne shalt thou bee,
For thanne agayne shalle come to thee
Sighes and pleyntes with newe woo,
That no yechyng prikketh soo.   2450
Who wote it nought, he may go lere,
Of hem that bien love so dere.
No thyng thyn herte appesen may,
That ofte thou wolt goon and assay,
If thou maist seen by aventure
Thi lyves joy, thine hertis cure,
So that bi grace, if thou myght
Atteyne of hire to have a sight.
Thanne shalt thou done noon other dede,
But with that sight thyne eyen fede.   2460
That faire freshe whanne thou maist see,
Thyne herte shalle so ravysshed be,
That nevere thou woldest, thi thankis, lete
Ne remove, for to see that swete.
The more thou seest in sothfastnesse,
The more thou coveytest of that swetnesse,

The more thine herte brenneth in fier,
The more thine herte is in desire.
For who considreth every deelle,
It may be likned wondir welle,   2470
The peyne of love unto a fere ;
For evermore thou neighest nere
Thought, or whoo so that it bee,
For verray sothe I telle it thee,
The hatter evere shalle thou brenne,
As experience shalle thee kenne.
Where so comest in ony coost,
Who is next fuyre he brenneth moost.
And yitt forsothe for alle thine hete,
Though thou for love swelte and swete,   2480
Ne for no thyng thou felen may,
Thou shalt not willen to passen away.
And though thou go, yitt must thee, nede,
Thenke alle day, on hir fairhede,
Whom thou biheelde with so good wille ;
And holde thi-silf biguyled ille,
That thou ne haddest noon hardement,
To shewe hir ought of thyne entent.
Thyn herte fulle sore thou wolt dispise,
And eke repreve of cowardise,   2490
That thou so dulle in every thing,
Were domme for drede, withoute spekyng.
Thou shalt eke thenke thou didest folye,
That thou were hir so faste bye,
And durst not auntre thee to saye
Som thyng er thou cam awaye ;
For thou haddist nomore wonne,
To speke of hir whanne thou bigonne:
But yitt she wolde for thy sake,

In armes goodly thee have take,   2500
It shulde have be more worth to thee,
Than of tresour gret plenté.
  ' Thus shalt thou morne and eke compleyne,
And gete enchesoun to goone ageyne,
Unto thy walke, or to thi place,
Where thou biheelde her fleshly face.
And never for fals suspeccioun,
Thou woldest fynde *occasioun*,
For to gone unto hire hous.
So art thou thanne desirous,   2510
A sight of hir for to have,
If thou thine honour myghtist save,
Or ony erande myghtist make
Thider, for thi loves sake,
Fulle fayn thou woldist, but for drede
Thou gost not, lest that men take hede ;
Wherfore I rede in thi goyng,
And also in thyne ageyn-comyng,
Thou be welle ware that men ne wite ;
Feyne thee other cause than itte,   2520
To go that weye, or faste bye ;
To hele wel is no folye.
And if so be it happe thee,
That thou thi love there maist see,
In siker wise thou hir salewe,
Wherewith thy colour wole transmewe,
And eke thy blode shal al to quake,
Thyne hewe eke chaungen for hir sake.
But word and witte, with chere fulle pale,
Shulle wante for to telle thy tale.   2530
And if thou maist so fer forth wynne,
That thou resoun derst bigynne,

And woldist seyn thre thingis or mo,
Thou shalt fulle scarsly seyn the two.
Though thou bithenke thee never so welle,
Thou shalt foryete yit somdelle.
　　But if thou dele with trecherie.
For false lovers mowe alle folye
Seyn what hem lust withouten drede,
They be so double in her falshede,　　　　　2540
For they in herte cunne thenke a thyng
And seyn another, in her spekyng.
And whanne thi speche is eendid alle,
Ryght thus to thee it shalle byfalle;
If ony word thanne come to mynde,
That thou to seye hast left bihynde,
Thanne thou shalt brenne in gret martire;
For thou shalt brenne as ony fiere,
This is the stryf and eke the affray,
And the batelle that lastith ay.　　　　　2550
This bargeyn eende may never take,
But if that she thi pees wille make.
　　' And whanne the nyght is comen, anoon
A thosande angres shalle come uppon.
To bedde as fast thou wolt thee dighte,
Where thou shalt have but smal delite;
For whanne thou wenest for to slepe,
So fulle of peyne shalt thou crepe,
Sterte in thi bedde aboute fulle wide,
And turne fulle ofte on every side;　　　　　2560
Now dounward groff, and now upright,
And walowe in woo the longe nyght,
Thine armys shalt thou sprede abrode,
As man in werre were forweriede.
Thanne shalle thee come a remembraunce

Of hir shappe and hir semblaunce,
Whereto none other may be pere.
And wite thou wel withoute were,
That thee shal *seme* somtyme that nyght,
That thou hast hir that is so bright,   2570
Naked bitwene thyne armes there,
Alle sothfastnesse as though it were.
Thou shalt make castels thanne in Spayne,
And dreme of joye, alle but in vayne,
And thee deliten of right nought,
While thou so slomrest in that thought,
That is so swete and delitable,
The which in soth nys but fable,
For it ne shalle no while laste.
Thanne shalt thou sighe and wepe faste, 2580
And say, 'Dere God, what thing is this?
My dreme is turned alle amys,
Which was fulle swete and apparent,
But now I wake it is al shent!
Now yede this mery thought away.
Twenty tymes upon a day
I wolde this thought wolde come ageyne,
For it aleggith welle my peyne.
It makith me fulle of joyfulle thought,
It sleth me that it lastith noght.   2590
A, Lord! why nyl ye me socoure?
The joye I trowe that I langoure,
The deth I wolde me shulde sloo,
While I lye in hir armes twoo.
Myne harme is harde withouten wene,
My gret unease fulle ofte I meene.
But wolde Love do so I myghte
Have fully joye of hir so brighte,

My peyne were quytte me rychely.
Allas, to grete a thing aske I ! 2600
Hit is but foly, and wrong wenyng,
To aske so outrageous a thyng.
And who so askith folily,
He mote be warned hastily;
And I ne wote what I may saye,
I am so fer out of the waye;
For I wolde have fulle gret likyng,
And fulle gret joye of lasse thing.
For wolde she of hir gentylnesse,
Withoute more, me oonys kysse, 2610
It were to me a grete guerdoun,
Relees of alle my passioun.
But it is harde to come therto;
Alle is but folye, that I do,
So high I have myne herte sette,
Where I may no comfort gette.
I wote not where I seye welle or nought;
But this I wote wel in my thought,
That it were better of hir alloone,
For to stynte my woo and moone, 2620
A loke on hir i-caste goodly,
That for to have al utterly,
Of an other alle hoole the pley.
A Lord, where I shalle byde the day
That evere she shalle my lady be?
He is fulle cured, that may hir see.
A ! God ! whanne shal the dawnyng springe ?
To liggen thus is an angry thyng ;
I have no joye thus heere to lye,
Whanne that my love is not me bye. 2620
  A man to lyen hath gret disese,

Which may not slepe ne reste in ese.
I wolde it dawed, and were now day,
And that the nyght were went away,
For were it day, I wolde uprise.
A ! slowe sonne, shewe thine enprise !
Spede thee to sprede thy beemys right*e*,
And chace the derknesse of the nyght*e*,
To putte away the stoundes stronge,
Whiche in me lasten alle to longe.'   2640
    ' The nyght shalt thou contene soo,
Withoute rest, in peyne and woo ;
If evere thou knewe of love distresse,
Thou sha*l*t mowe lerne in that sijknesse.
And thus enduryng shalt thou lye
And ryse on morwe up erly,
Out of thy bedde, and harneyse thee
Er evere dawnyng thou maist see.
Alle pryvyly thanne sha*l*t thou goon,
What whider it be, thy silf alloon,   2650
For reyne, or hayle, for snowe, for slete,
Thider she dwellith that is so swete,
The which may falle a-slepe be,
And thenkith but lytel upon thee.
Thanne shalt thou goon, ful foule a-feerd,
Loke if the gate be unspered,
And waite without in woo and peyne,
Fulle yvel a-coolde in wynde and reyne.
Thanne sha*l*t thou go the dore bifore,
If thou maist fynde*n* ony score,   2660
Or hoole, or reeft, what evere it were ;
Thanne shalt thou stoupe, and lay to ere,
If they withynne a slepe be ;
I mene alle save the lady free.

Whom wakyng if thou maist aspie,
Go putte thi silf in jupartie,
To aske grace, and thee bimene,
That she may wite, withoute wene,
That thou *al* nyght no rest hast hadde,
So sore for hir thou were bystadde.   2670
Wommen wel oughte pité to take
Of hem that sorwen for her sake.
And loke, for love of that relyke,
That thou thenke noon other lyke.
For whanne thou hast so gret annoy,
Shalle kysse thee er thou go away,
And holde that in fulle gret deynté.
And for that no man shal thee see
Bifore the hous, ne in the way,
Loke thou be goone ageyn er day. .   2680
Such comyng, and such goyng,
Such hevynesse, and such walkyng,
Makith lovers, withouten ony wene,
Under her clothes pale and lene,
For Love leveth colour ne cleernesse;
Who loveth trewe hath no fatnesse.
Thou shalt wel by thy silfe see
That thou must nedis assaid be.
For men that shape hem other weye
Falsly her ladyes for to bitraye,   2690
It is no wonder though they be fatte;
With false othes her loves they gatte;
For ofte I see suche losengours
Fatter than abbatis or priours.
  'Yit with o thing I charge thee,
That is to seye, that thou large be
Unto the mayde, that hir doith serve,

So best hir thanke thou shalt deserve.
Yeve hir yiftes, and gete hir grace,
For so thou may thanke purchace,   2700
That she thee worthy holde and free.
Thi lady, and alle that may thee see,
Also hir servauntes worshipe ay,
And please as mych*el* as thou may;
Grete good thorough hem may come to thee,
Bi-cause with hir they ben pryvé.
They shal hir telle hou they thee fande
Curteis and wys, and welle doande,
And she shalle preise welle thee more.
Loke oute of londe thou be not fore;   2710
And if such cause thou have, that thee
Bihoveth to gone out of contree,
Leve hoole thin herte in hostage,
Tille thou ageyn make thi passage.
Thenke longe to see the swete thyng
That hath thine herte in hir kepyng.
   ' Now have I tolde thee, in what wise
A lovere shalle do me servise.
Do it thanne, if thou wolt have
The meede that thou aftir crave.'   2720
   Whanne Love alle this hadde boden me,
I seide hym:—' Sire, how may it be
That lovers may in such manere,
Endure the peyne ye have seid heere?
I merveyle me wonder faste,
How ony man may lyve or laste
In suche peyne, and suche brennyng,
In sorwe and thought, and such sighing,
Aye unrelesed woo to make,
Whether so it be they slepe or wake.   2730

In such annoy contynuely,
As helpe me God this merveile I
How man, but he were maad of stele,
Myght*e* lyve a monthe, such peynes to fele.'
    The God of Love thanne seide me,
' Freend, by the feith I owe to thee,
May no man have good, but he it bye.
A man loveth more tendirly
The thyng that he hath bought most dere,
For wite thou welle, withouten were,   2740
In thanke that thyng is taken more,
For which a man hath suffred sore.
Certis no wo ne may atteyne,
Unto the sore of loves peyne.
Noon yvel ther-to ne may amounte,
No more than a man *may* counte
The dropes that of the water be.
For drye as welle the greet*e* see
Thou myghtist, as the harmes telle
Of hem that with Love dwelle   2750
In servyse; for peyne hem sleeth,
And that ech man wolde fle the deeth,
And trowe thei shulde nevere escape,
Nere that Hope couthe hem make,
Glad as man in prisoun sett*e*,
And may not geten for to ete
But barly breed, and watir pure,
And lyeth in vermyn and in ordure;
With alle this yitt can he lyve,
Good-hope such comfort hath hym yeve,   2760
Which maketh wene that he shalle be
Delyvered and come to liberté;
In fortune is *his* fulle trist.

Though he lye in strawe or dust,
In Hoope is alle his susteynyng.
And so for lovers in her wenyng,
Whiche love hath shitte in his prisoun ;
Good-hope is her salvacioun.
Good-hope, how sore that they smerte,
Yeveth hem bothe wille and herte   2770
To profre her body to martire ;
For Hope so sore doith hem desire
To suffre ech harme that men devise,
For joye that aftirward shalle aryse.
　Hope in desire cacche victorie,
In hope of love is alle the glorie,
For Hope is alle that love may yeve ;
Nere Hope, ther shulde no lover lyve,
Blessid be Hope, which with desire,
Avaunceth lovers in such manere.   2780
Good-hope is curteis for to please,
To kepe lovers from alle disese.
Hope kepith his londe, and wole abide,
For ony perille that may be-tyde ;
For Hope to lovers, as most cheef,
Doth hem endure alle myscheef ;
Hope is her helpe whanne myster is.
And I shalle yeve thee eke iwys,
Three other thingis, that gret solas
Doith to hem that be in my las.   2790
　' The firste good that may be founde,
To hem that in my lace be bounde,
Is Swete-thought, for to recorde
Thing wherwith thou canst accorde
Best in thyne herte ; where she be,
Thenkyng in absence is good to thee. '

Whanne ony lover doth compleyne,
And lyveth in distresse and in peyne,
Thanne Swete-thought shal come as blyve,
Awey his angre for to dryve.   2800
It makith lovers to have remembraunce
Of comfort, and of high plesaunce,
That Hope hath hight hym for to wynne.
For Thought anoon thanne shalle bygynne,
As ferre, God wote, as he can fynde,
To make a mirrour of his mynde,
For to biholde he wole not lette.
Hir persone he shalle a-fore hym sette,
 Hir laughing eyen, persaunt and clere,
Hir shappe, hir fourme, hir goodly chere,   2810
Hir mouth that is so gracious,
So swete, and eke so saverous,
Of alle hir fetures he shalle take heede,
His eyen with alle hir lymes fede.
 'Thus Swete-thenkyng shalle aswage
The peyne of lovers, and her rage.
Thi joye shalle double, withoute gesse,
Whanne thou thenkist on hir semlynesse,
Or of hir laughing, or of hir chere,
That to thee made thi lady dere.   2820
This comfort wole I that thou take,
And if the nexte thou wolt forsake
Which is not lesse saverous,
Thou shuldist not ben to daungerous.
 'The secounde shal be Swete-speche,
That hath to many oon be leche,
To bringe hem out of woo and were,
And helpe many a bachilere,
And many a lady sent socoure,

That have loved paramour,   2830
Thorough spekyng, whanne they myght*en* heere,
Of her lovers to hem so dere.
To me it voidith alle her smerte,
The which is closed in her herte.
In herte it makith hem glad and light,
Speche, whanne they mowe have sight.
And therfore now it cometh to mynde,
In olde dawes as I fynde,
That clerkis writen that hir knewe,
Ther was a lady fresh of hewe,   2840
Which of hir love made a songe
On hym, for to remembre amonge,
In which she seide, 'Whanne that I here
Speken of hym that is so dere,
To me it voidith alle smerte,
Iwys he sittith so nere myne herte.
To speke of hym at eve or morwe,
It cureth me of alle my sorwe.
To me is noon so high plesaunce
As of his persone dalyaunce.'   2850
She wist*e* fulle welle that Swete-spekyng
Comfortith in fulle myche thyng.
Hir love she hadde fulle welle assaid,
Of hem she was fulle welle apaied;
To speke of hym hir joye was sette.
Therfore I rede thee that thou gett*e*
A felowe that can welle concele,
And kepe thi counselle, and welle hele,
To whom go shewe hoolly thine herte,
Bothe welle and woo, joye and smerte: 2860
To gete comfort to hym thou goo,
And pryvyly bitwene yow twoo,

Yee shalle spoke of that goodly thyng,
That hath thyne herte in hir kepyng;
Of hir beauté and hir semblaunce,
And of hir goodly countenaunce;
Of alle thi state, thou shalt hym seye,
And aske hym counseille how thou may
Do ony thyng that may hir plese,
For it to thee shalle do gret ese,   2870
That he may wite thou trust hym soo,
Bothe of thi wele and of thi woo.
And if his herte to love be sett,
His companye is myche the bett,
For resoun wole he shewe to thee
Alle uttirly his pryvyté,
And what she is he loveth so
To thee pleynly he shal undo,
Withoute drede of ony shame,
Bothe telle hir renoun and hir name.   2880
Thanne shalle he forther ferre and nere,
And namely to thi lady dere,
In syker wise, yee, every other
Shalle helpen as his owne brother,
In trouthe withoute doublenesse,
And kepen cloos in sikernesse.
For it is noble thing in fay*e*,
To have a man thou darst say*e*
Thy pryvé counselle every deelle,
For that wole comforte thee right welle,   2890
And thou shalt holde thee welle apayed,
Whanne such a freend thou hast assayed.
  'The thridde good of gret comforte
That yeveth to lovers most disporte,
Comyth of sight and of biholdyng,

That clepid is Swete-lokyng,
The whiche may noon ese do,
Whanne thou art fer thy lady fro ;
Wherfore thou prese alwey to be
In place, where thou maist hir see.   2900
For it is thyng most amerous,
Most delytable and faverous,
For to a-swage a mannes sorowe,
To sene his lady by the morwe.
For it is a fulle noble thing
Whanne thyne eyen have metyng
With that relike precious,
Wherof they be so desirous.
But al day after, soth it is,
They have no drede to faren amysse,   2910
They dreden neither wynde ne reyne,
Ne noon other maner peyne.
For whanne thyne eyen were thus in blisse,
Yit of hir curtesie, ywysse,
Alloone they can not have her ioye,
But to the herte they conveye,
Parte of her blisse ; to hym thou sende,
Of alle this harme to make an ende.
The eye is a good messangere,
Which can to the herte in such manere   2920
Tidyngis sende, that *he* hath sene
To voide hym of his peynes clene.
Wherof the herte rejoiseth soo
That a gret partye of his woo
Is voided, *and* putte awey to flight.
Right as the derknesse of the nyght
Is chased with clerenesse of the mone,
Right so is al his woo fulle soone

Devoided clene, whanne that the sight
Biholden may that freshe wight   2930
That the herte desireth soo,
That al his derknesse is a-goo;
For thanne the herte is alle at ese,
Whanne they sene that may hem plese.
  'Now have I declared thee alle oute,
Of that thou were in drede and doute;
For I have tolde thee feithfully,
What thee may curen utterly,
And alle lovers that wole be
Feithfulle, and fulle of stabilité.   2940
Good-hope alwey kepe bi thi side,
And Swete-thought make eke abide,
Swete-lokyng and Swete-speche,
Of alle thyne harmes thei shalle be leche.
Of every thou shalt have gret plesaunce,
If thou canst bide in suffraunce,
And serve wel withoute feyntise,
Thou shalt be quyte of thyne emprise,
With more guerdoun, if that thou lyve;
But alle this tyme this I thee yeve.'   2950
    The God of Love, whanne al the day,
Hadde taught me, as ye have herd say,
And enfourmed compendiously,
He vanyshide awey alle sodeynly,
And I alloone lefte alle soole,
So fulle of compleynt and of doole,
For I sawe no man there me by.
My woundes me grevede wondirly;
Me for to curen no thyng I knewe,
Save the bothom bright of hewe,   2960
Wheron was sett hoolly my thought;

Of other comfort knewe I nought.
But it were thorugh the God of Love,
I knew not elles to my bihove
That myght*e* me ease or comfort gete,
But if he wolde hym entermete.
The roser was, withoute doute,
I-closed with an hegge withoute,
As ye toforn have herd me seyne;
As fast I bisiede, and wolde fayne   2970
Have passed the hay, if I myght*e*
Have geten ynne by ony slight*e*
Unto the bothom so faire to see.
But evere I dradde blamed to be,
If men wolde have suspeccioun
That I wolde of entencioun
Have stole the roses that there were;
Therfore to entre I was in fere.
But at the last, as I bithought*e*
Whether I shulde passe or nought*e*,   2980
I sawe come with a glad*e* chere
To me, a lusty bachelere,
Of good stature, and of good hight*e*,
And Bialacoil forsothe he hight*e*.
Sone he was *un*to Curtesie,
And he me grauntide fulle gladly,
The passage of the outter hay*e*,
And seide:—' Sir, how that yee may*e*
Passe, if youre wille be,
The fresh*e* roser for to see,   2990
And yee the swete savour fele.
Youre warrans may *I be* right wele,
So thou thee kepe fro folye,
Shalle no man do thee vylanye.

If I may helpe you in ought,
I shalle not feyne, dredeth nought;
For I am bounde to youre servise,
Fully devoide of feyntise.'
Thanne unto Bialacoil saide I,
'I thanke you, sir, full hertely,   3000
And youre biheeste take at gre,
That ye so goodly profer me;
To you it cometh of gret fraunchise,
That ye me profer youre servise.'
Thanne aftir fully delyverly,
Thorough the breres anoon wente I,
Wherof encombred was the haye.
I was wel plesed, the soth to saye,
To se the bothom faire and swote,
So freshe sprange out of the rote.   3010
    And Bialacoil me servede welle,
Whanne I so nygh me myghte fele
Of thilke bothom the swete odour,
And so lusty hewed of colour.
But thanne a cherle (foule hym bityde!)
Biside the roses gan hym hyde,
To kepe the roses of that roser,
Of whom the name was Daunger.
This cherle was hid there in the greves,
Kovered with gras and with leves,   3020
To spie and take whom that he fonde
Unto that roser putte an honde.
He was not soole, for ther was moo;
For with hym were other twoo
Of wikkid maners, and yvel fame.
That oon was clepid by his name,
Wykked-tonge, God yeve hym sorwe!

For neither at eve ne at morwe,
He can of no man goode speke ;
On many a just man doth he wreke.   3030
Ther was a womman eke, that highte
Shame, that, who can reken righte,
Trespace was hir fadir name,
Hir moder Resoun ; and thus was Shame
Brought of these ilke twoo.
And yitt hadde Trespasse never adoo
With Resoun, ne never ley hir bye,
He was so hidous and so oughlye,
I mene this that Trespas highte ;
But Resoun conceyveth, of a sighte,   3040
Shame, of that I spake aforne.
And whanne that Shame was thus borne,
It was ordeyned, that Chastité
Shulde of the roser lady be,
Which, of the bothoms more and lasse,
With sondré folk assailed was,
That she ne wiste what to doo.
For Venus hir assailith soo,
That nyght and day from hir she stale
Bothoms and roses over alle.   3050
To Resoun thanne praieth Chastité,
Whom Venus hath flemed over the see,
That she hir doughter wolde hir lene,
To kepe the roser fresh and grene.
Anoon Resoun to Chastité
Is fully assented that it be,
And grauntide hir, at hir request,
That Shame, by-cause she is honest,
Shalle keper of the roser be.
And thus to kepe it ther were three,   3060

That noon shulde hardy be ne bolde,
Were he yong or were he olde
Ageyn hir wille awey to bere
Bothoms ne roses, that there were.
I hadde wel spedde, hadde I not bene
Awayted with these three, and sene.
For Bialacoil, that was so faire,
So gracious and so debonaire,
 Quytt hym to me fulle curteislye,
And me to please bade that I   3070
Shulde drawe me to the bothom nere;
Prese in to touche the rosere
Which bare the roses, he yaf me leve;
This graunte ne myghte but lytel greve.
And for he sawe it likede me,
Ryght nygh the bothom pullede he
A leef alle grene, and yaff me that,
The whiche fulle nygh the bothom sat;
I made of that leefe fulle queynte.
And whanne I felte I was aqueynte   3080
With Bialacoil, and so pryvé,
I wende alle at my wille hadde be,
Thanne waxe I hardy for to telle
To Bialacoil hou me bifelle,
Of Love, that toke and wounded me;
And seide: ' Sir, so mote I thee,
I may no joye have in no wise,
Uppon no side, but it rise;
For sithe (if 1 shalle not feyne)
In herte I have hadde so gret peyne   3090
So gret annoy, and such affray,
That I ne wote what I shalle say;
 I drede youre wrath to disserve.

Lever me were, that knyves kerve
My body shulde in pecys smalle,
Than in any wise it shulde falle,
That ye wratthed shulde ben with me.'
' Sey boldely thi wille,' quod he,
' I nyl be wroth, if that I may,
For nought that thou shalt to me say.'   3100
    Thanne seide I, ' Sir, not you displease,
To knowen of myn gret unnese,
In which oonly love hath me brought;
For peynes gret, disese and thought,
Fro day to day he doth me drye;
Supposeth not, sir, that I lye.
In me fyve woundes dide he make,
The soore of whiche shalle nevere slake,
But ye the bothom graunte me,
Which is moost passaunt of beauté,   3110
My lyf, my deth, and my martire,
And tresour that I moost desire.'
Thanne Bialacoil, affrayed alle,
Seyde, ' Sir, it may not falle;
That ye desire it may not arise.
What! wolde ye shende me in this wise?
A mochel foole thanne I were,
If I suffride you awey to bere
The freshe bothom, so faire of sight.
For it were neither skile ne right,   3120
Of the roser ye broke the rynde,
Or take the rose aforn his kynde;
Ye are not curteys to asken it.
Late it stille on the roser sitte,
And late it growe til it amended be,
And perfytly come to beauté.

I nolde not that it pulled were,
Fro th*ilke* roser that it bere,
To me it is so leef and deere.'
    With that sterte oute anoon Daungere,   3130
Out of the place *where* he was hidde.
His malice in his chere was kidde;
Fulle grete he was and blak of hewe,
Sturdy, and hidous, who-so hym knewe,
Like sharp urchouns his here was growe,
His eyes rede sparkling as the fire glowe,
His nose frounced fulle kirked stoode,
He come criande as he were woode,
And seide, ' Bialacoil, telle me why
Thou bryngest hider so boold*ely*   3140
Hym that so nygh *cam* the roser?
Thou worchist in a wrong maner;
He thenkith to dishonoure thee,
Thou art wel worthy to have maugree,
To late hym of the roser wite;
Who serveth a feloun is yvel quitte.
Thou woldist have doon gret bounté,
And he with shame wolde quyte thee.
Fle hennes felowe! I rede thee goo!
It wanteth litel *I* wole thee sloo;   3150
For Bialacoil ne knewe thee nought,
Whanne thee to serve he sette his thought;
For thou wolt shame hym if thou myght,
 Bothe ageyn*es* resoun and right.
I wole no more in thee affye,
That comest so slyghly for tespye;
For it preveth wonder welle,
Thy slight and tresoun every deelle.'
I durst*e* no more there make abode,

For thi*lke* cherl he was so wode; 3160
So gan he threte and manace,
And thurgh the haye he dide me chace.
For feer of hym I tremblyde and quoke,
So cherlishly his heed it shoke;
And seide, if eft he myght*e* me take,
I shulde not from his hondis scape.
  Thanne Bialacoil is fledde and mate,
And I alle soole disconsolate,
Was left aloone in peyne and thought,
For shame to deth I was nygh brought. 3170
Thanne thought I on myn high*e* foly,
How that my body, utterly,
Was yeve to peyne and to martire;
And therto hadde I so gret ire,
That I ne durst*e* the hayes passe;
There was noon hope, there was no grace.
I trowe nevere man wiste of peyne,
But he were laced in Loves cheyne;
Ne no man *wiste*, and sooth it is,
But if he love, what anger is. 3180
Love holdith his heest to me right wele,
Whanne peyne he seide I shulde fele.
Noon herte may thenke, ne tunge seyne,
A quarter of my woo and peyne.
I myght*e* not with the anger laste;
Myn herte in poynt was for to barste,
Whanne I thought on the rose, that soo
That was thurgh Daunger cast me froo.
  A longe while stode I in that state,
Til that me saugh so madde and mate 3190
The lady of the high*e* warde,
Which from hir tour lokide thiderward.

Resoun men clepe that lady,
Which from hir tour delyverly,
Come doun to me withoute more.
But she was neither yong, ne hoore,
No high ne lowe, ne fat ne lene,
But best, as it were in a mene.
Hir eyen twoo were cleer and lighte
As ony candelle that brenneth brighte ;   3200
And on hir heed she hadde a crowne.
Hir semede wel an high persoune;
For rounde enviroun hir crownet
Was fulle of riche stonys frett.
Hir goodly semblaunt, by devys,
I trowe were maad in paradys ;
For nature hadde nevere such a grace,
 To forge a werk of such compace.
For certeyn, but-if the letter lye,
God hym-silf, that is so high,   3210
Made hir aftir his ymage,
And yaff hir sith sich avauntage,
That she hath myght and seignurie
To kepe men from alle folye ;
Who-so wole trowe hir lore,
Ne may offenden nevermore.

   And while I stode thus derk and pale,
Resoun bigan to me hir tale,
She seide : ' Alhayle, my swete freende !
Foly and childhoode wole thee sheende,   3220
Which ye have putt in gret affray ;
Thou hast bought deere the tyme of May,
That made thyn herte mery to be.
In yvelle tyme thou wentist to see
The gardyne, wherof Ydilnesse

Bare the keye, and was maistresse
Whanne thou *yedest* in the daunce
With hir, and hadde a-queyntaunce :
Hir aqueyntaunce is perilous,
First softe, and aftir noious ;   3230
She hath *the* trasshed, withoute wene ;
The God of Love hadde the not sene,
Ne hadde Ydilnesse thee conveyed
In the verger where Myrthe hym pleyed.
If Foly have supprised thee,
Do so that it recovered be ;
And be wel ware to take nomore
Counsel, that greveth aftir sore ;
He is wise that wole hym silf chastise.
And though a yong man in ony wise   3240
Trespace amonge, and do foly,
Late hym not tarye, but hastily
Late hym amende what so be mys.
And eke I counseile thee, iwys,
Tho god of love hoolly foryete,
That hath thee in sich peyne sette,
And thee in herte tourmented soo.
I can*not* sene how thou maist goo
Other weyes to garisoun ;
For Daunger, that is so feloun,   3250
Felly purposith thee to werye,
Which is ful cruel the soth to seye.
  ' And yitt of Daunger cometh no blame,
In rewarde of my doughter Shame,
Which hath the roses in hir warde,
As she that may be no musarde.
And Wikked-tunge is with these two,
That suffrith no man thider goo ;

For er a thing be do he shalle,
Where that he cometh, over alle,   3260
In fourty places, if it be sought,
Seye thyng that nevere was don ne wrought;
So moche tresoun is in his male,
Of falsnesse for to seyne a tale.
Thou delest with angry folk, ywis;
Wherfore to thee bettir *it* is,
From th*ilke* folk awey to fare,
For they wole make thee lyve in care.
This is the yvelle that love they calle,
Wherynne ther is but foly alle,   3270
For love is foly everydelle;
Who loveth, in no wise may do welle,
Ne sette his thought on no good werk.
His scole he lesith, if he be a clerk;
Or other craft eke, if he be,
He shal not thryve therynne; for he
In love shal have more passioun,
Than monke, hermyte, or chanoun.
The peyne is hard out of mesure,
The joye may eke no while endure;   3280
And in the possessioun,
Is myche tribulacioun;
The joye it is so short lastyng,
And but in happe is the getyng;
For I see there many in travaille,
That atte laste foule fayle.
I was no thyng thi counseler,
Whanne thou were maad the omager
Of God of Love to hastily;
Ther was no wisdom but foly.   3290
Thyne herte was joly, but not sage,

Whanne thou were brought in sich arrage,
To yelde thee so redily,
And to Love of his grete maistrie.
  ' I rede thee Love awey to dryve,
That makith thee recche not of thi lyve.
The foly more fro day to day
Shal growe, but thou it putte away.
Take with thy teeth the bridel faste,
To daunte thyne herte ; and eke thee caste, 3300
If that thou maist, to gete thee defence
For to redresse thi first offence.
Who-so his herte alwey wole leve,
Shal fynde amonge that shal hym greve.'
    Whanne I hir herde thus me chastise,
I answerd in ful angry wise.
I prayed hir ceessen of hir speche,
Outher to chastise me or teche,
To bidde me my thought refreyne,   3309
Which Love hath caught in his demeyne :—
' What ! wene ye love wole consente,
That me assailith with bowe bente,
To drawe myne herte out of his honde,
Which is so qwikly in his bonde ?
That ye counseyle, may nevere be ;
For whanne he firste arestide me,
He took myne herte so hoole hym tille,
That it is no thyng at my wille ;
He thought it so hym for to obey,
That he it sparrede with a key.   3320
I pray yow late me be alle stille,
For ye may welle, if that ye wille,
Youre wordis waste in idilnesse ;
For utterly withouten gesse,

Alle that ye seyn is but in veyne.
Me were lever dye in the peyne,
Than Love to meward shulde arette
Falsheed, or tresoun on me sette.
I wole me gete prys or blame,
And love trewe to save my name; 3330
Who that me chastisith, I hym hate.'
  With that word Resoun wente hir gate,
Whanne she saugh for no sermonynge
She myghte me fro my foly brynge.
Thanne dismaied, I, lefte alle sool,
Forwery, for-wandred as a fool,
For I ne knewe no cherisaunce,
Thanne felle into my remembraunce,
How Love bade me to purveye
A felowe, to whom I myghte seye 3340
My counselle and my pryveté,
For that shulde moche availe me.
With that bithought I me, that I
Hadde a felowe faste by,
Trewe and siker, curteys, and hende,
And he was called by name a freende;
A trewer felowe was no-wher noon.
In haste to hym I wente anoon,
And to hym alle my woo I tolde,
Fro hym right nought I wolde witholde. 3350
I tolde hym alle withoute were,
And made my compleynt on Daungere.
How for to see he was hidous,
And to me-ward contrarious;
The whiche thurgh his cruelté,
Was in poynt to *have* meygned me;
With Bialacoil whanne he me sey

Withynne the gardeyn walke and pley,
Fro me he made hym for to go,
And I bilefte aloone in woo ;   3360
I durste no lenger with hym speke,
For Daunger seide he wolde be wreke,
Whanne than he sawe how I wente,
 The freshe bothom for to hente,
If I were hardy to come neer,
Bitwene the hay and the roser.
    This freend whanne he wiste of my thought,
He discomfortede me right nought,
But seide, ' Felowe, be not so madde,
Ne so abaysshed nor bystadde.   3370
My silf I knowe fulle welle Daungere,
And how he is feers of his cheere,
At prime temps, Love to manace ;
Ful ofte I have ben in his caas.
A feloun firste though that he be,
Aftir thou shalt hym souple se.
Of longe passed I knewe hym welle ;
Ungoodly first though men hym feele,
He wole meke aftir in his beryng
Been, for service and obeyssyhng.   3380
I shal thee telle what thou shalt doo·:—
Mekely I rede thou go hym to,
Of herte pray hym specialy
Of thy trespace to have mercy,
And hote hym welle, here to plese,
That thou shalt nevermore hym displese.
Who can best serve of flaterie,
Shalle please Daunger most uttirly.'
    Mi freend hath seid to me so wel,
That he me esid hath somdelle,   3390

And eke allegged of my torment ;
For thurgh hym had I hardement
Agayn to Daunger for to go,
To preve if I myghte meke hym soo.
To Daunger came I alle ashamed,
The which aforn me hadde blamed,
Desiryng for to pese my woo ;
But over hegge durst I not goo,
For he forbede me the passage.
I fonde hym cruel in his rage,   3400
And in his honde a gret burdoun.
To hym I knelide lowe a-doun,
Ful meke of port, and symple of chere,
And seide, ' sir, I am comen heere
Oonly to aske of you mercy.
That greveth me fulle gretely
That evere my lyf I wratthede you,
But for to amenden I am come now ;
With alle my myght, bothe loude and stille,
To doon right at youre owne wille ;   3410
For Love made me for to doo
That I have trespassed hidirto ;
Fro whom I ne may withdrawe myne herte ;
Yit shalle *I* never, for joy ne smerte,
What so bifalle good or ille,
Offende more ageyn youre wille.
Lever I have endure disese,
Than do that you shulde displese.
    I you require, and pray that ye
Of me have mercy and pitee,   3420
To stynte your ire that greveth soo,
That I wole swere for ever mo
To be redressid at youre likyng,

If I trespasse in ony thyng;
Save that, I pray thee, graunte me
A thyng that may not warned be;
That I may love alle oonly,
Noon other thyng of you aske I.
I shalle doon elles welle iwys,
If of youre grace ye graunte me this.   3430
And ye *ne* may not letten me,
For wel wot ye that love is free,
And I shalle loven sichen that I wille,
Who evere like it welle or ille;
And yit ne wold I for alle Fraunce
Do thyng to do you displesaunce.'
  Thanne Daunger fille in his entent
For to foryeve his male-talent;
But alle his wratthe yit at*te* laste
He hath relesed, I preyde so faste: 3440
' Shortly,' he seide, ' thy request
Is not to mochel dishonest;
Ne I wole not wernen it thee,
For yit no thyng engreveth me.
For though thou love thus evermore,
To me is neither softe ne soore.
Love where that the list; what recchith me,
So *thou* fer fro my roses be?
Trust not on me for noon assay,
In ony tyme to passe the hay.'   3450
Thus hath he graunted my praiere.
  Thanne wente I forth withouten were
Unto my freend, and tolde hym alle,
Which was right joyfulle of my talle.
He seide, ' Now goth wel thyn affere,
He shalle to thee be debonaire.

Though he aforn was dispitous,
He shalle heere-aftir be gracious.
If he were touchid on somme good veyne,
He shulde yit rewen on thi peyne.   3460
Suffre, I rede, and no boost make,
Tille thou at goodnes maist hym take.
By sufferaunce, and wordis softe,
A man may overcomen ofte   .
Hym that aforn he hadde in drede,
In bookis sothly as I rede.'
    Thus hath my freend with gret comfort
Avaunced *me* with high disport,
Which wolde me good as mych as I.
And thanne anoon fulle sodeynly   3470
I toke my leve, and streight I wente
Unto the hay; for gret talente
I hadde to sene the freshe bothom,
Wherynne lay my salvacioun;
And Daunger toke kepe, if that I
Kepe hym covenaunt trewely.
So sore I dradde his manasyng,
I durste not breke his biddyng;
For lest that I were of hym shent,
I brake not his comaundement,   3480
For to purchase his good wille.
It was *hard* for to come ther-tille,
His mercy was to ferre bihynde;
I wepte, for I ne myght it fynde.
I compleyned and sighede sore,
And langwisshed evermore,
For I durste not over goo,
Unto the rose I lovede soo,
Thurgh-out my demyng outerly,

That he had*de* knowlege certeinly,   3490
Thanne Love me ladde in sich a wise,
That in me ther was no feyntise,
Falsheed, ne no trecherie.
And yit he, fulle of vylanye,
Of disdeyne and *of* cruelté,
On me ne wolde have pité,
His cruel wille for to refreyne,
Thou*gh* I wepe alwey, and me compleyne.
  And while I was in this torment,
Were come of grace, by God sent,   3500
Fraunchise, and with hir Pité,
Fulfild the bothom of bounté.
They go to Daunger anoon right
To forther me with alle her myght,
And helpe in worde and *ek* in dede,
For welle they saugh that it was nede.
First of hir grace dame Fraunchise
Hath taken of this emprise :
She seide, ' Daunger, gret wrong ye do
To worche this man so myche woo,   3510
Or pynen hym so angerly,
It is to you gret villanye.
I can not see why ne how
That he hath trespassed ageyn you,
Save that he loveth ; wherfore ye shulde
The more in chereté of hym holde.
The force of love makith hym do this ;
Who wolde hym blame he dide amys ?
He leseth more than ye may do ;
His peyne is harde, ye may see, lo !   3520
And Love in no wise wolde consente
That *he* have power to repente ;

For though that quyk ye wolde hym sloo,
Fro Love his herte may not goo.
Now, swete sir, is it youre ese
Hym forto angre or disese?
Allas, what may it you avaunce
To done to hym so gret grevaunce?
What worship is it agayn hym take,
Or on youre man a werre make,   3530
Sith he so lowly every wise
Is redy, as ye luste devise?
If Love hath caught hym in his lace,
You for to beye in every caas,
And ben youre suget at youre wille,
Shulde ye therfore willen hym ille?
Ye shulde hym spare more alle oute,
Than hym that is bothe proude and stoute.
Curtesie wole that ye socour
Hem that ben meke undir youre cure.   3540
His herte is hard that wole not meke,
Whanne men of mekenesse hym biseke.'
    'That is certeyn,' seide Pité;
'We se ofte that humilité,
Bothe ire, and also felonye
Venquyssheth, and also malencolye;
To stonde forth in such duresse
Is cruelté and wikkidnesse.
Wherfore I pray you, sir Daungere,
 For to mayntene no lenger heere   3550
Such cruel werre agayn youre man,
As hoolly youres as ever *he* can;
Nor that ye worchen no more woo
Upon this caytif that langwisshith soo,
Which wole no more to you trespasse,

But putte hym hoolly in youre grace.
His offense ne was but lite;
The God of Love it was to wite,
That he youre thralle so gretly is,
And if ye harme hym, ye done amys;   3560
For he hath hadde fulle hard penaunce,
Sith that ye refte hym thaqueyntaunce
Of Bialacoil, his moste joye,
Which alle hise peynes myght acoye.
He was biforn anoyed sore,
But thanne ye doubled hym welle more;
For he of blis hath ben fulle bare,
Sith Bialacoil was fro hym fare.
Love hath to hym do gret distresse,
He hath no nede of more duresse.   3570
Voideth from hym your ire, I rede;
Ye may not wynnen in this dede.
Makith Bialacoil repeire ageyn,
And haveth pité upon his peyne;
For Fraunchise wole, and I Pité,
That mercyful to hym ye be;
And sith that she and I accorde,
Have upon hym misericorde;
For I you pray, and eke moneste,
Nought to refusen oure requeste;   3580
For he is hard and felle of thought,
That for us twoo wole do right nought.'
   Daunger ne myghte no more endure,
He mekede hym unto mesure.
   ' I wole in no wise,' seith Daungere,
' Denye that ye have asked heere;
It were to gret uncurtesie.
I wole ye have the companye

Of Bialacoil, as ye devise:
I wole hym lette in no wise.'   3580
    To Bialacoil thanne wente in high
Fraunchise, and seide fulle curteislye:—
' Ye have to longe be deignous
Unto this lover, and daungerous,
[Fro hym to withdrawe your presence,
Whyche hath do to hym great offence,
That ye not wolde upon hym se;
Wherfore a sorouful man is he.
Shape ye to paye hym, and to please,
Of my love yf ye wol have ease.   3590
Fulfyl his wyl, sythe that ye knowe
Daunger is daunted and brought lowe
Through helpe of me and of Pyté:
You dare no more aferde be.'
    ' I shal do right as ye wylle,'
Saythe Bialacoil, ' for it is skylle,
Sythe Daunger wol that it so be.'
Than Fraunchyse hath hym sent to me.
    Byalacoil at the begynnyng
Saluede me in his commyng,   3600
No straungenesse was in him sene,
No more than he ne hadde wrathed bene.
As fayre semblaunt than shewed he me,
And goodly, as aforne dyd he;
And by the honde, withoute doute,
Wythin the haye ryght al aboute,
He ladde me, with right good chere,
Al envyron thilke vergere,
That Daunger hadde me chased fro.
Nowe have I leave overal to goo: 3610
Now am I raysed, at my devyse,

Fro helle unto paradyse.
Thus Bialacoil of gentylnesse
With al his payne and besynesse,
Hathe shewed me onely of grace
The extres of the swote place.
I sawe the rose whan I was nygh,
Was greatter woxen, and more high,
Fresshe, roddy, and fayre of hewe,
Of coloure ever yliche newe. 3520
And whan I hadde it longe sene,
I sawe that through the leves grene
The rose spredde to spannyshinge;
To sene it was a goodly thynge.
But it ne was so sprede on brede,
That men withyn myghte knowe the sede;
For it covert was and close
Bothe with the leves and with the rose.
The stalke was even and grene upright,
It was theron a goodly syght; 3540
And wel the better withoute wene,
For the sede was nat i-sene.
Ful fayre it spradde, the god of blesse!
For suche another, as I gesse,
Aforne ne was, ne more vermayle.
I was abawed for marveyle,
For ever the fayrer that it was,
The more I am bounden in Loves laas.

   Longe I abode there, sothe to saye,
Tyl Bialacoil I ganne to praye, 3550
Whan that I sawe him in no wyse
To me warnen his servyse,
That he me wolde graunt a thynge,
Whiche to remembre is wel syttynge;

This is to sayne, that of his grace
He wolde me yeve leysar and space
To me that was so desyrous
To have a kyssynge precious
Of thilke goodly freshe rose,
That so swetely smelleth in my nose ;   3660
' For if it you displeasede nought,
I wolde gladly, as I have sought,
Have a cosse therof freely.
Of your yefte ; for certainly
I wol none have but by your leve,
So lothe me were you for to greve.'
He sayde, ' Frend, so God me spede,
Of Chastité I have such drede,
Thou shuldest nat warned be for me,
But I dare nat for Chastyté.   3670
Agayne her dare I nat mysdo,
For alwaye byddeth she me so
To yeve no lover leave to kysse ;
For who therto maye wynnen, ywisse,
He of the surplus of the praye
May lyve in hoope to gette some daye.
For who-so kyssynge may attayne,
Of loves payne hath, sothe to sayne,
The best and most avenaunt.'
And ernest of the remenaunt.'   3680
    Of hys answere I sighede sore ;
I durst assaye him tho no more,
I hadde suche drede to greve hym aye.
A man shulde nat to moche assaye
To chafe hys frende out of measure,
Nor putte his lyfe in aventure ;
For no man at the fyrste stroke

Ful many, hir wille for to doo.
　Thanne Drede hadde in hir baillie
The kepyng of the conestablerye,
Toward the north, I undirstonde,
That openyde upon the lyfte honde,　　　4220
The which for no thyng may be sure
But-if she do *hir* bisy cure
Erly on morowe and also late,
Strongly to shette and barre the gate.
Of every thing that she may see,
Drede is aferd, wher-so she be;
For with a puff of litelle wynde,
Drede is a-stonyed in hir mynde.
Therfore, for stelyng of the rose,
I rede hir nought the yate unclose.　　　4230
A foulis flight wole make hir flee,
And eke a shadowe if she it see.
　Thanne Wikked-tunge fulle of envye,
With soudiours of Normandye,
As he that causeth alle the bate,
Was keper of the fourthe gate,
And also to the tother three,
He wente fulle ofte for to see.
Whanne his lotte was to wake a-nyght*e*,
His instrumentis wolde he digh*te*,　　　4240
For to blowe and make sowne,
Ofte*r* thanne he hath enchesoun;
And walken oft upon the walle,
Corners and wikettis over alle
Fulle narwe serchen and espie;
Though he nought fonde, yit wol*de* he lye.
Discordaunt ever fro armonye,
And distoncd from melodie,

Controve he wolde, and foule fayle,
With hornepipes of Cornewaile.   4250
In floytes made he discordaunce,
And in his musyk, with myschaunce,
He wolde seyn with notes newe,
That he *ne* fonde no womman trewe,
Ne that he saugh never in his lyf,
Unto hir husbonde a trewe wyf;
Ne noon so ful of honesté,
That she nyl laughe and mery be,
Whanne that she hereth, or may espie,
A man spoken of leccherie.   4260
Everiche of hem hath somme vice;
Oon is dishonest, another is nyce;
If oon be fulle of vylanye,
Another hath a likerous ighe;
If oon be fulle of wontonesse,
Another is a chideresse.
Thus Wikked-tunge, (God yeve him shame!)
Can putt hem everychone in blame;
Withoute dissert and causeles,
He lieth, though they ben gilteles.   4270
I have pité to sene the sorwe,
That walketh bothe eve and morwe,
To innocentis doith such grevaunce;
I pray God yeve him evel chaunce,
That he ever so bisie is,
Of ony womman to seyn amys!
    Eke Jelousie God confounde!
That hath i-maad a tour so rounde,
And made aboute a garisoun,
So sette Bealacoil in prisoun;   4280
The which is shette there in the tour,

Ful longe to holde there sojour,
There for to lyven in penaunce,
And for to do hym more grevaunce.
Which hath ordeyned Jelousie,
An olde vekke for to espye
The maner of his governaunce;
The whiche devel, in hir enfaunce
Hadde lerned of Loves arte,
And of his pleyes toke hir parte ;   4290
She was except in his servise.
She knewe eche wrenche and every gise
Of love, and every wile,
It was harder hir to gile.
Of Bealacoil she toke ay hede,
That evere he lyveth in woo and drede.
He kepte hym koy and eke pryvé,
Lest in hym she hadde see
Ony foly countenaunce,
For she knewe alle the olde daunce.   4300
And aftir this, whanne Jelousie
Hadde Bealacoil in his baillie,
An shette hym up that was so fre,
For seure of hym he wolde be,
He trusteth sore in his castelle ;
The stronge werk hym liketh welle.
He dradde not that no glotouns
Shulde stele his roses or bothoms.
The roses weren assured alle
Defenced with the stronge walle.   4310
Now Jelousie fulle wel may be
Of drede devoide in liberté,
Whether that he slepe or wake,
For his roses may noon be take.

But I, allas, now morne shalle;
Bi-cause I was withoute the walle,
Fulle moche doole and moone I made.
Who hadde wist what woo I hadde,
I trowe he wolde have had pité.
Love to deere hadde soolde to me   4320
The good that of his love hadde I.
I wente aboute it alle queyntely;
But now thurgh doublyng of my peyne
I see he wolde it selle ageyne,
And me a newe bargeyn leere,
The which alle oute the more is deere,
For the solace that I have lorn,
Thanne I hadde it never a-forn.
Certayn I am ful like in deede
To hym that caste in erthe his seede;   4330
And hath joie of the newe spryng,
Whanne it greneth in the gynnyng,
And is also faire and fresh of flour,
Lusty to seen, swoote of odour.
But er he it in his sheves shere,
May falle a weder that shal it dere,
And maken it to fade and falle,
The stalke, the greyne, and floures alle;
That to the tylyers is fordone
The hope that he hadde to soone.   4340
I drede certeyn that so fare I;
For hope and travaile sikerlye
Ben me byraft alle with a storme;
The floure nel seeden of my corne.
For Love hath so avaunced me,
Whanne I bigan my pryvité
To Bialacoil alle for to telle,

Whom I ne fonde ne froward no felle,
But toke a-gree alle hool my play;
But Love is of so hard assay, 4350
That alle at oonys he revede me,
Whanne I wente best aboven to have be.
It is of Love, as of Fortune,
That chaungeth ofte, and nyl contune;
Which whilom wole on folke smyle,
And glowmbe on hem another while;
Now freend, now foo, *thou* shalt hir feele,
For a twynklyng turne hir wheele.
She can writhe hir hood a-wey,
This is the concours of hir pley; 4360
She canne arise that doth morne,
And whirle adown, and over-turne
Who sittith hieghst, but as hir luste;
A foole is he that wole hir truste.
For it is I that am come down
Thurgh charge and revolucioun!
Sith Bealacoil mote fro me twynne,
Shette in the prisoun yonde withynne,
His absence at myn herte I fele;
For alle my joye and alle myne hele 4370
Was in hym and in the rose,
That but thoue wole, which hym doth close,
Opene, that I may hym see,
Love nyl not that I cured be
Of the peynes that I endure,
Nor of my cruel aventure.

 A, Bialacoil, myn owne deere!
Though thou be now a prisonere,
Kepe atte leste thyne herte to me,
And suffre not that it daunted be, 4380

Ne late not Jelousie in his rage,
Putten thine herte in no servage.
Al-though he chastice thee withoute,
And make thy body unto hym loute,
Have herte as hard as dyamaunt,
Stedefast, and nought pliaunt.
In prisoun though thi body be
At large kepe thyne herte free.
A trewe herte wole not plie
For no manace that it may drye.   4390
If Jelousie doth thee payne,
Quyte hym his while thus agayne,
To venge thee atte leest in thought,
If other way thou maist nought;
And in this wise sotilly
Worche, and wynne the maistrie.
But yit I am in gret affray,
Lest thou do not as I say;
I drede thou canst me gret maugre,
That thou enprisoned art for me;   4400
But that not for my trespas,
For thurgh me never discovred was
Yit thyng that oughte be secree.
Wel more anoy is in me,
Than is in thee of this myschaunce;
For I endure more harde penaunce
Than ony can seyn or thynke,
That for the sorwe almost I synke.
Whanne I remembre me of my woo,
Fulle nygh out of my witt I goo.   4410
Inward myn herte I feele blede,
For comfortles the deth I drede.
Owe I not wel to have distresse,

Whanne false, thurgh hir wikkednesse,
And traitours, that arn envyous,
To noyen me be so coragious?
   A, Bialacoil! fulle wel I see,
That they hem shape to disceyve thee,
To make thee buxom to her lawe,
And with her corde thee to drawe   4420
Where so hem lust, right at her wille;
I drede they have thee brought thertille.
Withoute comfort, thought me sleeth;
This game wole brynge me to my deeth.
For if youre good wille I leese,
I mote be deed; I may not chese.
And if that thou foryete me,
Myne herte shal nevere in likyng be;
Nor elles-where fynde solace,
If I be putt out of youre grace,   4430
As it shal never been, I hope;
Thanne shulde I falle in wanhope.
   Allas, in wanhope—nay, pardee!
For I wole never dispeired be.
If Hope me faile, thanne am I
Ungracious and unworthy;
In Hope I wole comforted be,
For Love, whanne he bitaught hir me,
Seide, that Hope, where-so I goo,
Shulde ay be reles to my woo.   4440
   But what and she my baalis beete,
And be to me curteis and sweete?
She is in no thyng fulle certeyne.
Lovers she putt in fulle gret peyne,
And makith hem that woo to deele.
Hir faire biheeste disceyveth feele,

For she wole byhote sikirly,
And failen aftir outrely.
A, that is a fulle noyous thyng !
For many a lover in lovyng   4450
Hangeth upon hir, and trusteth faste,
Whiche leese her travel at the laste.
Of thyng to comen she woot right nought :
Therfore, if it be wysely sought,
Hir counseille foly is to take.
For many tymes, whanne she wole make
A fulle good silogisme, I dreede
That aftirward ther shal in deede
Folwe an evelle conclusioun ;
This putte me in confusioun.   4460
For many tymes I have it seen,
That many have bigyled been,
For trust that they have sette in hope,
Which felle hem aftirward a-slope.
    But, nevertheles, yit gladly she wolde,
That he that wole hym with hir holde,
Hadde alle tymes *his* purpos clere,
Withoute deceyte or ony were.
That she desireth sikirly ;
Whanne I hir blamed, I dide foly.   4470
But what avayleth hir good wille,
Whanne she no may staunche my stounde ille ?
That helpith litel that she may doo,
Outake biheest unto my woo.
And heeste certeyn in no wise,
Withoute yift, is not to preise.
Whanne heest and deede a-sundry varie,
They doon a gret contrarie.
    Thus am I possed up and doun

With doole, thought, and confusioun ; 4480
Of my disese ther is no noumbre.
Daunger and Shame me encumbre,
Drede also, and Jelousie,
And Wikked-tunge fulle of envie,
Of whiche the sharpe and cruel ire
Fulle ofte me putte in gret martire.
They han my joye fully lette,
Sith Bialacoil they have bishette
Fro me in prisoun wikkidly,
Whom I love so entierly, 4490
That it wole my bane bee,
But I the sonner may hym see.
And yit more-over wurst of alle,
Ther is sette to kepe, foule hir bi-falle,
A rympled vekke, ferre ronne in age,
Frownyng and yelowe in hir visage,
Which in a-wayte lyth day and nyght,
That noon of hem may have a sight.
  Now mote my sorwe enforced be ;
Fulle soth it is, that Love yaf me 4500
Three wonder yiftes of his grace,
Whiche I have lorn, now in this place,
Sith they ne may withoute drede
Helpen but lytel, who taketh heede.
For here availeth no Swete-thought,
And Sweete-speche helpith right nought.
The thridde was called Swete-lokyng,
That now is lorn withoute lesyng.
Yiftes were faire, but not forthy
They helpe me but symply, 4510
But Bialacoil loosed be,
To gon at large and to be free.

For hym my lyf lyth alle in doute,
But-if he come the rather oute.
Allas! I trowe it wole not bene!
For how shuld I evermore hym sene?
He may not oute, and that is wronge,
By-cause the tour is so stronge.
How shulde he oute? by whos prowesse,
Oute of so stronge a forteresse?   4520
By me certeyn it nyl be doo;
God woot I have no witte therto!
But wel I woot I was in rage,
Whonne I to Love dide homage.
Who was in cause, in sothfastnesse,
But hir-silf, dame Idelnesse,
Which me conveiede thurgh faire praiere
To entre into that faire verger?
She was to blame me to leve,
The which now doth me soore greve,   4530
A foolis word is nought to trowe,
Ne worth an appel for to lowe;
Men shulde hym snybbe bittirly,
At pryme temps of his foly.
I was a fool, and she me leevede,
Thurgh whom I am right nought releeved.
Sheo accomplisshid alle my wille,
That now me greveth wondir ille;
Resoun me seide what shulde falle.
    A fool my-silf I may wel calle,   4540
That love *a-syde* I hadde *not* leyde,
And trowede that dame Resoun seide.
Resoun hadde bothe skile and ryght,
Whanne she me blamede, with alle hir myght,
To medle of love, that hath me shent;

But certeyn now I wole repente.
  'And shulde I repente? Nay, pardé!
A fals traitour thanne shulde I be.
The develle engynnes wolde me take,
If I my Love wolde forsake,   4550
Or Bialacoil falsly bitraye.
Shulde I at myscheef hate hym? nay,
Sith he now for his curtesie
Is in prisoun of Telousie.
Curtesie certeyn dide he me,
So mych that may not yolden be,
Whanne he the hay passen me lete,
To kisse the rose, faire and swete;
Shulde I therfore cunne hym mawgre?
Nay, certeynly, it shal not be,   4560
For Love shalle nevere, yeve Good wille,
Here of me, thurgh word or wille,
Offence or complaynt more or lesse,
Neither of Hope nor Idilnesse;
For certis, it were wrong that I
Hated hem for her curtesie.
Ther is not ellys, but suffre and thenke,
And waken whanne I shulde wynke;
Abide in hope, til Love, thurgh chaunce,
Sende me socour or allegeaunce,   4570
Expectant ay tille I may mete,
To geten mercy of that swete.
    Whilom I thenke how Love to me
Seide he wolde take atte gree
My servise, if unpacience
Causede me to done offence.
He seide, 'In thank I shal it take,
And high maister eke thee make,

If wikkednesse ne reve it thee ;
But sone I trowe that shalle not be.' 4580
These were his wordis by and by ;
It semede he lovede me trewely.
Now is ther not but serve hym wele,
If that I thenke his thanke to fele.
My good, myne harme, lyth hool in me :
In Love may no defaute be ;
For trewe Love ne failide never man.
Sothly the faute mote nedys than
(As God forbede !) be founde in me,
And how it cometh, I can not see. 4590
Now late it goon as it may goo ;
Whether Love wole socoure me or sloo,
He may do hool on me his wille.
I am so sore bounde hym tille,
From his servise I may not fleen,
For lyf and deth, withouten wene,
Is in his hande ; I may not chese ;
He may me doo bothe wynne and leese.
And sith so sore he doth me greve,
Yit, if my lust he wolde acheve, 4600
To Bialacoil goodly to be,
I yeve no force what felle on me.
For though I dye, as I mote nede,
I praye Love, of his goodlyhede,
To Bialacoil do gentylnesse,
For whom I lyve in such distresse,
That I mote deyen for penaunce.
But first, withoute repentaunce,
I wole me confesse in good entent,
And make in haste my testament, 4610
As lovers doon that feelen smerte :—

To Bialacoil leve I myne herte
Alle hool, withoute departyng,
Or doublenesse of repentyng.

COMENT RAISOUN VIENT A LAMANT.

Thus as I made my passage
In compleynt, and in cruel rage,
And I not where to fynde a leche,
That couthe unto myne helpyng eche,
Sodeynly agayn comen doun
Out of hir tour I saugh Resoun,	4620
Discrete and wijs, and fulle plesaunt,
And of hir porte fulle avenaunt.
The righte weye she tooke to me,
Which stode in gret perplexité,
That was posshed in every side,
That I nyste where I myght abide,
Tille she demurely sad of chere
Seide to me as she come nere :—
' Myne owne freend, art thou yit greved?
How is this quarelle yit acheved	4630
Of Loves side ? Anoon me telle,
Hast thou not yit of love thi fille ?
Art thou not wery of thy servise
That the hath in siche wise ?
What joye hast thou in thy lovyng ?
Is it swete or bitter thyng ?
Canst thou yit chese, late me see,
What best thi socour myghte be ?
Thou servest a fulle noble lorde,
That maketh thee thralle for thi rewarde,
Which ay renewith thi turment,	4641
With foly so he hath thee blent ;

Thou felle in myscheef thilke day.
Whanne thou didist, the sothe to say,
Obeysaunce and eke homage,
Thou wroughtest no thyng as the sage.
Whanne thou bicam his liege man,
Thou didist a gret foly than;
Thou wistest not what felle therto,
With what lord thou haddist to do.   4650
If thou haddist hym wel knowe
Thou haddist nought be brought so lowe;
For if thou wistest what it were,
Thou noldist serve hym half a yeer,
Not a weke, nor half a day,
Ne yit an hour withoute delay,
Ne never ilovede paramours,
His lordshippe is so fulle of shoures.
Knowest hym ought?'
    Lamaunt. Yhe, dame, pardé!   4660
    Raisoun. Nay, nay.
    Lamaunt. Yhis, I.
    Raisoun.   Wherof, late se?
    Lamaunt. Of that he seide I shulde be
Glad to have sich lord as he,
And maister of sich seignorie.
    Raisoun. Knowist hym no more?
    Lamauut.   Nay, certis, I,
Save that he yaf me rewles there,
And wente his wey, I nyste where,
And I aboode bounde in balaunce.   4670
    Raisoun. Lo, there a noble conisaunce!
    But I wille that thou knowe hym now
Gynnyng and eende, sith that thou
Art so anguisshous and mate,
Diffigured oute of a-state;

Ther may no wrecche have more of woo,
Ne caityfe noon enduren soo.
It were to every man sittyng,
Of his lord have knowleching.
For if thou knewe hym oute of doute,   4680
Lightly thou shulde escapen oute
Of the prisoun that marreth thee.
   Lamaunt. Yhe, dame! sith my lord is he,
And I his man maad with myn honde,
I wolde right fayne undirstonde
To knowe of what kynde he by
If ony wolde informe me.
   Raisoun. I wolde, seide Resoun, thee lere,
Sith thou to lerne hast sich desire,
And shewe thee withouten fable   4690
A thyng that is not demonstrable.
Thou shalt, withouten science,
And knowe, withouten experience,
The thyng that may not knowen be,
Ne wist ne shewid in no degré.
Thou maist the sothe of it not witen
Though in thee it were writen.
Thou shalt not knowe therof more,
While thou art reuled by his lore.
But unto hym that love wole flee,   4700
The knotte may unclosed bee,
Which hath to thee, as it is founde,
So long be knette and not unbounde
Now sette wel thyne entencioun,
To here of love discripcioun.
   Love it is an hatefulle pees,
A free acquitaunce withoute relees,
A trouthe frette fulle of falsheede,

A sikernesse alle sette in drede,
In herte is a dispeiryng hope,   4710
And fulle of hope it is wanhope,
Wise woodnesse, and wode resoun,
A swete perelle in to droune,
An hevy birthen lyght to bere,
A wikked wawe awey to were.
It is Karibdous perilous,
Disagreable and gracious.
It is discordaunce that can accorde,
And accordaunce to discorde.
It is kunnyng withoute science,   4720
Wisdome withoute sapience,
Witte withoute discrecioun,
Havoire withoute possessioun.
It is sike hele and hool sekenesse,
A thrust drowned in dronknesse,
And helth fulle of maladie,
And charité fulle of envie,
And anger fulle of habundaunce,
And a gredy suffisaunce ;
Delite right fulle of hevynesse,   4730
And drerihed fulle of gladnesse ;
Bitter swetnesse and swete errour,
Right evelle savoured good savour ;
Sin that pardoun hath withynne,
And pardoun spotted withoute *with* synne ;
A peyne also it is joious,
And felonye right pitous ;
Also pley that selde is stable,
And stedefast right movable ;
A strengthe weyked to stonde upright,   4740
And feblenesse fulle of myght ;

Witte unavised, sage folie,
And joie fulle of turmentrie;
A laughter it is weping ay,
Reste that traveyleth nyght and day,
Also a swete helle it is,
And a soroufulle Paradys;
A plesaunt gayl and esy prisoun,
And fulle of froste somer sesoun;
Pryme temps fulle of frostes white,   4750
And May devoide of al delite;
With seer braunches, blossoms ungrene,
And newe fruyt fillid with wynter tene.
It is a slowe may not for-bere
Ragges ribaned, with gold, to were;
For also welle wole love be sette
Under ragges as riche rochette;
And eke as wel be amourettes
In mournyng blak, as bright burnettes.
For noon is of so mochel pris,   4760
Ne no man founden _is_ so wys,
Ne noon so high is of parage,
Ne no man founde of witt so sage;
No man so hardy ne so wight,
Ne no man of so mychel myght;
Noon so fulfilled of bounté,
That he with love may daunted be.
Alle the world holdith this way;
Love makith alle to goon myswey.
But it be they of yvel lyf,   4770
Whom genius cursith, man and wyf,
That wrongly werke ageyn nature.
Noon such I love, ne have no cure
Of sich as loves servauntes bene,

And wole not by my counsel flene.
For I ne preise that lovyng
Wherthurgh men, at the laste eendyng,
Shalle calle hem wrecchis fulle of woo,
Love greveth hem and shendith soo.
But if thou wolt wel love eschewe,   4780
For to escape out of his mewe,
And make al hool thi sorwe to slake,
No bettir counsel maist thou take,
Than thynke to fleen ; wel iwis,
May nought helpe elles ; for wite thou this :—
If thou fle it, it shal flee thee ;
Folowe it, and folowen shal it thee.'
    Lamant.—Whanne I hadde herde alle Resoun
        seyne,
Which hadde spilt hir speche in veyne :
' Dame,' seide I, ' I dar wel sey   4790
Of this avaunt me wel I may
That from youre scole so devyaunt
I am, that never the more avaunt
Right nought am I thurgh youre doctrine ;
I dulle under youre discipline ;
I wote no more than *I* wist ever,
To me so contrarie and so fer
Is every thing that ye me lere ;
And yit I can it alle by parcuere.
Myne herte foryetith therof right nought,   4800
It is so writen in my thought ;
And depe graven it is so tendir
That alle by herte I can it rendre,
And rede it over comunely ;
But to my silf lewedist am I.
   ' But sith ye love discreven so,
And lak and preise it bothe twoo,

Defyneth it into this letter,
That I may thenke on it the better,
For I herde never diffyned heere, 4310
And wilfully I wolde it lere.'
    Raisoun.—' If love be serched wel and sought
It is a sykenesse of the thought
Annexed and kned bitwixt tweyne,
With male and female, with oo cheyne,
So frely that byndith, that they nylle twynne,
Whether so therof they leese or wynne.
The roote springith thurgh hoote brennyng
Into disordinat desiryng,
For to kissen and enbrace 4320
And at her lust *hem* to solace.
Of other thyng love recchith nought,
But setteth her herte and alle her thought
More for delectacioun
Than ony procreacioun
Of other fruyt by engendrure ;
Which love, to God is not plesyng ;
For of her body fruyt to gete
They yeve no force, they are so sette
Upon delite to pley in feere. 4330
And somme have also this manere,
To feynen hem for love seke ;
Sich love I preise not at a leke.
For paramours they do but feyne ;
To love truly they disdeyne.
They falsen ladies traitoursly,
And swerne hem othes utterly,
With many a lesyng, and many a fable,
And alle they fynden deceyvable.
And whanne they han her lust geten 4340

The hoote ernes they al foryeten.
Wymmen the harme they bien fulle sore;
But men this thenken evermore,
That lasse harme is, so mote I the,
Deceyve *hem*, than deceyved be;
And namely where they ne may
Fynde none other mene wey.
For I wote wel, in sothfastnesse,
That who doth now his bisynesse
With ony womman for to dele, 4850
For ony lust that he may fele,
But if it be for engendrure,
He doth trespasse, I you ensure.
For he shulde setten alle his wille
To geten a likly thyng hym tille,
And to sustene, if he myght*e*,
And kepe forth, by Kyndes right*e*,
His owne lyknesse and semblable.
For because alle is corumpable,
And faile shulde successioun, 4860
Ne were their generacioun,
Oure sectis strene for to save,
Whanne fader or moder arn in grave,
Her children shulde, whanne they ben deede,
Fulle diligent ben, in her steede,
To use that werke on such a wise,
That oon may thurgh another rise.
Therfore sette Kynde therynne delite,
For men therynne shulde hem delite,
And of that deede be not erke, 4870
But ofte sithes haunt*e* that werke.
For noon wolde drawe therof a draught
Ne were delite, which hath hym kaught.

This hadde sotille dame Nature ;
For noon goth right, I thee ensure,
Ne hath entent hool ne parfight,
For hir desir is for delyte,
The which fortened crece and eke
The pley of love, for ofte seke,
And thralle hem-silf they be so nyce   4880
Unto the prince of every vice.
For of ech synne it is the rote
Unlefulle lust, though it be sote,
And of alle yvelle the racyne,
As Tulius can determyne,
Which in his tyme was fulle sage,
In a boke he made of age,
Where that more he preyseth Eelde
Though he be croked and unweelde,
And more of commendacioun,   4890
Than youthe in his discripcioun.
For youthe sette bothe man and wyf
In alle perelle of soule and lyf;
And perelle is, but men have grace,
The perelle of yougth for to pace,
Withoute ony deth or distresse,
It is so fulle of wyldenesse ;
So ofte it doth shame or damage
To hym or to his lynage.
It ledith man now up now doun   4900
In mochel dissolucioun,
And makith hym love yvelle companye,
And lede his lyf disrewlilye,
And halt hym payed with noon estate.
Withynne hym-silf is such debate,
He chaungith purpos and entente,

And yalte into somme covente,
To lyven aftir her emprise,
And lesith fredom and fraunchise,
That Nature in hym hadde sette, 4910
The which ageyne he may not gette,
If he there make his mansioun,
For to abide professioun.
Though for a tyme his herte absente,
It may not fayle, he shal repente,
And eke abide thilke day,
To leve his abite, and gone his way,
And lesith his worshippe and his name,
And dar not come ageyn for shame,
But al his lyf he doth so morne, 4920
By-cause he dar not hom retourne.
Fredom of kynde so lost hath he
That never may recured be,
But if that God hym graunte grace
That he may, er he hennes pace,
Conteyne undir obedience
Thurgh the vertu of pacience.
For youthe sett man in alle folye,
In unthrift and ribaudie,
In leccherie, and in outrage, 4930
So ofte it chaungith of corage.
Youthe gynneth ofte sich bargeyne,
That may not eende withouten peyne.
In gret perelle is sett youthede,
Delite so doth his bridil leede.
Delite thus hangith, drede thee nought,
Bothe mannys body and his thought,
Oonly thurgh youthes chamber*ere*,
That to done yvelle is custommere,

And of nought elles taketh hede, 4940
But oonly folkes for to lede
Into disporte and wyldenesse,
So is *he* frowarde from sadnesse.
But eelde drawith hem therfro ;
Who wote it nought he may wel goo,
And moo of hem that now arn olde,
That whilom youthe hadde in holde,
Which yit remembreth of tendir age
Hou it hem brought in many a rage,
And many a foly therynne wrought. 4950
But now that Eelde hath hym thurgh sought
They repente hem of her folye,
That youthe hem putte in jupardye,
In perelle and in myche woo,
And made hem ofte amys to do.
And suen yvelle companye
Riot and avoutrie.
  ‘ But Eelde gan ageyn restreyne
From siche foly, and refreyne,
And sette men, by her ordinaunce, 4960
In good reule and governaunce.
But yvelle she spendith hir servise,
For no man wole hir love, neither preise ;
She is *i*-hated, this wote I welle.
Hir acqueyntaunce wolde no man fele,
Ne han of Elde companye,
Men hate to be of·hir alye :
For no man wolde bicomen olde,
Ne dye, whanne he is yong and bolde.
And Eelde merveilith right gretlye, 4970
Whanne thei remembre hem inwardly
Of many a perelous emprise,

Whiche that they wrought in sondry wise,
Hou evere they myght, withoute blame,
Escape awey withoute shame,
In youthe withoute damage
Or repreef of her lynage,
Losse of membre, shedyng of blode,
Perelle of deth, and losse of good.
  'Woste thou nought where Youthe abit, 4980
That men so preisen in her witt?
With Delite she halt sojour,
For bothe they dwellen in oo tour.
As longe as Youthe is in sesoun,
They dwellen in oon mansioun.
Delite of Youthe wole have servise
To do what so he wole devise;
And Youthe is redy evermore
For to obey, for smerte of sore,
Unto Delite, and hym to yeve   4990
Hir servise, while that she may lyve.
  'Where Elde abit, I wole thee telle
Shortely, and no while dwelle,
For thidir byhoveth thee to goo.
If Deth in youthe thee not sloo,
Of this journey thou maist not faile.
With hir Labour and Travaile
Logged ben with Sorwe and Woo,
That never out of hir court goo.
Peyne and Distresse, Syknesse, and Ire, 5000
And Malencoly, that angry sire,
Ben of hir paleys senatours.
Gronyng and Grucchyng, hir herbejours,
The day and nyght, hir to turmente,
With cruelle Deth they hir presente.

And tellen hir, erliche and late,
That Deth stondith armed at hir gate.
Thanne brynge they to her remembraunce
The foly dedis of hir infaunce,
Whiche causen hir to mourne in woo   5010
That Youthe hath hir bigiled so,
Which sodeynly awey is hasted.
She wepe*th* the tyme that she hath wasted,
Compleynyng of the preterit,
And the present, that not abit,
And of hir olde vanité,
That but aforn hir she may see
In the future somme socour,
To leggen hir of hir dolour,
To graunte hir tyme of repentaunce,   5020
For her synnes to do penaunce,
And atte the laste so hir governe
To wynne the joy that is eterne,
Fro which go bakward Youthe he made
In vanité to droune and wade.
For present tyme abidith nought,
It is more swift than any thought;
So litel while it doth endure
That ther nys compte ne mesure.
    'But hou that evere the game go   5030
Who list to love joie and mirth also
Of love, be it he or she,
High or lowe who it be,
In fruyt they shulde hem delyte,
Her part they may not elles quyte,
To save hem-silf in honesté.
And yit fulle many one I se
Of wymmen, sothly for to seyne,

That desire and wolde fayne
The pley of love, they be so wilde;   5040
And not coveite to go with childe.
And if with child they be perchaunce,
They wole it holde a gret myschaunce,
But what-som-ever woo they fele,
They wole not pleyne, but concele;
But if it be ony fool or nyce,
In whom that shame hath no justice.
For to delyte echone they drawe,
That haunte this werke, bothe high and lawe,
Save siche that arn worth right nought,   5050
That for money wole be bought.
Such love I preise in no wise,
Whanne it is goven for coveitise.
I preise no womman, though sho be wood,
That yeveth hir-silf for ony good.
For litel shulde a man telle
Of hir, that wole hir body selle,
Be she mayde, be she wyf,
That quyk wole selle hir bi hir lyf.
Hou faire chere that evere she make,   5060
He is a wrecche I undirtake
That lovede such one, for swete or soure,
Though she hym calle hir paramoure,
And laugheth on hym, and makith hym feeste.
For certeynly no such beeste
To be loved is not worthy,
Or bere the name of drurie.
Noon shulde hir please, but he were woode,
That wole dispoile hym of his goode.
Yit nevertheles I wole not sey   5070
That she, for solace and for pley,

May a jewel or other thyng
Take of her loves fre yevyng;
But that she aske it in no wise,
For drede of shame *or* coveitise.
And she of hirs may hym, certeyn,
Withoute sclaundre, yeven ageyn,
And joyne her hertes to-gidre so
In love, and take and yeve also.
Trowe not that I wolde hem twynne,   5080
 Whanne in her love ther is no synne;
I wole that they to-gedre go,
And don al that they han ado,
As certeis shulde and debonaire,
And in her love beren hem faire,
Withoute vice, bothe he and she;
So that al-wey in honesté,
Fro foly love to kepe hem clere
That brenneth hertis with his fere;
And that her love, in ony wise,   5090
Be devoide of coveitise.
Good love shulde engendrid be
Of trewe herte, just, and secré,
And not of such as sette her thought
To have her lust, and ellis nought,
So are they caught in Loves lace,
Truly, for bodily solace.
Fleshly delite is so present
With thee, that sette alle thyne entent,
Withoute more what shulde I glose?   5100
For to gete and have the rose,
Which makith *thee* so mate and woode
That thou desirest noon other goode.
But thou art not an inche the nerre,

But evere abidist in sorwe and werre,
As in thi face it is *i*-scne;
It makith thee bothe pale and lene,
Thy myght, thi vertu goth away.
A sory geste in goode fay,
Thou herberest hem in thyne inne,   5110
The God of Love whanne thou let inne!
Wherfore I rede thou shette hym oute,
Or he shalle greve thee, oute of doute;
For to thi profit it wole turne,
Iff he nomore with thee sojourne.
In gret myscheef and sorwe sonken
Ben hertis, that of love are dronken,
As thou peraventure knowen shalle,
Whanne thou hast lost the tyme alle,
And spent *thy* thought in ydilnesse,   5120
In waste, and wofulle lustynesse;
If thow maist lyve the tyme to se
Of love for to delyvered be,
Thy tyme thou shalt biwepe sore
The whiche never thou maist restore.
(For tyme lost, as men may see,
For no thyng may recured be)
And if thou scape, yit atte laste,
Fro Love that hath thee so faste
I-knytt and bounden in his lace,   5130
Certeyn I holde it but a grace.
For many oon, as it is seyne,
Have lost, and spent also in veyne,
In his servise withoute socour,
Body and soule, good, and tresour,
Witte, and strengthe, and eke richesse,
Of which they hadde never redresse.'

Lamant.—Thus taught and preched hath Resoun,
But Love spilte hir sermoun,
That was so ymped in my thought,   5140
That hir doctrine I sette at nought.
And yitt ne seide she never a dele,
That I ne undirstode it wele,
Word by word the mater alle.
But unto Love I was so thralle,
Which callith over alle his pray,
And chasith so my thought ay,
And holdith myne herte undir his sele,
As trust and trew as ony stele;
So that no devocioun   5150
Ne hadde I in the sermoun
Of dame Resoun; ne of hir rede
I toke no sojour in myne hede.
For alle yede oute at oon ere
That in that other she dide lere;
Fully on me she lost hir lore.
Hir speche me grevede wondir sore,
That unto hir for ire I seide,
For anger, as I dide abraide :—
' Dame, and is it youre wille algate,   5160
That I not love, but that I hate
Alle men, as ye me teche ?
For if I do aftir youre speche,
Sith that ye seyne love is not good,
Thanne must I nedis say with mood
If I it leve, in hatrede ay
Lyven, and voide love away,
From me a synfulle wrecche,
Hated of alle that tecche
I may not go noon other gate,   5170

For other must I love or hate.
And if I hate men of newe,
More than love it wole me rewe,
As by youre preching semeth me,
For Love no thing ne preisith thee.
Ye yeve good counsel, sikirly,
That prechith me al day, that I
Shulde not Loves lore alowe;
He were a foole wolde you not trowe!
In speche also ye han me taught,   5180
Another love that knowen is naught,
Which I have herd you not repreve,
To love ech other, by youre leve.
If ye wolde diffyne it me,
I wolde gladly here, to se,
Atte the leest, if I may lere
Of sondry loves the manere.'

   Raisoun.—' Certis, freend, a fool art thou
Whan that thou no thyng wolt allowe,
That I for thi profit say.   5190
Yit wole I sey thee more, in fay,
For I am redy, at the leste,
To accomplisshe thi requeste,
But I not where it wole avayle:
In veyn perauntre I shal travayle.
Love ther is in sondry wise,
As I shal thee heere devise.
For somme love leful is and good;
I mene not that which makith thee wood,
And bringith thee in many a fitte,   5200
And ravysshith fro thee al thi witte,
It is so merveilouse and queynte;
With such love be no more aqueynte.'

COMMENT RAISOUN DIFFINIST AUNSETE.

' Love of freendshippe also ther is,
Which makith no man done amys,
Of wille knytt bitwixe two,
That wole not breke for wele ne woo ;
Which long is likly to contune,
Whanne wille and goodis ben in comune,
Grounded by Goddis ordinaunce,   5210
Hoole withoute discordaunce ;
With hem holdyng comunté
Of alle her goode in charité,
That ther be noon excepcioun,
Thurgh chaungyng of entencioun,
That ech helpe other at her neede,
And wisely hele bothe word and dede,
Trewe of menyng, devoide of slouthe,
For witt is nought withoute trouthe ;
So that the ton dar alle his thought   5220
Seyn to his freend, and spare nought,
As to hym-silf withoute dredyng
To be discovered by wreying.
For glad is that conjunccioun,
Whanne ther is noon susspecioun,
Whom they wolde prove
That trewe and parfit weren in love.
For no man may be amyable,
But-if he be so ferme and stable,
That fortune chaunge hym not, ne blynde, 5230
But that his freend alle wey hym fynde,
Bothe pore and riche, in oo state.
For if his freend, thurgh ony gate,
Wole compleyne of his poverté,

He shulde not bide so long, til he
Of his helpyng hym requere ;
For goode dede done thurgh praiere
Is sold, and bought to deere iwys,
To her*te* that of grete valour is.
For her*te* fulfilled of gentilnesse,   5240
Can yvel demene his distresse.
And man that worthy is of name,
To asken often hath gret shame.
A good man brenneth in his thought
For shame, whanne he axeth ought.
He hath gret thought, and dredeth ay
For his disese, whanne he shal pray
His freend, lest that he warned be,
Til that he preve his stabilté.
But whanne that he hath founden oon   5250
That trusty is and trewe as stone,
And assaied hym at alle,
And founde hym stedefast as a walle,
And of his freendshippe be certeyne,
He shal hym shewe bothe joye and peyne,
And alle that *he* dar thynke or sey,
Withoute shame, as he wel may.
For how shulde he a-shamed be,
Of sich one as I tolde thee ?
For whanne he woot his secré thought,   5260
The thridde shal knowe therof right nought ;
For tweyne of noumbre is bet than thre,
In every counselle and secré.
Repreve he dredde never a dele,
Who that bisett his wordis wele ;
For every wise man, out of drede,
Can kepe his tunge til he se nede ;

And fooles can not holde her tunge;
A fooles belle is soone runge.
Yit shal a trewe freend do more   5270
To helpe his felowe of his sore,
And socoure hym, whanne he hath neede,
In alle that he may done in deede;
And gladder that he hym plesith
Than his felowe that he esith.
And if he do not his requeste,
He shal as mochel hym moleste
As his felow, for that he
May not fulfille his volunté
Fully, as he hath requered.   5280
If bothe the hertis Love hath fered,
Joy and woo they shulle departe,
And take evenly ech his parte.
Half his anoy he shal have ay,
And comfort, what that he may;
And of this blisse parte shal he,
If love wole departed be.
    And whilom of this unyté
Spake Tulius in a ditee;
And shulde maken his requeste   5290
Unto his freend, that is honeste;
And he goodly shulde it fulfille,
But it the more were out of skile,
And other-wise not graunte therto,
Except oonly in cause twoo.
If men his freend to deth wolde drife
Late hym be bisy to save his lyve.
Also if men wolen hym assayle,
Of his wurshippe to make hym faile,
And hyndren hym of his renoun,   5300

Late hym, with fulle entencioun,
His dever done in eche degre
That his freend ne *i*-shamed be,
In this two caas with his myght,
Taking no kepe to skile nor right,
As ferre as love may hym excuse;
This oughte no man to refuse.
This love that I have tolde to thee
Is no thing contrarie to me;
This wole I that thou folowe wele,   5310
And leve the tother everydele.
This love to vertu alle entendith,
The tothir fooles blent and shendith.

 'Another love also there is,
That is contrarie unto this,
Which desire is so constreyned
That *it* is but wille feyned;
Awey fro trouthe it doth so varie
That to good love it is contrarie;
For it.maymeth, in many wise,   5320
Sike hertis with coveitise;
Alle in wynnyng and in profit,
Sich love settith his delite.
This love so hangeth in balaunce
That if it lese his hope, perchaunce,
Of lucre, that he is sett upon,
It wole faile, and quenche anoon;
For no man may be amerous,
Ne in his lyvyng vertuous,
But he love more, in moode,   5330
Men for hem-silf than for her goode.
For love that profit doth abide,
Is fals, and bit not in no tyde.

Love cometh of dame Fortune,
That litel while wole contune,
For it shal chaungen wonder soone,
And take eclips right as the moone,
Whanne he is from us *i*-lett
Thurgh erthe, that bitwixe is sett
The sonne and hir, as it may falle,   5340
Be it in partie, or in alle;
The shadowe maketh her bemys merke,
And hir hornes to shewe derke,
That part where she hath lost hir lyght
Of Phebus fully, and the sight;
Til whanne the shadowe is overpaste,
She is enlumyned ageyn as faste,
Thurgh the brightnesse of the sonne bemes
That yeveth to hir ageyne hir lemes.
That love is right of sich nature;   5350
Now is faire, and now obscure,
Now bright, now elipsi of manere,
And whilom dymme, and whilom clere.
As soone as Poverte gynneth take,
With mantel and with wedis blake
Hidith of Love the light awey,
That into nyght it turneth day;
It may not see Richesse shyne,
Tille the blake shadowes fyne.
For, whanne Richesse shyneth brighte,   5360
Love recovereth ageyn his lighte;
And whanne it failith, he wole flit*te*,
And as she greveth, so greveth it*te*.
Of this love here what I sey:—
The riche men are loved ay,
And namely tho that sparand bene,

That wole not wasshe her hertes clene
Of the filthe, nor of the vice
Of gredy brennyng avarice.
The riche man fulle fonned is, y-wys,   5370
That weneth that he loved is.
If that his herte it undirstode,
It is not he; it is his goode.
He may wel witen in his thought,
His good is loved, and he right nought.
For if he be a nygard eke,
Men wole not sette by hym a leke,
But haten hym; this is the sothe.
Lo, what profit this catell doth!
Of every man that may hym see,   5380
It geteth hym nought but enmyté.
But he amende hym-silf of that vice,
And knowe hym-silf, he is not wys.
Certys he shulde ay freendly be,
To gete hym love also ben free,
Or ellis he is not wise ne sage
No more than is a gote ramage.
That he not loveth his dede proveth,
Whan he his richesse so wel loveth,
That he wole hide it ay, and spare,   5390
His pore freendis sene forfare,
To kepen ay his purpose,
Til for drede his iyen close,
And til a wikked deth hym take;
Hym hadde lever a-sondre shake,
And late alle hise lymes a-sondre ryve,
Than leve his richesse in his lyve.
He thenkith parte it with no man;
Certayn no love is in hym than.

How shulde love withynne hym be,   5400
Whanne in his herte is·no pité?
That he trespasseth wel I wote,
For ech man knowith his estate;
For wel hym ought to be reproved
That loveth nought, ne is not loved.
  ' But *sen* we arn to Fortune comen,
And hath oure sermoun of hir nomen,
A wondir wille Y telle thee nowe,
Thou herdist never sich oon, I trowe.
I note where thou me leven shalle,   5410
Though sothfastnesse it be *in* alle,
As it is writen, and is soth,
That unto men more profit doth
The froward Fortune and contraire,
Than the swote and debonaire :
And if thee thynke it is doutable,
It is thurgh argument provable.
For the debonaire and softe
Falsith and bigilith ofte;
For lyche a moder she can cherishe   5420
And mylken as doth a norys,
And of hir goode to hym deles
And yeveth hym parte of her Ioweles,
With grete richesse and dignité,
And hem she hoteth stabilité,
In a state that is not stable,
But chaungynge ay and variable;
And fedith hym with glorie and veyne,
And worldly blisse non certeyne.
Whanne she hym settith on hir whele,   5430
Thanne wene they to be right wele,
And in so stable state with-alle,

That never they wene for to falle.
And whanne they sette so highe be,
They wene to have in certeynté
Of hertly freendis so grete noumbre,
That no thyng myght her state encombre;
They trust hem so on every side,
Wenyng with hym they wolde abide,
In every perelle and myschaunce,   5440
Withoute chaunge or variaunce,
Bothe of catelle and of goode;
And also for to spende her bloode,
And alle her membris for to spille,
Oonly to fulfille her wille.
They maken it hole in many wise,
And hoten hem her fulle servise,
How sore that it do hem smerte;
Into her *veray* naked sherte,
Herte and alle, so hole they yeve,   5450
For the tyme that they may lyve,
So that with her flaterie,
They maken foolis glorifie
Of her wordis spekyng,
And han cheer of a rejoysyng,
And trowe hem as the evangile;
And it is alle falsheede and gile,
As they shal aftirwardes se,
Whanne they arn falle in poverté,
And ben of good and catelle bare;   5460
Thanne shulde they sene who freendis ware.
For of an hundred certeynly,
Nor of a thousande fulle scarsly,
Ne shal they fynde unnethis oon,
Whanne poverte is comen upon.

For thus Fortune that I of telle,
With men whanne hir lust to dwelle,
Makith men to leese her conisaunce,
And norishith hem in ignoraunce.
'But froward Fortune and perverse, 5470
Whanne high estatis she doth reverse,
And maketh hem to tumble doune
Of with hir whele, with sodeyn tourne,
And from her Richesse doth hem fle,
And plongeth hem in poverté,
As a stepmoder envyous,
And leieth a plastre dolorous
Unto her hertis wounded egre,
Which is not tempred with vynegre,
But with poverte and indigence, 5480
For to shewe by experience,
That she is Fortune verelye
In whom no man shulde affye,
Nor in hir yeftis have fiaunce,
She is so fulle of variaunce.
Thus kan she maken high and lowe,
Whanne they from richesse arn *i*-throwe,
Fully to knowen, withou*te* were,
Freend of affect, and freend of chere;
And which in love weren trewe and stable, 5490
And whiche also weren variable,
After Fortune her goddes*se*,
In poverte, outher in richesse;
For alle that yeveth here out of drede,
Unhappe bereveth it in dede;
For In-fortune late not oon
Of freendis, whanne Fortune is gone;
I mene tho freendis that wole fle

Anoon as entreth poverté.
And yit they wole not leve hem so,   5500
But in ech place where they go
They calle hem 'wrecche,' scorne and blame,
And of her myshappe hem diffame,
And, namely, siche as in richesse,
Pretendith moost of stablenesse,
Whanne that they sawe hym sett on-lofte,
And weren of hym socoured ofte,
And·most i-holpe in alle her neede :
But now they take no maner heede,
But seyn in voice of flaterie,   5510
That now apperith her folye,
Over-alle where so they fare,
And synge, Go, fare wel feldfare.
Alle suche freendis I beshrewe,
For of trowe ther be to fewe ;
But sothfaste freendis, what-so bitide,
In every fortune wolen abide ;
Thei han her hertis in suche noblesse
That they nyl love for no richesse,
Nor for that Fortune may hem sende   5520
Thei wolen hem socoure and defende,
And chaunge for softe ne for sore.
For who his freend loveth evermore
Though men drawe swerde his freend to slo,
He may not hewe her love a-two.
But in case that I shalle sey,
For pride and ire lese it he may,
And for reprove by nyceté,
And discovering of privité,
With tonge woundyng, as feloun,   5530
Thurgh venemous detraccioun.

Frende in this case wole gone his way,
For no thyng greve hym more ne may,
And for nought ellis wole he fle,
If that he love in stabilité.
And certeyn he is wel bigone
Among a thousand that fyndith oon.
For ther *ne* may be no richesse
Ageyns frendshipp of worthynesse,
For it ne may so high atteigne,   5540
As may the valoure, soth to seyne,
Of hym that loveth trew and welle;
Frendshipp is more than is catelle.
For freend in court ay better is
Than peny in purs, certis;
And Fortune myshappyng,
Whanne upon men she is fablyng,
Thurgh mysturnyng of hir chaunce,
And caste hem oute of balaunce,
She makith, thurgh hir adversité,   5550
Men fulle clerly for to se
Hym that is freend in existence
From hym that is by apparence.
For yn-fortune makith anoon,
To knowe thy freendis fro thy foon,
By experience, right as it is.
The which is more to preise, ywis,
Than in myche richesse and tresour,
For more depe profit and valour,
Poverte, and such adversité   5560
Bifore, than doth prosperité;
For the toon yeveth conysaunce,
And the tother ignoraunce.
    ‘ And thus in poverte is in dede

Trouthe declared fro falseheed,
For feynte frendis it wole declare,
And trewe also, what wey they fare.
For whanne he was in his richesse,
These freendis, ful of doublenesse,
Offrid hym in many wise   5570
Hert and body, and servise.
What wolde he thanne ha *yove* to ha bought,
To knowen openly her thought,
That he now hath so clerly seen?
The lasse bigiled she shulde have bene
And he hadde thanne perceyved it,
But richesse nolde not late hym witte.
Wel more avauntage doth hym thanne,
Sith that it makith hym a wise man,
The grete myscheef that he perceyveth,   5580
Than doth richesse that hym deceyveth.
Richesse riche ne makith nought
Hym that on tresour sette his thought;
For richesse stonte in suffisaunce,
And no thyng in habundaunce;
For suffisaunce alle oonly
Makith men to lyve richely.
   For he that hath mycches tweyne,
Ne value in his demeigne,
Lyveth more at ese, and more is riche,   5590
Than doth he that is chiche,
And in his berne hath, soth to seyn,
An hundred mauis of whete greyne,
Though he be chapman or marchaunte,
And have of golde many besaunte.
For in the getyng he hath such woo,
And in the kepyng drede also,

And sette evermore his bisynesse
For to encrese, and not to lesse,
For to aument and multiplie.   5600
And though on hepis that lye hym bye,
Yit never shal make his richesse,
Asseth unto his gredynesse.
But the povre that recchith nought,
Save of his lyflode, in his thought,
Which that he getith with his travaile,
He dredith nought that it shalle faile,
Though he have lytel worldis goode,
Mete and drynke, and esy foode,
Upon his travel and lyvyng,   5610
And also suffisaunt clothyng.
Or if in syknesse that he falle,
And lothe mete and drynke withalle,
Though he have not his mete to bye,
He shal bithynke hym hastely,
To putte hym oute of alle daunger,
That he of mete hath no myster;
Or that he may with lytel eke
Be founden, while that he is seke;
Or that men shulle hym berne in haste,   5620
To lyve, til his syknesse be paste,
To somme maysondewe biside;
He caste nought what shal hym bitide.
He thenkith nought that evere he shalle
Into ony syknesse falle.
   ' And though it falle, as it may be,
That alle be-tyme spare shalle he
As mochel as shal to hym suffice,
While he is sike in ony wise,
He doth for that he wole be   5630

Contente with his poverté
Withoute nede of ony man.
So myche in litel have he can,
He is apaied with his fortune;
And for he nyl be importune
Unto no wi*ght*te, ne honerous,
Nor of her goodes coveitous;
Therfore he spareth, it may wel bene,
His pore estate for to sustene.
    'Or if hym lust not for to spare,   5640
But suffrith forth, as not ne ware,
Atte last it hapneth, as it may,
Right unto his las*te* day,
And take the world as it wolde be;
For evere in herte thenkith he
The sonner that Deth hym slo,
To paradys the sonner go
He shal, there for to lyve in blisse,
Where that he shal noo good*e* misse.
Thider he hopith God shal hym sende,   5650
Aftir his wrecchid lyves ende.
Pictigoras hym-silf reherses,
In a book that the Golden Verses
Is clepid, for the nobilité
Of the honourable ditee:—
Thanne whanne thou goste thy body fro,
Fre in the eir thou shalt up go,
And leven al humanité,
And purely lyve in deité,
He is a foole withouten were   5660
That trowith have his countré heere.
In erthe is not oure countré,
That may these clerkis seyn and see

In Boice of Consolacioun,
Where it is maked mencioun
Of oure countré pleyn at the eye,
By teching of philosophie,
Where lewid men myghte lere witte,
Who-so that wolde translaten it.
If he be sich that can wel lyve   5670
Aftir his rente may hym yeve,
And not desireth more to have,
Than may fro poverte hym save.
A wise man seide, as we may seen,
Is no man wrecched, but he it wene,
Be he kyng, knyght, or ribaude.
And many a ribaude is mery and baude,
That swynkith, and berith, bothe day and nyght,
Many a burthen of grete myght,
The whiche doth hym lasse offense,   5680
For he suffrith in pacience.
They laugh and daunce, trippe and synge,
And leye not up for her lyvyng,
But in the taverne alle dispendith
The wynnyng that God hem sendith.
Thanne goth he fardeles for to bere,
With as good chere as he dide ere,
To swynke and traveile he not feyntith,
For for to robben he disdeyntith;
But right anoon, aftir his swynke,   5690
He goth to taverne for to drynke.
Alle these ar riche in abundaunce,
That can thus have suffisaunce
Wel more than can an usurere,
As God wel knowith, withoute were.
For an usurer, so God me se,

Shal nevere for richesse riche be,
But evermore pore and indigent,   5700
Scarce, and gredy in his entent.
    'For soth it is, whom it displese,
Ther may no marchaunt lyve at ese,
His herte in sich a were is sett,
That it brenneth quyke to gete,
Ne never shal, though he hath geten,
Though he have gold in gerners yeten,
For to be nedy he dredith sore.
Wherfore to geten more and more
He sette his herte and his desire;
So hote he brennyth in the fire
Of coveitise, that makith hym woode   5710
To purchace other mennes goode.
He undirfongith a gret peyne,
That undirtakith to drynke up Seyne;
For the more he drynkith, ay
The more he leveth, the soth to say.
Thus is thurst of fals getyng,
That laste ever in coveityng,
And the angwisshe and distresse
With the fire of gredynesse.
. She fightith with hym ay, and stryveth,   5720
That his herte a-sondre ryveth;
Such gredynesse hym assaylith,
That whanne he most hath, most he failith.
    'Phiciciens and advocates
Gone right by the same yates.
They selle her science for wynnyng,
And haunte her crafte for gret getyng.
Her wynnyng is of such swetnesse,
That if a man falle in sikenesse,

They are fulle glad, for ther encrese ;   5730
For by her wille, withoute lees,
Everiche man shulde be seke,
And though they die, they sette not a leke.
After whanne they the gold have take,
Fulle litel care for hem they make.
They wolde that fourty were seke atonys,
Yhe, .ij. hundred, in flesh and bonys,
And yit .ij. thousand, as I gesse,
For to encrecen her richesse.
They wole not worchen in no wise,   5740
But for lucre and coveitise,
For fysic gynneth first by fy,
The phicicien also sothely ;
And sithen it goth fro fy to sy ;
To truste on hem is foly ;
For they nyl in no maner gre,
Do right nought for charité.
  ' Eke in the same secte ar sette
Alle tho that prechen for to gete
Worshipes, honour, and richesse.   5750
Her hertis arn in grete distresse,
That folk lyve not holily.
But aboven alle specialy,
Sich as prechen veynglorie,
And toward God have no memorie,
But forth as ypocrites trace,
And to her soules deth purchace,
And outward shewing holynesse,
Though they be fulle of cursidnesse.
Not liche to the apostles twelve,   5760
They deceyve other and hem-selve ;
Bigiled is the giler thanne.

For prechyng of a cursed man,
Though to other may profite,
Hymsilf it availeth not a myte;
For ofte goode predicacioun
Cometh of evel entencioun.
To hym not vaileth his preching
Alle helpe he other with his teching;
For where they good ensaumple take,   5770
There is he with veynglorie shake.

  ‘ But late us leven these prechoures,
And speke of hem that in her toures
Hepe up her gold, and faste shette,
And sore theron her herte sette.
They neither love God, ne drede;
They kepe more than it is nede,
 And in her bagges sore it bynde;
Out of the sonne, and of the wynde,
They putte up more than nede were,   5780
Whanne they seen pore folk forfare,
For hunger die, and for cold quake;
God can wel vengeaunce therof take.
Thre grete myscheves hem assailith,
And thus in gadring ay travaylith;
With myche peyne they wynne richesse,
And drede hem holdith in distresse,
To kepe that they gadre faste;
With sorwe they leve it at the laste;
With sorwe they bothe dye and lyve,   5790
That unto richesse her hertis yive,
And in defaute of love it is,
As it shewith ful wel, iwys;
For if this gredy, the sothe to seyn,
Loveden, and were loved ageyn,

And goode love regned over-alle,
Such wikkidnesse ne shulde falle;
But he shulde yeve that most good hadde
To hem that weren in nede bistadde,
And lyve withoute false usure,   5800
For charité, fulle clene and pure.
If they hem yeve to goodnesse,
Defendyng hem from ydelnesse,
In alle this world thanne pore noon
We shulde fynde, I trowe not oon.
But chaunged is this world unstable,
For love is over-alle vendable.
We se that no man loveth nowe
But for wynnyng and for prowe;
And love is thralled in servage   5810
Whanne it is sold for avauntage;
Yit wommen wole her bodyes selle;
Suche soules goth to the devel of helle.'

  *   *   *   *   *

Whanne Love hadde told hem his entente,
The baronage to councel wente;
In many sentences they fille,
And dyversely they seide hir tille:
But aftir discorde they accordede,
And her accord to Love recordede.
'Sir,' seiden they, ' we ben atone,   5820
Bi evene accorde of everichone,
Outake Richesse al oonly,
That sworne hath ful hauteynly,
That she the castelle nyl not assaile,
Ne smyte a stroke in this bataile,
With darte, ne mace, spere, ne knyf,
For man that spekith or berith the lyf,

And blameth youre emprise, iwys,
And from oure hoost departed is,
Atte lest*e* wey, as in this plyte,   5830
So hath she this man in dispite;
For she seith he ne loved hir never,
And therfore she wole hate hym evere.
For he wole gadre no tresoure,
He hath hir wrath for evermore.
He agylte hir never in other caas,
Lo, heere alle hoolly his trespas!
She seith wel, that this other day
He axide hir leve to gone the way
That is clepid To-moche-yevyng,   5840
And spak fulle faire in his praiyng;
But whanne he praiede hir, pore was he.
Therfore she warned hym the entre.
Ne yit is he not thryven so
That he hath geten a peny or two,
That quytely is his owne in holde.
Thus hath Richesse us alle tolde;
And whanne Richesse us this recorded,
Withouten hir we ben accorded.

And we fynde in oure accordaunce,   5850
That False-semblant and Abstinaunce,
With alle the folk of her bataille,
Shulle at the hyndre gate assayle,
That Wikkid-tunge hath in kepyng,
With his Normans fulle of janglyng.
And with hem Curtesie and Largesse,
That shulle shewe her hardynesse,
To the olde wyf that kepte so harde
Fair-welcomyng withynne her warde.
Thanne shal Delite and Wel-heelynge   5860

Fonde Shame adowne to brynge,
With alle her oost erly and late ;
They shulle assailen that ilke gate.
Agaynes Drede shalle Hardynesse
Assayle, and also Sikernesse,
With alle the folk of her ledyng,
That never wiste what was fleyng.
    Fraunchise shalle fight, and eke Pité,
With Daunger fulle of cruelté.
Thus is youre hoost ordeyned wele ;   5870
Doune shalle the castelle every dele,
If everiche do his entent,
So that Venus be present,
Youre modir, fulle of vesselage,
That can ynough of such usage ;
Withouten hir may no wight spede
This werk, neithir for word ne deede.
Therfore is good ye for hir sende,
For thurgh hir may this werk amende.'
    Amour. Lordynges, my modir, the goddesse, 5880
That is my lady, and my maistresse,
Nis not alle at my willyng,
Ne doth not alle my desiryng.
Yit can she some tyme done labour,
Whanne that hir lust, in my socour,
As my nede is for to a-cheve,
But now I thenke hir not to greve.
My modir is she, and of childehede
I bothe worshipe hir, and eke drede ;
For who that dredith sire ne dame,   5890
Shal it abye in body or name.
And, netheles, yit kunne we
Sende aftir hir, if nede be,

And were she nygh, she comen wolde,
I trowe that no thyng myght hir holde.
  Mi modir is of gret prowesse;
She hath tan many a fortresse,
That cost hath many a pounde er this,
There I nas not present, ywis;
And yit men seide it was my dede;   5900
But I come never in that stede;
Ne me ne likith, so mote I the,
That such toures ben take withoute me.
For-why me thenkith that in no wise
It may bene clepid but marchandise.
  'Go bye a courser blak or white,
And pay therfore; than art thou quyte.
The marchaunt owith thee right nought,
Ne thou hym whanne thou it *hast* bought.
I wole not sellyng clepe yevyng,   5910
For sellyng axeth no guerdonyng;
Here lith no thank, ne no merite,
That oon goth from that other al quyte.
But this sellyng is not semblable;
For, whanne his hors is in the stable,
He may it selle ageyn, pardé,
And wynnen on it, such happe may be;
Alle may the man not leese, iwys,
For at the leest the skynne is his.
Or ellis, if it so bitide   5920
That he wole kepe his hors to ride,
Yit is he lord ay of his hors*e*.
But thilk*e* chaffare is wel worse,
There Venus entremetith ought;
For who-so such chaffare hath bought,
He shal not worchen so wisely,

That he ne shal leese al outerly
Bothe his money and his chaffare;
But the seller of the ware,
The prys and profit have shalle.   5930
Certeyn the bier shal leese alle,
For he ne can so dere it bye
To have lordship and fulle maistrie,
Ne have power to make lettyng,
Neithir for yift ne for prechyng,
That of his chaffare maugre his,
Another shal have as moche iwis,
If he wole yeve as myche as he,
Of what contrey so that he be;
Or for right nought, so happe may,   5940
If he can flater hir to hir pay.
Ben thanne siche marchauntz wise?
No, but fooles in every wise,
Whanne they bye sich thyng wilfully,
There as they leese her good folyly.
But natheles, this dar I say,
My modir is not wont to pay,
For she is neither so fool ne nyce,
To entremete hir of sich *vice*.
But trust*e* wel, he shal pay alle,   5950
That repent of his bargeyn shalle,
Whanne Poverte putte hym in distresse,
Alle were he scoler to Richesse;
That is for me in gret yernyng,
Whanne she assentith to my willyng.
    ‘ But, *by* my modir seint Venus,
And by hir fader Saturnus,
That hir engendride by his lyf,
But not upon his weddid wyf!

Yit wole I more unto you swere,   5960
To make this thyng the seurere
Now by that feith, and that leauté
That I owe to alle my britheren fre,
Of which ther nys wight undir heven
That kan her fadris names neven,
So dyverse and so many ther be,
That with my modir have be privé !
Yit wolde I swere, for sikirnesse,
The pole of helle to my witnesse,
Now drynke I not this yeere clarré,   5970
If that I lye, or forsworne be!
For of the goddes the usage is,
That who-so hym forswereth amys,
Shal that yeer drynke no clarré.
Now have I sworne ynough, pardee ;
If I forswere me, thanne am I lorne,
But I wole never be forsworne ;
Syth Richesse hath me failed heere,
She shal abye that trespas ful dere,
Atte leeste wey, but *she* hir arme   5980
With swerd, or sparth, or gysarme.
For certis sith she loveth not me,
Fro thilk tyme that she may se
The castelle and the tour to shake.
In sory tyme she shal a-wake.
If I may grepe a riche man
I shal so pulle hym, if I can,
That he shal, in a fewe stoundes,
Lese alle his markis and his poundis.
I shal hym make his pens outslynge,   5990
But they in his gerner sprynge ;
Oure maydens shal eke pluk hym so,

That hym shal neden fetheres mo,
And make hym selle his londe to spende,
But he the bet kunne hym defende.
  ' Pore men han maad her lord of me ;
Al-though they not so myghty be,
That they may fede me in delite,
I wole not have hem in despite.
No good man hateth hem, as I gesse,   6000
For chynche and feloun is Richesse,
That so can chase hem and dispise,
And hem defoule in sondry wise.
They loven fulle bet, so God me spede,
Than doth the riche chynchy grede,
And ben in good feith, more stable
And trewer, and more serviable.
And therfore it suffisith me
Her goode herte and her beauté.   6010
They han on me sette alle her though
And therfore I forgete hem nought.
I wole hem bringe in grete noblesse,
If that I were God of Richesse,
As I am God of Love sothely,
Sich routhe upon her pleynt have I.
Therfore I must his socour be,
That peyneth hym to serven me,
For if he deide for love of this,
Thanne semeth in me no love ther is.'
  ' Sir,' seide they, ' soth is every deel   6020
That ye reherce, and we wote wel
Thilk oth to holde is resonable ;
For it is good and covenable,
That ye on riche men han sworne.
For, sir, this wote we wel biforne ;

If riche men done you homage,
That is as fooles done outrage;
But ye shulle not forsworne be,
Ne lette therfore to drynke clarré,
Or pyment makid fresh and newe.   6030
Ladies shulle hem such pepir brewe,
If that they falle into her laas,
That they for woo mowe seyn ' Allas!'
Ladyes shullen evere so curteis be,
That they shal quyte youre oth alle free.
Ne sekith never othir vicaire,
For they shal speke with hem so faire
That ye shal holde you paied fulle wele.
Though ye you medle never a dele,
Late ladies worthe with her thyngis,   6040
They shal hem telle so fele tidynges,
And moeve hem eke so many requestis
Bi flateri, that not honest is,
And therto yeve hem such thankynges,
What with kissyng, and with talkynges,
That certis, if they trowed be,
Shal never leve hem londe ne fee
That it nyl as the moeble fare,
Of which they first delyverid are.
Now may ye telle us alle youre wille,   6050
And we youre heestes shal fulfille.

  ' But Fals-semblant dar not, for drede
Of you, sir, medle hym of this dede,
For he seith that ye ben his foo;
He note, if ye wole worche hym woo.
Wherfore we pray you alle, beau sire,
That ye forgyve hym now your ire,
And that he may dwelle, as your man,

With Abstinence his dere lemman ;
This oure accord and oure wille nowe.'   6060
' Parfay,' seide Love, ' I graunte it yowe ;
I wole wel holde hym for my man ;
Now late hym come :' and he forth ran.
' Fals-semblant,' quod Love, ' in this wise
I take thee heere to my servise,
That thou oure freendis helpe alway,
And hyndreth hem neithir nyght ne day,
But do thy myght hem to releve,
And eke oure enemyes that thou greve.
Thyne be this myght, I graunte it thee,   6070
My kyng of harlotes shalt thou be ;
We wole that thou have such honour.
Certeyne thou art a fals traitour,
And eke a theef ; sith thou were borne,
A thousand tyme thou art forsworne.
But, netheles, in oure heryng,
To putte oure folk out of doutyng,
I bidde thee teche hem, wostowe howe ?
Bi somme general signe nowe,
In what place thou shalt founden be,   6080
If that men hadde myster of thee,
And how men shal thee best espye,
For thee to knowe is gret maistrie ;
Telle in what place is thyn hauntyng.'
    F. Sem.—' Sir I have fele dyverse wonyng,
That I kepe not rehersed be,
So that ye wolde respiten me.
For if that I telle you the sothe,
I may have harme and shame bothe.
If that my felowes wisten it,   6090
My talis shulden me be quytt ;

For certeyne they wolde hate me,
If ever 1 knewe her cruelté ;
For they wolde overalle holde hem stille
Of trouthe that is ageyne her wille ;
Suche tales kepen they not here.
I myght eftsoone bye it fulle deere,
If I seide of hem ony thing.
That ought displesith to her heryng.
For what word that hem prikke or biteth,   6100
In that word noon of hem deliteth,
Al were it gospel the evangile,
That wolde reprove hem of her gile,
For they are cruel and hauteyne.
And this thyng wote I welle certeyne,
If I speke ought to peire her loos,
Your court shal not so welle be cloos,
That they ne shalle wite it atte last.
Of goode men am I nought agast,
For they wole taken on them no thyng,   6110
Whanne that they knowe al my menyng ;
But he that wole it on hym take,
He wole hym-silf suspecious make,
That he his lyf let covertly,
In Gile and in Ipocrisie,
That me engendred and yaf fostryng.'
    ' They made a fulle good engendryng,'
Quod Love, 'for who-so sothly telle,
They engendrede the devel of helle.
But nedely, how-so-evere it be,'   6120
Quod Love, ' I wole and charge thee,
To telle anoon thy wonyng places,
Heryng ech wight that in this place is ;
And what lyf that thou lyvest also,

Hide it no lenger now; wherto?
Thou most discovere alle thi wurchyng,
How thou servest, and of what thyng,
Though that thou shuldist for thi sothe sawe
Ben al to-beten and to-drawe;
And yit art thou not wont, pardee.   6130
But natheles, though thou beten be,
Thou shalt not be the first, that so
Hath for soth sawe suffred woo.'

   F'. Sem.—'Sir, sith that it may liken you,
Though that I shulde be slayne right now,
I shal done youre comaundement,
For therto have I gret talent.'

   Withouten wordis mo, right thanne,
Fals-semblant his sermon biganne,
And seide hem thus in audience:—   6140
' Barouns, take heede of my sentence!
That wight that list to have knowing
Of Fals-semblant fulle of flatering,
He must in worldly folk hym seke,
And, certes, in the cloistres eke;
I wone no where but in hem twey;
But not lyk even, soth to sey;
Shortly, I wole herberwe me,
There I hope best to hulstred be;
And certeynly, sikerest hidyng,   6150
Is undirnethe humblest clothing.

   ' Religiouse folk ben fulle covert;
Seculer folk ben more appert.
But natheles, I wole not blame
Religious folk, ne hem diffame,
In what habit that ever they go:
Religioun umble, and trewe also,

Wole I not blame, ne dispise,
But I nyl love it in no wise.
I mene of fals religious,   6160
That stoute ben, and malicious ;
That wolen in an abit goo,
And setten not her herte therto.
Religious folk ben al pitous ;
Thou shalt not seen oon dispitous.
They loven no pride, ne no strif,
But humbÌ€ely they wole lede her lyf,
With which folk wole I never be.
And if I dwelle, I feyne me
I may wel in her abit go ;   6170
But me were lever my nekke a-two,
Than lette a purpose that I take,
What covenaunt that ever I make.
I dwelle with hem that proude be,
And fulle of wiles and subtilité ;
That worship of this world coveiten,
And grete nede kunnen espleiten ;
And gone and gadren gret pitauncez,
And purchace hem the acqueyntauncez
Of men that myghty lyf may leden ;   6180
And feyne hem pore, and hem-silf feden
With gode morcels delicious,
And drinken *goode* wyne precious,
And preche us povert and distresse,
And fisshen hem-silf gret richesse,
With wily nettis that they caste :
It wole come foule out at the laste.
They ben fro clene riligioun went ;
They make the world an argument,
That *hath* a foule conclusioun.   6190

' I have a robe of religioun,
Thanne am I alle religious ;'
This argument is alle roignous ;
It is not worth a croked brere ;
Abit ne makith neithir monk ne frere,
But clene lyf and devocioun,
Makith gode men of religioun.
Netheles, ther kan noon answere,
How high that evere his heed he shere
With *rasour* whetted never so kene,   6200
That Gile in braunches kut thrittene,
Ther can no wight distincte it so,
That he dare sey a word therto.
    ' But what herberwe that ever I take,
Or what semblant that evere I make,
I mene but gile, and folowe that ;
For right no mo than Gibbe oure cat,
That awayteth mice and rattes to kyllen,
Ne entende I but to bigilyng ;   6210
    Ne no wight may, by my clothing,
Wite with what folk is my dwellyng
Ne by my wordis yit, pardé,
So softe and so plesaunt they be.
Biholde the dedis that I do ;
But thou be blynde thou oughtest so ;
For varie her wordis fro her deede,
They thenke on gile, withoute dreede,
What maner clothing that they were,
Or what estate that evere they bere,   6220
Lered or lewde, lord or lady,
Knyght, squyer, burgeis, or bayly.'
    Right thus while Fals-semblant sermoneth ;
Eftsones Love hym aresoneth,

And brake his tale in his spekyng
As though he had hym tolde lesyng.
And seide: 'What devel is that I here?
What folk hast thou us nempned heere?
May men fynde religioun
In worldly habitacioun?'
   F. Sem.—'Yhe, sir; it folowith not that they
Shulde lede a wikked lyf, parfey,   6231
Ne not therfore her soules leese,
That hem to worldly clothes chese;
For, certis, it were gret pitee.
Men may in seculer clothes see,
Florishen hooly religioun.
Fulle many a seynt in feeld and toune,
With many a virgine glorious,
Devoute, and fulle religious,
Han deied, that comyn cloth ay beeren,   6240
Yit seyntes nevere-the-lesse they weren.
I cowde reken you many a ten;
Yhe, wel nygh *alle* these hooly wymmen,
That men in chirchis herie and seke,
Bothe maydens, and these wyves eke,
That baren fulle many a faire child heere,
Wered alwey clothis seculere,
And in the same dieden they
That seyntes weren, and ben alwey.
The .xj. thousand maydens deere,   6250
That beren in heven her ciergis clere,
Of whiche men rede in chirche, and synge,
Were take in seculer clothing,
Whanne they resseyved martirdome,
And wonnen hevene unto her home.
Good herte makith the goode thought;

The clothing yeveth ne reveth nought.
The goode thought and the worching,
That makith the religioun flowryng ;
Ther lyth the goode religioun,   6260
Aftir the right entencioun.
  ' Who-so took a wethers skynne,
And wrapped a gredy wolf therynne,
For he shulde go with lambis whyte,
Wenest thou not he wolde hem bite ?
Yhis ! neverthelasse, as he were woode,
He wolde hem wery, and drinke the bloode ;
And wel the rather hem disceyve,
For sith they cowde not perceyve
His treget, and his cruelté,   6270
They wolde hym folowe, al wolde he fle.
  ' If ther be wolves of siche hewe,
Amonges these apostlis newe,
Thou, hooly chirche, thou maist be wailed !
Sith that thy citee is assayled
Thourgh knyghtis of thyn owne table,
God wote thi lordship is doutable !
If thei enforcen it to wynne,
That shulde defende it fro withynne,
Who myghte defense ayens hem make ?   6280
Withoute stroke it mote be take,
Of trepeget or mangonel ;
Withoute displaiyng of pensel.
And if God nyl done it socour,
But lat renne in this colour,
Thou most thyn heestis laten be.
Thanne is ther nought, but yelde thee,
Or yeve hem tribute, doutlees,
And holde it of hem to have pees :

But gretter harme bitide thee,   6290
That they al maister of it be.
Wel konne they scorne thee withal;
By day stuffen they the walle,
And al the nyght they mynen there.
Nay, thou planten most elles where
Thyn ympes, if thou wolt fruyt have.
Abide not there thi-silf to save.
    'But now pees! heere I turne ageyne;
I wole nomore of this thing seyne,
If I may passen me herby,   6300
For I myghte maken you wery.
But I wole heten you al-way,
To helpe youre freendis what I may,
So they wollen my company;
For they be shent al outerly,
But if so falle, that I be
Ofte with hem, and they with me.
And eke my lemman mote they serve,
Or they shulle not my love deserve.
Forsothe I am a fals traitour;   6310
God juggede me for a theef trichour;
Forsworne I am, but wel nygh none
Wote of my gile, til it be done.
    'Thourgh me hath many oon deth resseyved,
That my treget nevere aperceyved;
And yit resceyveth, and shal resseyve,
That my falsnesse shal nevere a-perceyve:
But who-so doth, if he wise be,
Hym is right good be warre of me.
But so sligh is the a-perceyvyng   6320
That al to late cometh knowyng.
For Protheus that cowde hym chaunge,

In every shape homely and straunge,
Cowde nevere sich gile ne tresoune
As I; for I come never in toune
There as I myghte knowen be,
Though men me bothe myght here and see.
Fulle wel I can my clothis chaunge,
Take oon, and make another straunge.
Now am I knyght, now chasteleyne;   6330
Now prelat, and now chapeleyne;
Now prest, now clerk, and now forstere;
Now am I maister, now scolere;
Now monke, now chanoun, now baily;
What ever myster man am I.
Now am I prince, now am I page,
And kan by herte every langage.
Somme tyme am I hore and olde;
Now am I yonge, stoute, and bolde;
Now am I Robert, now Robyn;   6340
Now frere menour, now jacobyn;
And with me folwith my loteby,
To done me solas and company,
That hight dame Abstinence, and reyned
In many a queynte array feyned.
Ryght as it cometh to hir lykyng,
I fulfille al hir desiryng.
Somtyme a wommans cloth take I;
Now am I a mayde, now lady.
Somtyme I am religious;   6350
Now lyk an anker in an hous.
Somtyme am I *a* prioresse,
And now a nonne, and now abbesse;
And go thurgh alle regiouns,
Sekyng alle religiouns.

But to what ordre that I am sworne,
I take the strawe and bete the corne ;
To joly folk I enhabite,
I axe nomore but her abite.
What wole ye more ? in every wise   6360
Right as me lyst I me disgise.
Wel can I were me undir wede :
Unlyk is my word to my dede.
Thus make *I* into my trappis falle,
Thurgh my pryveleges, alle
That ben in Cristendome alyve.
I may assoile, and I may shryve,
That no prelat may lette me,
Alle folk, where evere thei founde be :
I note no prelate may done so,   6370
But it the pope be, and no mo,
That made thilk establisshing.
Now is not this a propre thing ?
But were my sleightis a-perceyved,
Ne shulde I more ben receyved
As I was wont; and wostow whye?
For I dide hem a *tregetrie* ;
But therof yeve I a lytel tale,
I have the silver and the male,
So have I prechid and eke shreven,
So have I take, so have I yeven,   6380
Thurgh her foly, husbonde and wyf,
That I lede right a joly lyf,
Thurgh symplesse of the prelacye ;
They knowe not al my tregettrie.
    ‘ But for asmoche as man and wyf
Shulde shewe her paroche prest her lyf
Onys a yeer, as scith the book,

Er ony wight his housel took,
Thanne have I pryvylegis large,
That may of myche thing discharge,   6390
For he may seie right thus pardé:
' Sir Preest, in shrift I telle it thee,
That he to whom that I am shryven
Hath me assoiled, and me yeven
For penaunce sothly for my synne,
Which that I fonde me gilty ynne;
Ne I ne have nevere entencioun
To make double confessioun,
Ne reherce efte my shrift to thee;
O shrift is right ynough to me.   6400
This oughte thee suffice wele,
Ne be not rebel never a dele;
For certis, though thou haddist it sworne,
I wote no prest ne prelat borne
That may to shrift efte me constreyne.
And if they done I wole me pleyne;
For I wote where to pleyne wele.
Thou shalt not streyne me a dele,
Ne enforce me, ne not me trouble,
To make my confessioun double.   6410
Ne I have none affeccioun
To have double absolucioun.
The firste is right ynough to me;
This latter assoilyng quyte I thee.
I am unbounde; what maist thou fynde
More of my synnes me to unbynde?
For he that myght hath in his honde,
Of alle my synnes me unbonde.
And if thou wolt me thus constreyne,
That me mote nedis on thee pleyne,   6420

There shalle no jugge imperial,
Ne bisshop, ne official,
Done jugement on me; for I
Shal gone and pleyne me openly
Unto my shriftefadir newe,
That highte Frere Wolf untrewe,
And he shal cheveys hym for me,
For I trowe he can hampre thee.
But, lord! he wolde be wrooth withalle,
If men hym wolde Frere Wolf calle!　　6430
For he wolde have no pacience,
But done al cruel vengeaunce!
He wolde his myght done at the leeste,
No thing spare for Goddis heeste.
And, God so wys be my socour,
But thou yeve me my savyour
At Ester, whanne it likith me,
Withoute presyng more on thee,
I wole forth, and to hym gone,
And he shal housele me anoon,　　6440
For I am out of thi grucching;
I kepe not dele with thee no thing.'
Thus may he shryve hym, that forsaketh
His paroche prest, and to me takith.
And if the prest wole hym refuse,
I am fulle redy hym to accuse,
And hym punysshe and hampre so,
That he his chirche shal forgo.
　' But who-so hath in his felyng
The consequence of such shryvyng,　　6450
Shal sene that prest may never have myght
To knowe the conscience a-right
Of hym that is undir his cure.

And this ageyns holy scripture,
That biddith every heerde honeste
Have verry knowing of his beeste.
But pore folk that gone by strete,
That have no gold, ne sommes grete,
Hem wolde I lete to her prelates,
Or lete her prestis knowe her states,   6460
For to me right nought yeve they;
' And why is it?' ' For they ne may.
They ben so bare, I take no kepe;
But I wole have the *fatte* sheepe;
Lat parish prestis have the lene,
I yeve not of her harme a bene!
And if that prelates grucche it,
That oughten wroth be in her witt,
To leese her *fatte* beestes so,
I shal yeve hem a stroke or two,   6470
That they shal leesen with *the* force,
Yhe, bothe her mytre and her crocc.
Thus jape I hem, and have do longe,
My pryveleges ben so stronge.'
    Fals-semblant wolde have stynted heere,
But Love ne made hym no such cheere,
That he was wery of his sawe;
But for to make hym glad and fawe,
He seide:—' Telle on more specialy,
Hou that thou servest untrewely.   6480
Telle forth, and shame thee never a dele
For, as thyn abit shewith wele,
Thou servest an hooly heremyte.'
    ' Sothe is; but I am but an ypocrite.'
    ' Thou goste and prechest poverté?'
    ' Yhe, sir; but Richesse hath pousté.'

'Thou prechest abstinence also?'
'Sir, I wole fillen, so mote I go,
My paunche of goode mete and wyne,
As shulde a maister of dyvyne;
For how that I me pover feyne,
Yit alle pore folk I disdeyne.
I love bettir that queyntaunce,
Ten tyme, of the kyng of Fraunce,
Than of a pore man of mylde mode,
Though that his soule be al-so gode.
For whanne I see beggers quakyng,
Naked on myxnes al stynkyng,
For hungre crie, and eke for care,
I entremete not of her fare.
They ben so pore, and ful of pyne,
They myghte not oonys yeve me a dyne,
For they have no thing but her lyf;
What shulde he yeve that likketh his knyf?
It is but foly to entremete,
To seke in houndes nest fat mete.
Lete bere hem to the spitel anoon,
But, for me, comfort gete they noon.
But a riche sike usurere
Wolde I visite and drawe nere.
Hym wole I comforte and rehete,
For I hope of his gold to gete.
And if that wikkid Deth hym have,
I wole go with hym to his grave.
And if ther ony reprove me,
Why that I lete the pore be,
Wostow how I not a-scape?
I sey and swere hym ful rape,
That riche men han more tecches

Of synne, than han pore wreeches,   6520
And han of counsel more mister ;
And therfore I wole drawe hem ner.
But as grete hurt, it may so be,
Hath a soule in right grete poverté,
As soule is grete richesse, forsothe,
Al be it that they hurten bothe.
For richesse and mendicitees
Ben clepid .ij. extremytees ;
The mene is cleped suffisaunce,
Ther lyth of vertu the aboundaunce.   6530
For Salamon fulle wel I wote,
In his parablis us wrote,
As it is knowe to many a wight,
In his thrittene chapitre right ;—
God thou me kepe, for thi pousté,
Fro richesse and mendicité ;
For if a riche man hym dresse,
To thenke to myche on richesse,
His herte on that so fer is sett,
That *he* his creatour foryett ;   6540
And hym that beggith, wole ay greve.
How shulde I bi his word hym leve ?
Unnethe that he nys a mycher,
Forsworne, or ellis Goddis lyer.
Thus seith Salamon*es* sawes.
Ne we fynde writen in no lawis,
And namely in oure Cristen lay,
Whoso seith, ' yhe,' I dar sey, ' nay '
That Crist, ne his apostlis dere,
While that they walkide in ertho heere,   6550
Were never seen her bred beggyng,
For they nolden beggen for no thing.

And right thus was men wont to teche ;
And in this wise wolde it preche,
The maistres of divinité
Somtyme in Parys the citee.
  ' And if men wolde ther geyn appose
The nakid text, and lete the glose,
It myghte soone assoiled be ;
 For men may wel the sothe see,   6560
That, pardé, they myght aske a thing
Pleynly forth withoute begging.
For they weren Goddis herdis decre,
And cure of soules hadden heere,
They nolde no thing begge her fode ;
For aftir Crist was done on rode,
With *her* propre handis they wroughte,
And with travel, and ellis nought,
They wonnen alle her sustenaunce,
And lyveden forth in her penaunce,   6570
And the remenaunt yaf awey
To other poore folkis alwey.
They neither bilden tour ne halle,
But they in houses smale with alle.
A myghty man that can and may,
Shulde with his honde and body alway,
Wynne hym his fode in laboring,
If he ne have rent or sich a thing,
Al-though he be religious,
And God to serven curious.   6580
Thus mote he done, or do trespas,
 But if it be in certeyn cas,
That I can rcherce, if myster be,
 Right wel, whanne I the tyme se.
  ' Seke the book of Seynt Austyne,

Be it in papir or perchemyne,
There as he writ of these worchynges,
Thou shalt seen that noon excusynges
A parfit man ne shulde seke
Bi wordis, ne bi dedis eke,   6590
Al-though he be religious,
And God to serven curious,
That he ne shal, so mote I go,
With propre hondis and body also,
Gete his fode in laboryng,
If he ne have proprete of thing.
Yit shulde he selle alle his substaunce,
And with his swynk have sustenaunce,
If he be parfit in bounté.
Thus han tho bookes tolde me: 6600
For he that wole gone ydilly,
And usith it ay *besily*
Go haunten other mennes table,
He is a trechour ful of fable,
Ne he ne may, by gode resoun,
Excuse hym by his orisoun.
For men bihoveth, in somme gise,
Ben somtyme in Goddis servise,
To gone and purchasen her nede.
Men mote eten, that is no drede,   6610
And slepe, and *ek* do other thing,
So longe may they leve praiyng.
So may they eke her praier blynne,
While that they werke her mete to wynne.
Seynt Austyn wole therto accorde,
In thilke book that I recorde.
Justinian eke, that made lawes,
Hath thus forboden by olde *dawes*:

' No man, up peyne to be dede,
Mighty of body, to begge his brede,   6620
If he may swynke it for to gete ;
Men shulde hym rather mayme or bete,
Or done of hym aperte justice,
Than suffren hym in such malice.'
' They done not wel, so mote I go,
That taken such almesse so,
But if they have somme pryvelege,
That of the peyne hem wole allege.
But how that is, can I not see,
But if the prince disseyved be ;   6630
Ne I ne wene not sikerly,
That they may have it rightfully.
But I wole not determine
Of prynces power, ne defyne,
Ne by my word comprende, iwys,
If it so ferre may streeche in this.
I wole not entremete a dele ;
But I trowe that the book seith wele,
Who that takith almessis, that be
Dewe to folk that men may se   6640
Lame, feble, wery, and bare,
Pore, or in such maner care,
That konne wynne hem never mo,
For they have no power therto,
He etith his owne dampnyng,
But if He lye that made al thing.
And if ye such a truaunt fynde,
. Chastise hym wel, if ye be kynde.
But they wolde hate you, per cas,
And if ye fillen in her laas.   6650
They wolde eftsoonys do you scathe,

If that they myghte, late or rathe;
For they be not fulle pacient,
That han the world thus foule blent.
And witeth wel, that *as* God bad
The good-man selle al that he had*de*,
And folowe hym, and to pore it yeve,
He wolde not therfore that he lyve,
To serven hym in mendience,
For it was nevere his sentence;   6660
But he bad wirken whanne that neede is,
And folwe hym in goode dedis.
Seynt Poule that loved al hooly chirche,
He bade thappostles for to wirche,
And wynnen her lyflode in that wise,
And hem defendede truaundise,
And seide, 'wirketh with youre honden;'
Thus shulde the thing be undirstonden.
He nolde, iwys, have bidde hem begging,
Ne sellen gospel, ne prechyng,   6670
Lest they berafte, with her askyng,
Folk of her catel or of her thing.
For in this world is many a man
That yeveth his good, for he ne can
Werne it for shame, or ellis he
Wolde of the asker delyvered be;
And for he hym encombrith so,
He yeveth hym good to late hym go:
But it can hym no thyng profite,
They lese the yift and the meryte.   6680
The goode folk that Poule to prechede,
Profred hym ofte, whan he hem techede,
Somme of her good in charité;
But therfore right no thing toke he;

But of his hondwerk wolde he gete
Clothes to wryne hym, and his mete.
  'Telle me thanne how a man may lyven,
That al his good to pore hath yiven,
And wole but oonly bidde his bedis,
And never with hondes laboure his nedis.   6690
May he do so?' 'yhe, sir.'   'And how?'
'Sir, I wole gladly telle yow:—
Seynt Austyn seith, a man may be
In houses that han propreté,
As templers and hospitelers,
And as these chanouns regulers,
Or white monkes, or these blake,
I wole no mo ensamplis make,
And take therof his sustenyng,
For therynne lyth no begging,   6700
But other weyes not, ywys;
Yit Austyn gabbith not of this.
And yit fulle many a monke laboreth,
That God in hooly chirche honoureth
For whanne her swynkyng is agone,
They rede and synge in chirche anone.
  'And for ther hath ben gret discorde,
As many a wight may bere recorde,
Upon the estate of mendiciens,
I wole shortly, in youre presence,   6710
Telle how a man may begge at nede,
That hath not wherwith hym to fede,
Maugre his felones jangelyngis,
For sothfastnesse wole none hidyngis;
And yit percas I may abeye,
That I to yow sothly thus seye.
  Lo heere the caas especial:—

If a man be so bestial,
That he of no craft hath science,
And nought desireth ignorence,   6720
Thanne may he go a begging yerne,
Til he somme maner crafte kan lerne,
Thurgh which, withoute truaundyng,
He may in trouthe have his lyvyng.
Or if he may done no labour,
For elde, or sykenesse, or langour,
Or for his tendre age also,
Thanne may he yit a begging go.
Or if he have peraventure,
Thurgh usage of his norture,   6730
Lyved over deliciously,
Thanne oughten good folk comunly
Han of his myscheef somme pitee,
And suffren hym also, that he
May gone aboute and begge his breed,
That he be not for hungur deed.
Or if he have of craft kunnyng,
And strengthe also, and desiryng
To wirken, as he had*de* what,
But he fynde neithir this ne that,   6740
Thanne may he begge til that he
Have geten his necessité.
Or if his wynnyng be so lite,
That his labour wole not acquyte
Sufficiantly al his lyvyng,
Yit may he go his breed begging;
Fro dore to dore, he may go trace,
Til he the remenaunt may purchace.
Or if a man wolde undirtake
Ony emprise for to make,   6750

In the rescous of oure lay,
And it defenden as he may,
Be it with armes or lettrure,
Or other covenable cure,
If it be so he pore be,
Thanne may he begge, til that he
May fynde in trouthe for to swynke
And gete hym clothe, mete, and drynke.
Swynke he with his hondis corporelle,
And not with hondis espirituelle.   6760

    In al this caas, and in semblables,
If that ther ben mo resonables,
He may begge, as I telle you heere,
And ellis nought in no manere,
As William Seynt Amour wolde preche,
And ofte wolde dispute and teche
Of this mater alle openly
At Parys fulle solempnely.
And also God my soule blesse
As he had in this stedfastnesse   6770
The accorde of the université,
And of the puple, as semeth me.
    " No good man oughte it to refuse,
Ne ought hym therof to excuse,
Be wrothe or blithe, who-so be ;
For I wole speke, and telle it thee,
Al shulde I dye, and be putt doun,
As was seynt Poule, in derke prisoun ;
Or be exiled in this caas
With wrong, as maister William was,   6780
That my moder Ypocrysie
Banysshed for hir gret envye.
    ' Mi modir flemed hym, Seynt Amour :

The noble dide such labour
To susteyne evere the loyalté,
That he to moche agilte me.
He made a book, and lete it write,
Wherein his lif he did al write,
And wolde ich reneyede begging,
And lyvede by my traveylyng,   6790
If I ne hadde rent ne other goode.
What? wened he that I were woode?
For labour myghte me never plese,
I have more wille to bene at ese;
And have wel lever, soth to seye,
Bifore the puple patre and preye,
And wrie me in my foxerie
Under a cope of papelardie.'
Quod Love, 'What devel is this that I heere?
What wordis tellest thou me heere?'   6800
     'What, sir? Falsnesse, that apert is.
'Thanne dredist thou not God?' 'No, certis:
For selde in grete thing shal he spede
In this worlde, that God wole drede;
For folk that hem to vertu yeven,
And truely on her owne lyven,
And hem in goodnesse ay contene,
On hem is lytel thrift *i*-sene;
Suche folk drinken gret mysese;
That lyf *ne* may me never plese.   6810
But se what gold han usurers,
And silver eke in *her* garners,
Taylagiers, and these monyours,
Bailifs, bedels, provost, countours;
These lyven wel nygh by ravyne,
The smale puple hem mote enclyne,

And they as wolves wole hem eten.
Upon the pore folk they geten
Fulle moche of that they spende or kepe;
Nis none of hem that he nyl strepe,   6820
And wrine hem-silfe wel at fulle;
Withoute scaldyng they hem pulle.
The stronge the feble overgoth;
But I, that were my symple cloth,
Robbe bothe robbyng and robbours,
And gile giling, and gilours.
By my treget, I gadre and threste
The grete tresour into my cheste,
That lyth with me so faste bounde.
Myn highe paleys do I founde,   6830
And my delites I fulfille,
With wyne at feestes at my wille,
And tables fulle of entremees;
I wole no lyf, but ese and pees,
And wynne gold to spende also.
For whanne the grete bagge is go,
It cometh right with my japes.
Make I not wel tumble myn apes?
To wynnen is alwey myn entente;
My purchace is bettir than my rente;   6840
For though I shulde beten be,
Over al I entremete me;
Withoute me may no wight dure.
I walke soules for to cure;
Of al the world cure have I
In brede and lengthe; boldly
I wole bothe preche and eke counceilen;
With hondis wille I not traveilen,
For of the pope I have the bulle.

I ne holde not my wittes dulle; 6350
I wole not stynten, in my lyve,
These emperours for to shryve,
Or kyngis, dukis, *or* lordis grete;
But pore folk al quyte I lete.
I love no such shryvyng, pardé,
But it for other cause be.
I rekke not of pore men,
Her astate is not worth an hen.
Where fyndest thou a swynker of labour
Have me unto his confessour? 6360
But emperesses, and duchesses,
Thise queenes, and eke countesses,
Thise abbessis, and eke bygyns,
These grete ladyes palasyns,
These joly knyghtis, and baillyves.
Thise nonnes, and thise burgeis wyves,
That riche ben, and eke plesyng,
And thise maidens welfaryng,
Wher-so they clad or naked be,
Uncounceiled goth ther noon fro me. 6370
And, for her soules saveté,
At lord and lady, and her meyné,
I axe, whanne thei hem to me shryve,
The propreté of al her lyve,
And make hem trowe, bothe meest and leest,
Hir paroche prest nys but a beest
Ayens me and my companye,
That shrewis ben as gret as I;
For whiche I wole not hide in holde,
No pryveté that me is tolde, 6380
That I by word or signe, y-wis,
Wole make hem knowe what it is,

And they wolen also tellen me;
They hele fro me no pryvyté.
.And for to make yow hem perceyven,
That usen folk thus to disceyven,
I wole you seyn, withouten drede,
What men may in the Gospel rede,
Of Seynt Mathew, the gospelere,
That seith, as I shal you sey heere.   6890
  ' Uppon the chaire of Moyses'
(Thus is it glosed douteles :—
That is the olde testament,
For ther by is the chaire ment)
' Sitte scribes and pharisen ;'
(That is to seyn, the cursid men,
Whiche that we ypocritis calle)
' Doth that they preche, I rede you alle,
But doth not as they don a dele,
That ben not wery to seye wele,   6900
But to do wel, no wille have they;
And they wolde bynde on folk al-wey,
That ben to be giled able,
Burdons that ben importable ;
On folkes shuldris thinges they couchen,
That they nyl with her fyngris touchen.'
  ' And why wole they not touche it ?'—'Why?'
For hem ne lyst not, sikirly ;
For sadde burdons that men taken,
Make folkes shuldris aken.   6910
And if they do ought that good be,
That is for folk it shulde se :
Her burdons larger maken they,
And make her hemmes wide alwey,
And loven setes at the table

The firste and most honourable;
And for to han the firste chaieris
In synagogis, to hem fulle decre is;
And willen that folk hem loute and grete,
Whanne that they passen thurgh the strete, 6920
 And wolen be cleped Maister also.'
But they ne shulde not willen so;
The gospel is ther ageyns I gesse:
That shewith wel her wikkidnesse.
 ' Another custome use we:—
Of hem that wole ayens us be,
We hate hym deedly everichone,
And we wole werrey hym, as oon.
Hym that oon hatith, hate we alle,
And congecte hou to done hym falle.   6930
 And if we seen hym wynne honour.
Richesse or preis, thurgh his valour,
Provende, rent, or dignyté,
Fulle fast, iwys, compassen we
Bi what ladder he is clomben so;
And for to maken hym doun to go,
With traisoun we wole hym defame,
And done hym leese his goode name.
Thus from his ladder we hym take,
And thus his freendis foes we make;   6940
But word ne wite shal he noon,
Tille alle hise freendis ben his foon.
For if we dide it openly,
We myght have blame redily;
For hadde he wist of oure malice,
He hadde hym kept, but he were nyce.
 ' Another is this, that if so falle,
That ther be oon amonge us alle

That doth a good turne, out of drede,
We seyn it is oure alder deede.
Yhe, sikerly, though he it feynede,
Or that hym list, or that hym deynede
A man thurgh hym avaunced be,
Therof alle parseners, be we,
And tellen folk where-so we go,
That man thurgh us is sprongen so.
And for to have of men preysyng,
We purchace, thurgh oure flateryng,
Of riche men of gret pousté,
Lettres, to witnesse oure bounté,
So that man weneth that may us see,
That alle vertu in us be.
And al-wey pore we us feyne ;
But how-so that we begge or pleyne,
We ben the folk, withoute lesyng,
That alle thing have without havyng ;
Thus be we dred of the puple, iwis.
And gladly my purpos is this :—
I dele with no wight, but he
Have gold and tresour gret plenté ;
Her acqueyntaunce wel love I ;
This is moche my desire shortly.
I entremete me of brokages,
I make pees and mariages,
I am gladly executour,
And many tymes a procuratour ;
I am somtyme messager,
That fallith not to my myster.
And many tymes I make enquestes ;
For me that office not honest is ;
To dele with other mennes thing.

That is to me a gret lykyng.
And if that ye have ought to do
In place that I repeire to,
I shal it speden thurgh my witt,
As soone as ye have told me it.
So that ye serve me to pay,
My servyse shal be youre alway.
But who-so wole chastise me,
 Anoon my love lost hath he;   6990
For I love no man in no gise,
That wole me repreve or chastise;
But I wolde al folk undirtake,
And of no wight no teching take;
For I that other folk chastie,
Wole not be taught fro my folie.
 'I love noon hermitage more;
Alle desertes and holtes hore
And grete wodes everichon,
I lete hem to the Baptist John.   7000
I quethe hym quyte, and hym relese
Of Egipt alle the wildirnesse;
To ferre were alle my mansiouns
Fro citees and goode tounes.
My paleis and myn hous make I
There men may renne ynne openly,
And sey that I the world forsake.
But al amydde I bilde and make
My hous, and swimme and pley therynne
 Bet than a fish doth with his fynne.   7010
Of Antecristes men am I,
Of whiche that Crist seith openly,
They have abit of hoolynesse,
And lyven in such wikkednesse.

Outward lambren semen we,
Fulle of goodnesse and of pitee,
And inward we, withouten fable,
Ben gredy wolves ravysable.
We enviroune bothe londe and se ;
With alle the world werrien we ;   7020
We wole ordeyne of al thing :
Of folkis good, and her lyvyng.
  ' If ther be castel or citee
Wherynne that ony begger be,
Al though that they of Milayne were,
For therof ben they blamed there ;
Or if a wight out of mesure,
Wolde lene his gold, and take usure,
For that he is so coveitous ;
Or if he be to leccherous,   7020
Or these that haunte symonye ;
Or provost fulle of trecherie,
Or prelat lyvyng jolily,
Or prest that halt his quene hym by,
Or olde horis hostilers,
Or other bawdes or bordillers,
Or elles blamed of ony vice,
Of whiche men shulden done justice :
Bi alle the seyntes that me pray,
But they defende *hem* with lamprey,   7040
With luce, with elys, with samons,
With tendre gees, and with capons,
With tartes, or with chessis fat*te*,
With deynté flawnes, brode and flat*t*
With caleweis, or with pullaylle,
With conynges, or with fyne vitaill(
That we undir our clothes wide,

Maken thurgh oure golet glide ;
Or but he wole do come in haste
 Roo venysoun *i*-bake in paste,   7050
Whether so that he loure or groyne,
He shal have of a corde a loigne,
With whiche men shal hym bynde and lede,
To brenne hym for his synful deede,
That men shulle here hym crie and rore
A myle wey aboute and more.
Or ellis he shal in prisoun dye,
But if he wole *oure* frendship bye,
Or smerten that that he hath do,
More than his gilt amounteth to.   7060
But and he couthe thurgh his sleght
Do maken up a tour of hight,
Nought rought I whethir of stone or tree,
Or erthe, or turves though it be,
Though it were of no rounde stone,
Wrought with squyre and scantilone,
So that the tour were stuffed welle
With alle richesse temporelle ;
And thanne that he wolde updresse
Engyns, bothe more and lesse,   7070
To cast at us, by every side,
To bere his good*e* name wide,
Such*e* sleghtes I shal yow nevene,
Barelles of wyne, by sixe or sevene,
Or gold in sakkis gret plenté,
He shulde soone delyvered be.
And if *he have* noon sich pitaunces,
Late hym study in equipolences,
And late lyes and fallaces,
If that he wolde deserve oure graces,   7080

Or we shal bere hym such witnesse
Of synne, and of his wrecchidnesse,
And done his loos so wide renne,
That al quyk we shulden hym brenne,
Or ellis yeve hym suche penaunce,
That is wel wors than the pitaunce.
   ' For thou shalt never for no thing
Kon knowen a-right by her clothing
The traitours fulle of trecherie,
But thou her werkis can a-spie.   7090
And ne hadde the good kepyng be
Whilom of the université,
That kepith the key of Cristendome,
We hadde turmented al and some.
Suche ben the stynkyng prophetis ;
Nys none of hem, that good prophete is ;
For they thurgh wikked entencioun,
The yeer of the incarnacioun
A thousand and two hundred yeer,
Fyve and fifty, ferther ne *nere*   7100
Broughten a book, with sory grace,
To yeven ensample in comune place,
That seide thus, though it were fable :—
' This is the gospel perdurable,
That fro the Holy Goost is sent.'
Wel were it worth to bene *i*-brent.
Entitled was in such manere
This book, of which I telle heere.
Ther nas no wight in alle Parys,
Biforne oure lady at parvys,   7110
That they ne myghte buye the booke,
To copy, if hem talent toke ;
There myght he se, by gret tresoun,

Fulle many fals comparisoun :—
'As moche as thurgh his grete myght,
Be it of hete or of lyght,
The *sonne* sourmounteth the mone,
That troublere is, and chaungith soone,
And the note kernelle the shelle,
(I scorne not that I yow telle)   7120
Right so withouten ony gile
Sourmounteth this noble evangile,
The word of ony evangelist.'
And to her title they token Crist ;
And many a such comparisoun,
Of which I make no mencioun,
Mighte men in that booke fynde,
Who-so coude of hem have mynde.
  'The université, that tho was a-slepe,
Gan for to braide, and taken kepe ;   7130
And at the noys the heed upcaste,
Ne never sithen slept it faste,
But up it stert, and armes toke
Ayens this false horrible boke,
Al redy bateil *for* to make,
And to the juge the book to take.
But they that broughten the boke there,
Hent it anoon awey for fere ;
They nolde shewe more a dele,
But thenne it kept, and kepen wille,   7140
Til such a tyme that they may see,
That they so stronge woxen be,
That no wyght may hem wel withstonde,
For by that book *they* durste not stonde.
Away they gonne it for to bere,
For they ne durste not answere

By exposicioun ne glose
To that that clerkis wole appose
Ayens the cursednesse, iwys,
That in that book *i*-writen is.   7150
Now wote I not, ne I can not see
What maner ende that there shal be
Of al*le* this that they *may* hyde;
But yit algate they shal abide,
Til that they may it bet defende;
This trowe I best wole be her ende.
    ' Thus Antecrist abiden we,
For we ben alle of his meyné,
And what man that wole not be so,
Right soone he shal his lyf forgo.   7160
We wole a puple upon hym areyse,
And thurgh oure gile done hym seise,
And hym on sharpe speris ryve,
Or other weyes brynge hym fro lyve,
But if that he wole folowe, iwys,
That in oure book *i*-writen is.
    Thus mych wole oure book signifie,
That while Petre hath maistrie
May never Iohn shewe welle his myght.
    ' Now have I you declared right,   7170
The menyng of the bark and rynde,
That makith the entenciouns blynde.
But now at erst I wole bigynne,
To expowne you the pith withynne :—
        *   *   *   *
And the seculers comprehende,
That cristes lawe wole defende,
And shulde it kepen and mayntenen
Ayens hem that alle sustenen,

And falsly to the puple techen,
That Iohn bitokeneth hem to prechen,   7180
That ther nys lawe covenable,
But thilke gospel perdurable,
That fro the Holy Gost was sent
To turne folk that ben myswent.
  The strengthe of Iohn they undirstonde,
The grace in whiche they seie they stonde,
That doth the synfulle folk converte,
And hem to Ihesu Crist reverte.
  ' Fulle many another orribilité,
May men in that booke se,   7190
That ben comaunded, douteles,
Ayens the lawe of Rome expres;
And alle with Antecrist they holden,
As men may in the book biholden.
And thanne comaunden they to sleen,
Alle tho that with Petre been;
But they shal nevere have that myghte.
And God to-forne, for strif to fighte,
That they ne shal ynough fynde,
That Petres lawe shal have in mynde,   7200
And evere holde, and so mayntene,
That at the last it shal be sene,
That they shal alle come therto,
For ought that they can speke or do.
And thilke lawe shal not stonde,
That they by Iohn have undirstonde,
But maugre hem it shal adowne,
And bene brought to confusioun.
But I wole stynt of this matere,
For it is wonder longe to here;   7210
But hadde that ilke book endured,

Of better estate I were ensured,
And freendis have I yit pardee,
That han me sett in gret degré.
    ' Of alle this world is emperour
Gyle my fadir, the trechour,
And emperis my moder is,
Maugre the Holy Gost, iwis.
Oure myghty lynage and owre rowte
Regneth in every regne aboute,   7220
And welle is worthy we mynystres be,
For alle this world governe we,
And can the folk so wel disceyve,
That noon oure gile can perceyve ;
And though they done, they dar not say*e* ;
The sothe dar no wight bywrey*e*.
But he in Cristis wrath hym ledith,
That more than Crist my britheren dredith.
He nys no fulle good champioun,
That dredith such similacioun,   7230
Nor that for peyne wole refusen,
Us to correcte and accusen.
He wole not entremete by right,
Ne have God in his iye-sight,
And therfore God shal hym punyshe ;
But me ne rekke of no vice,
Sithen men us loven comunably,
And holden us for so worthy,
That we may folk repreve echoon,
And we nyl have repref of noon.   7240
Whom shulden folk worshipen so,
But us that stynten never mo
To patren while that folk may us see,
Though it not so bihynde be ?

And where is more wode folye,
Than to enhaunce chyvalrie,
And love noble men and gay,
That ioly clothis weren alway?
If they be sich folk as they semen,
So clene, as men her clothis demen, 7250
And that her wordis folowe her dede,
It is gret pite, out of drede,
For they wole be noon ypocritis.
Of hym me thynketh gret spite is;
I can not love hym on no side.
But beggers with these hodes wide,
With streight and pale faces lene,
And greye clothis not fulle clene,
But fretted fulle of tatarwagges,
And highe shoos knopped with dagges, 7260
That frouncen lyke a quaile pipe,
Or botis revelyng as a gype;
To such folk as I you dyvyse,
Shulde princes and these lordis wise,
Take alle her londis and her thingis,
Bothe werre and pees, and governyngis;
To such folk shulde a prince hym yive,
That wolde his lyf in honour lyve.
 And if they be not as they seme,
That serven thus the world to queme, 7270
There wolde I dwelle to disceyve
The folk, for they shal not perceyve.
 ' But I ne speke in no such wise,
That men shulde humble abit dispise,
So that no pride ther undir be.
No man shulde hate, as thynkith me,
The pore man in sich clothyng.

But God ne preisith hym no thing,
That seith he hath the world forsake,
And hath to worldly glorie hym take, 7280
And wole of siche delices use.
Who may that begger wel excuse?
That papelard, that hym yeldith so,
And wole to worldly ese go,
And seith that he the world hath lefte,
And gredily it grypeth efte,
He is the hounde, shame is to seyn,
That to his castyng goth ageyn.

 ' But unto you dar I to lye.
But myght I felen or aspie, 7290
That ye perceyved it no thyng,
Ye shulde have a stark lesyng,
Right in youre honde thus to bigynne;
I nolde it lette for no synne.'

 The god lough at the wondir tho,
And every wight gan laugh also,
And seide :—' Lo, heere a man a-right,
For to be trusty to every wight!'

 ' Fals-semblant,' quod Love, ' sey to me,
Sith I thus have avaunced thee, 7300
That in my court is thi dwellyng,
And of ribawdis shalt be my kyng,
Wolt thou wel holden my forwordis ?'

 F. Sem. ' Yhe, sir, from hennes forewardis;
Hadde never youre fadir heere biforne,
Servaunt so trewe, sith he was borne.

 Amour. ' That is ayens alle nature.'

 F. Sem. ' Sir, putte you in that aventure;
For though ye borowes take of me,
The sikerer shal ye never be 7310

For ostages, ne sikernesse,
Or chartres, for to bere witnesse.
I take youre silf to recorde heere,
That men ne may in no manere
Teren the wolf out of his hide,
Til he be slayn, bak and side,
Though men hym bete and al to-defile;
What? wene ye that I wole bigile?
For I am clothed mekely,
Ther undir is alle my trechery;   7320
Myn herte chaungith never the mo
For noon abit, in which I go.
Though I have chere of symplenesse,
I am not wery of shrewidnesse.
Myn lemman, streyneth Abstinence,
Hath myster of my purveaunce;
She hadde ful longe a-go be deede,
Nere my councel and my rede;
Lete hir allone, and you and me.'
And Love answerde, 'I trust thee   7330
Withoute borowe, for I wole noon.'
And Fals-semblant, the theef, anoon,
Ryght in that ilke same place,
That hadde of tresoun al his face
Ryght blak withynne, and white withoute,
Thankith hym, gan on his knees loute.
    Thanne was there nought, but 'Every man
Now to assaut, that sailen can,'
Quod Love, 'and that fulle hardyly.'
Thanne armed they hem communly   7340
Of sich armour as to hem felle.
Whanne they were armed fers and felle,
They wente hem forth alle in a route,

And set the castel al aboute;
They wille nought away for no drede,
Tille it so be that they ben dede,
Or tille they have the castel take.
And foure batels they gan make,
And parted hem in foure anoon,
And toke her way, and forth they gone,   7350
The foure gates for to assaile,
Of whiche the kepers wole not faile;
For they ben neithir sike ne dede,
But hardy folk, and stronge in dede.

  Now wole I seyn the countynaunce
Of Fals-semblant, and Abstynaunce,
That ben to Wikkid-tonge went.
But first they heelde her parlement,
Whether it to done were,
To maken hem be knowen there,   7360
Or elles walken forth disgised.
But at the laste they devysed,
That they wolde gone in tapinage,
As it were in a pilgrimage,
Lyke good and hooly folk unfeyned.
 And dame Abstinence-streyned
Toke on a robe of kamelyne,
And gan hir graithe as a bygynne.
A large coverechief of threde,
She wrapped alle aboute hir heede,   7370
But she forgate not hir sawter.
A peire of bedis eke she bere
Upon a lace, alle of white threde,
On which that she hir bedes bede;
But she ne bought hem never a dele,
For they were geven her, I wote wele,

God wote, of a fulle hooly frere,
That seide he was hir fadir dere,
To whom she hadde ofter went,
Than ony frere of his covent. 7380
And he visited hir also,
And many a sermoun seide hir to;
He nolde lette for man on lyve,
That he ne wolde hir ofte shryve.
[And wyth so gret devotion
They made her confession,
That they had ofte, for the nones,
Two heedes in one hode at ones.

Of fayre shappe I devysed her the,
But pale of face sometyme was she; 7390
That false traytouresse untrewe,
Was lyke that salowe horse of hewe,
That in the Apocalips is shewed,
That signyfyeth *tho* folke beshrewed,
That bene al ful of trecherye,
And pale, through hypocrisye;
For on that horse no colour is,
But onely deed and pale, ywys.
Of such a colour enlangoured,
Was Abstinence, ywys, coloured; 7400
Of her estate she her repented*e*,
As her vysage representede.

She had a burdowne al of thefte,
That Gyle had yeve her of hys yefte;
And a skryppe of faynte distresse,
That ful was of elengenesse,
And forth she walked*e* sobrely:
And False-semblaunt saynt, je vous die,
And as it were for such mistere,

Done on the cope of a frere, 7410
With chere symple, and ful pytous,
Hys lookyng was not disdeynous,
Ne proude, but meke and ful pesyble.
About his necke he bare a Byble,
And squierly forth gan he gon;
And for to reste hys lymmes upon,
He had of Treason a potente;
As he were feble, hys way he wente.
But in hys sleve he gan to thrynge
A rasoure sharpe, and wel bytynge, 7420
That was *i*-forged in a forge,
Which that men clepen Coupe-gorge.
   So longe forth her waye they nomen,
Tyl they to Wycked-tonge comen,
That at hys gate was syttyng,
And sawe folke in the way passyng.
The pylgrymes sawe he faste by
That beren hem ful mekely,
And humbl*ely* they wyth hym mette.
Dame Abstinence fyrst hym grette, 7430
And syth hym False-semblant saluede,
And he hem; but he not remeuede,
For he ne dred hem not a dole.
For whan he sawe her faces wele,
Alwaye in herte hym thoughte so,
He shulde knowe hem both*e* two;
For wele he knewe dame Abstynaunce,
But he ne knewe not Constreynaunce.
He ne knewe nat that she was constreyned,
Ne of her theves lyfe fayned, 7440
But wende she come of wyl al fre;
But she come in another degré;

And yf of good wyl she beganne,
That wyl *i*-fayled was her thanne.
And False-semblant had he sene alse,
But he knewe nat that he was false.
Yet false was he, but his falsenesse
Ne coude he not espye, nor gesse ;
For Semblant was so slye wrought,
That falsenesse he ne espyede nought.   7450
But haddest thou knowen hym beforne,
Thow woldest on a boke have sworne,
Whan thou hym saugh in thylke araye
That he, that whylome was so gaye,
And of the daunce Joly Robyn,
Was tho become a Jacobyn.
But sothly, what-so men hym call*e*,
Frere preachours bene good*e* men all*e*;
Her order wyckedly they beren
Such Minstrel*es*, yf they weren.   7460
So bene Augustyns, and Cordylers,
And Carmes, and eke sacked freers,
And all*e* freres shodde and bare
(Though some of hem bene great and square)
Ful holy men, as I hem deme;
Everyche of hem wolde good man seme.
But shalt thou never of apparence
Sene conclude good consequence
In none argument, ywys,
If existence al fayled is.   7470
For men may fynde alwaye sopheme
The consequence to *e*nveneme,
Who-so that hath had the subtelté
The double sentence for to see.
    Whan the pylgrymes comen were

To Wycked-tonge that dwelled there,
(Her harneys nygh hem was algate)
By Wycked-tonge adowne they sate,
That badde hem nere hym for to come,
And of tidynges telle hym some,   7480
And sayde hem :—' What case maketh yow
To come to this place now?'
' Sir,' sayde Strayned-abstinaunce,
' We, for to dryen our penaunce,
With hertes pytous and devoute,
Are commen, as pylgrimes gon aboute ;
Wel nygh on fote alway we go ;
Ful doughty ben our heeles two ;
And thus bothe we ben i-sent
Throughoute this worlde that is myswent,   7490
To yeve ensample, and preche also.
To fyshen synful men we go,
For other fyshynge ne fyshe we.
And, syr, for that charité,
As we be wont, herborowe we crave,
Your lyfe to amende, Christ it save !
And so it shulde you nat displease,
We wolden, yf it were your ease,
A shorte sermon unto you sayne.
And Wicked-tonge answered agayne,   7500
' The house,' quod he, ' such as ye se,
Shal not be warned you for me,
Seye what you lyst, and I wol here.'
' Graunt mercy swete syr dere !'
Quod alderfirst, dame Abstynence,
And thus began she her sentence.
    Const. Abstinence. ' Sir, the fyrste vertue,
        certayne,

The greatest, and mooste soverayne
That may be founde in any man,
For havyng, or for wytte he can,   7510
That is hys tonge to refrayne;
Therto ought every wyght him payne.
For it is better stylle be,
Than for to speken harme, pardé!
And he that herkeneth it gladly,
He is no good man sykerly.
And, sir, aboven al other synne,
In that arte thou moost gylty inne.
Thou spake a jape not longe ago,
(And, sir, that was ryght yvel do)   7520
Of a yonge man that here repayrede,
And never yet thys place apayrede.
Thou saydest he awayted nothynge,
But to deceyve Fayre-welcomyng.
Ye sayde nothyng soth of that;
But, sir, ye lye; I tel you plat;
He ne cometh no more, ne goth, pardé!
I trowe ye shal hym never se.
Fayre-welcomynge in prison is,
That ofte hath played with you er thys   7530
The fayrest games that he coude,
Withoute fylthe styl or loude;
Nowe dare he not himselfe solace.
Ye han also the man do chase,
That he dare neyther come ne go.
What meveth you to hate hym so,
But properly your wycked thought,
That many a false leasyng hath thought?
That meveth youre foole eloquence,
That jangleth ever in audience,   7540

And on the folke areyseth blame,
And doth hem dishonour and shame,
For thyng that maye have no prevyng,
But lykelynesse, and contryvyng.
For I dare sayne, that Reason demeth,
It is not al soth thynge that semeth,
And it is synne to controve
Thyng*e* that is *for* to reprove ;
Thys wote ye wele.   And, syr, therfore
Ye arne to blame the more.   7550
And, nathlesse, he recketh lyte ;
He yeveth nat nowe therof a myte ;
For yf he thought*e* harme, parfaye,
He wolde come and gone al daye ;
He coude not himselfe abstene.
Nowe cometh he not, and that is sene,
For he ne taketh of it no cure,
But yf it be through aventure,
And lasse than other folke algate.
And thou her watchest at the gate,   7560
With speare in thyne arest alwaye ;
There muse, musard, al the daye ;
Thou wakest nyght and daye for thought;
Iwys thy traveyle is for nought.
And Jelosy, withouten fayle,
Shal never quyte the thy travayle.
And skath is that Fayre-welcomyng,
Wythoute any trespassyng,
Shal wrongfully in prison be,
There wepeth and languysheth he.   7570
And though thou never yet, ywys,
Agyltest man no more but thys,
(Take not a-greefe) it were worthy

To put*te* the out of thys bayly,
And afterwarde in prison lye,
And fettre the tyl that thou dye ;]
For thou shalt for this synne dwelle
Right in the devels ers of helle,
But-if that thou repente thee.'
' Mafay, thou liest falsly !' quod he.   7580
' What? welcome, with myschaunce nowe !
Have I therfore *i*-herberd yowe
To seye me shame, and eke reprove ?
With sory happe to youre bihove,
Am I to day youre herber*g*ere !
Go, herber yow elles-where than heere,
That han a lyer called*e* me.
Two tregetours art thou and he,
That in myn hous do me this shame,
And for my sothe-saugh ye me blame.   7590
Is this the sermoun that ye make ?
To alle the develles I me take,
Or elles, God, thou me confounde,
But er men diden this castel founde,
It passith not ten daies or twelve,
But it was tolde right to my selve,
And as they seide, right so tolde I,
He kyst*e* the rose pryvyly.
Thus seide I now, and have seid yore ;
I not where he dide ony more.   7600
Why shulde men sey me such a thyng,
If it *ne* hadde bene gabbyng ?
Ryght so seide I, and wole seye yit ;
I trowe I lied*e* not of it,   ·
And with my bemes I wole blowe
To alle neighboris a-rowe,

How he hath bothe comen and gone.'
    Tho spake Fals-semblant right anone,
' Alle is not gospel, oute of doute,
That men seyn in the towne aboute ;   7610
Ley no deef ere to my spekyng,
I swere yow, sir, it is gabbyng.
I trowe ye wote wel certeynly,
That no man loveth hym tenderly,
That seith hym harme, if he wote it,
Alle be he never so pore of wit.
And soth *it* is also sikerly,
This knowe ye, sir, as wel as I
That lovers gladly wole visiten
The places there her loves habiten.   7620
This man yow loveth and eke honoureth ;
This man to serve you laboureth ;
And clepith you his freend so deere,
And this man makith you good chere,
And every where that you meteth,
He yow saloweth, and he you greteth.
He preseth not so ofte, that ye
Ought of his come encombred be ;
Ther presen other folk on yow,
Fulle ofter than he doth now.   7630
And if his herte hym streynede so
Unto the rose for to go,
Ye shulde hym sene so ofte nede,
That ye shulde take hym with the dede ;
He cowde his comyng not forbere,
Though *ye* hym thrilled with a spere ;
I*t* nere not thanne as it is now.
But trustith wel, I swere it yow,
That it is clene out of his thought.

Sir, certis, he ne thenkith it nought; 7640
No more ne doth Faire-welcomyng,
That sore abieth al this thing.
And if they were of oon assent,
Fulle soone were the rose hent,
The maugre youres, wolde be.
And sir, of o thing herkeneth me:—
Sith ye this man, that loveth yow,
Han seid such harme and shame, now
Witeth wel, if he gessed it,
Ye may wel demen in youre wit, 7650
He nolde no thyng love you so,
Ne callen you his freende also,
But nyght and day he wole wake,
The castelle to destroie and take
If it were soth, as ye devise;
Or some man in some maner wise
Might it warne hym everydele,
Or by hym-silf perceyven wele.
For sith he myghte not come and gone
As he was whilom wont to done, 7660
He myght it sone wite and see;
But now alle other wise wote he.
Thanne have *ye* sir, al outerly
Deserved helle, and jolyly
The deth of helle douteles,
That thrallen folk so gilteles.'

    Fals-semblant proveth so this thing,
That he can noon answeryng,
And seth alwey such apparaunce,
That nygh he fel in repentaunce, 7670
And seide hym:—' Sir, it may wel be.
Semblant, a good man semen ye;

And, Abstinence, fulle wise ye seme;
Of o talent you bothe I deme.
What counceil wole ye to me yeven?'
    'Ryght heere anoon thou shalt be shryven
And sey thy synne withoute more;
Of this shalt thou repente sore;
For I am prest, and have pousté,
To shryve folk of most dignyté   7680
That ben as wide as world may dure.
Of alle this world I have the cure,
And that hadde never yit persoun,
Ne vicarie of no maner toun.
And, God wote, I have of thee,
A thosand tyme more pitee,
Than hath thi preest parochial,
Though he thy freend be special.
I have avauntage, in o wise,
That youre prelatis ben not so wise,   7690
Ne half so lettred as am I.
I am licenced boldely,
[In divinitie for to rede,
And to confessen, out of drede.
If ye wolle you nowe confesse,
And leave your synnes more and lesse,
Without abode, knele downe anon,
And ye shal have absolucion.']

EXPLICIT.

COMPLAYNTE OF A LOVERES LYFE;

OR, THE COMPLAINT OF THE

BLACK KNIGHT.

I.

IN May, when Flora, the fressh*e* lusty
        quene,
    The soyle hath clad in grene, rede, and
        white;
And Phebus gan to shede his stremes shene
Amyd the Bole, wyth al the bemes bryght*e*;
And Lucifer, to chace awey the nyght*e*,
Ayen the morowe our orysont hath take,
To byd*de* loveres oute of her slepe awake,

II.

And hertys hevy for to recomforte
From dreryhed of hevy nyghtis sorowe,
Nature bad hem ryse, and hem disporte,   10
Ageyn the goodly glad*e* grey*e* morowe;
And Hope also, with seint Johan to borowe,
Bad in dispite of daunger and dispeyre,
For to take the holsome lusty eyre.

III.

And wyth a sygh I gan for to abreyde
Out of my slombre, and sodenly out sterte,
As he, alas! that nygh for sorowe deyde,
My sekenes sat ay so nygh myn herte,
But for to fynde socoure of my smerte,
Or atte lest summe relesse of my peyn,   20
That me so sore halt in every veyn,

IV.

I rose anon, and thoght I wolde goon
Into the wode, to here the briddes singe,
When that the mysty vapour was agoon,
And clere and feyre was the morownyng;
The dewe also lyk sylver in shynynge
Upon the leves, as any baume swete,
Til firy Tytan with hys persaunt hete

V.

Hadde dried up the lusty lycour nywe,
Upon the herbes in the grene mede,   30
And that the floures of many dyvers hywe,
Upon the stalkes gunne for to sprede,
And for to splay out her leves on brede
Ageyn the sunne, golde-borned in hys spere,
That doun to hem caste hys bemes clere.

VI.

And by a ryver forth I gan costey,
Of water clere as berel or cristal,
Til at the last I founde a lytil wey,
Towarde a parke, enclosed with a wal
In compas rounde, and by a gate smal,   40
Who-so that wolde frely myghte goon,
Into this parke, walled with grene stoon.

VII.

And in I wont to here the briddes songe,
Which on the braunches, bothe in pleyn *and* vale,
So loude songe that al the *wode* ronge,
Lyke as hyt sholde shever in pesis smale;
And as me thoghte, that the nyghtyngale
Wyth so grete myght her voyse gan out wreste
Ryght as her herte for love wolde breste.

VIII.

The soyle was pleyne, smothe, and wonder softe,
Al oversprad with tapites that Nature   51
Hadde made her selfe; celured eke alofte
With bowys grene, the floures for to cure,
That in her beauté they may longe endure
Fro al assaute of Phebus fervent fere,
Which in his spere so hote shone and clere.

IX.

The eyre atempre, and the smothe wynde
Of Zepherus, amonge the blosmes whyte,
So holsomme was, and so nourysshing be kynde,
That smale buddes, and rounde blomes lyte,   60
In maner gan of her brethe delyte,
To yif us hope *her* frute shal take
Ayens autumpne, redy for to shake.

X.

I sawe ther Daphene closed under rynde,
Grene laurer, and the holsomme pyne,
The myrre also that wepeth ever of kynde,
The cedres high, upryght as a lyne,
The philbert eke, that lowe dothe enclyne
Her bowes grene to the erthe doune,
Unto her knyght ycalled Demophoune.   70

XI.

There saw I eke the fressh hawthorne
In white motele, that so soote doth smelle,
Asshe, firre, and oke, with many a yonge acorne,
And many a tre mo then I can telle;
And me beforne I sawe a litel welle,
That had his course, as I gan *tho* beholde,
Under an hille, with quyke stremes colde.

XII.

The gravel gold, the water pure as glas,
The bankys rounde, the welle environyng,
And softe as velvet the yonge gras   80
That thereupon ful lustely gan *spry*nge,
The sute of trees about*e* compassyng
Her shadowe cast*e*, closyng the wel*le* rounde,
And al the herbes grouyng on the grounde.

XIII.

The water was so holsom so vertuous,
Throgh myghte of herbes grouynge *ther* beside;
*N*at lyche the welle wher as Narcissus
Yslayn was throgh vengeaunce of Cupide,
Wher so covertely he did *ab*ide
The greyn of cruel deth upon eche brynke,   90
That deth mot folowe, who that ever drynke.

XIV.

Ne lyche the pitte of the Pegacé,
Under Pernaso, wher poetys slept*e*;
Nor lyke the welle of pure chastité,
Whiche as Dyane with her nymphes kept*e*,
When she naked into the water lepte,
That slowe Acteon with his houndes felle,
Oonly for he cam so nygh the welle.

XV.

But this welle that I her of reherse
So holsom was, that hyt wolde aswage   100
Bollyn hertis, and the venym *perse*
Of pensifhede, with al the cruel rage,
And evermore refresshe the visage
Of hem that were in eny werynesse
Of gret labour, or fallen in distresse.

XVI.

And I that throgh daungere and disdeyn,
So drye a-thruste, thoght I wolde assaye
To tast a draght of this welle or tweyn,
My bitter langour yf hyt myght alaye,
And on the banke anon adoune I lay,   110
And with myn hede unto the welle I raghte,
And of the water dranke I a good draghte.

XVII.

Wherof me thoght I was refresshed wel
Of the brynnyng that sate so nyghe my herte,
That verely anon I gan to fele
An huge part relesed of my smerte;
And therewithalle anoon up I sterte,
And thoght I wolde walken and se more,
Forth in the parke and in the holtys hore.

XVIII.

And thorgh a launde as I yede apace,   120
And gan aboute faste to beholde,
I fonde anon a delytable place,
That was beset with trees yong and olde,
Whos names her for me shal not be tolde,
Amyde of whiche stode an erber grene,
That benched was with *turves* nywe and clene.

XIX.

This herber was ful of floures *of inde*,
Into the whiche as I beholde gan,
Betwex an hulfere and a wodebynde,
As I was war, I sawe ther lye a man   130
In blake and white colour, pale and wan,
And wonder dedely also of his hiwe,
Of hurtes grene, and fresshe woundes ny*we*.

XX.

And overmore destreyned with sekenesse
Besyde al this he was ful grevously,
For upon him he had a hote accesse,
That day be day him shoke ful petously,
So that for constreynyng of hys malady,
And hertely wo, thus lyinge al alone,
It was a deth for to so here hym grone.   140

XXI.

Wherof astonied my fote I gan withdrawe,
Gretly wondring what hit myght*e* be,
That he so lay and had*de* no felowe,
Ne that I coude no wyght with him se;
Wherof I had*de* routhe, and eke pité,
And gan anon, so softly as I coude,
Amonge the busshes me prively to shroude;

XXII.

If that I myght in eny wise aspye,
What was the cause of his dedely woo,
Or why that he so pitously gan crie   150
On hys fortune, and on cure also,
With al my myght I leyde an ere to,
Every worde to marke what he sayed*e*,
Out of his swogh among as he abreyde.

XXIII.

But first, yf I shal make mensyoun
Of hys persone, and pleynly him diserive,
He was in sothe, without excepcioun,
To speke of manhod, oon the best on lyve ;
Ther may no man ayeines trouthe stryve,
For of hys tyme, and of his age also,   160
He proved was, ther men shuld have ado.

XXIV.

For oon the beste, ther of brede and lengthe
So wel ymade by good proporsioun,
Yf he hadde be in his delyver strengthe ;
But thoght and sekenesse wer occasion
That he thus lay in lamentacioun
Gruffe on the grounde, in place desolate,
Sole by hymself, awaped and amate.

XXV.

And for me semeth that hit ys fyttyng
His wordes alle *to* put in remembraunee,   170
To me that herde al his compleynyng
And all*e* the grounde of his woful chaunce,
Yf therwithal I may yow do plesaunce,
I wol to yow so as I can anone,
Lych as he seyde, rehersen everychone.

XXVI.

But who shal now helpe me for to compleyne ?
Or who shal now my stile guy or lede ?
O Nyobe, let now thi teres reyne
Into my penne, and eke helpe in this nede !
Thou woful Mirre that felist my hert*e* blede   180
Of pitouse wo, and my honde eke quake,
When that I write, for this mannys sake.

XXVII.

For unto wo acordeth compleynyng,
And delful chere unto hevynesse ;
To sorow also, sighing and wepyng,
And pitouse morenyng unto drerynesse ;
And whoso that shal writen of distresse,
In partye nedeth to knowe felyngly
Cause and rote of alle suche malady.

XXVIII.

But I alas ! that am of wytte but dulle,   190
And have no knowyng of such matere,
For to discryve, and wryten at the fulle
The woful compleynt, which that ye shul here,
But even-like as doth a skryvenere,
That can no more what that he shal write,
But as his maister beside dothe endyte ;

XXIX.

Ryght so fare I, that of no sentement
Sey ryght naught in conclusioun,
But as I herde, when I was present,
This man compleyne wyth a pytouse soun ;   2c0
For even-lych, wythout addisyoun,
Or disencrese, outher mor or lesse,
For to reherse anon I wol me dresse.

XXX.

And yf that eny now be in this place,
That fele in love brennyng or fervence,
Or hyndered were to his lady grace,
With false tonges, that with pestilence
Sle trewe men that never did offence
In worde nor dede, ne in here entent,—
If any suche be here now present,   210

XXXI.

Let hym of routhe ley to audyence,
With deleful chere, and sobre countenaunce,
To here this man, be ful high sentence,
His mortal wo, and his grete perturbaunce
Compleynyng, now lying in a traunce,
With loke upcast, and *with ful* reuful chere
Theffect of whiche was as ye shal here.

COMPLEYNT.

XXXII.

' The thought oppressed with inward sighes sore,
The peynful lyve, the body langwysshing,
The woful gost, the herte rent and tore,   220
The pitouse chere pale in compleynyng,
The dedely face, lyke asshes in shynyng,
The salte teres that fro myn yen falle,
Parcel declared grounde of my peynes alle.

XXXIII.

' Whos hert ys *b*ounde to blede on hevynesse;
The thoght resseyt of woo and of compleynt;
The brest is chest of dule and drerynesse;
The body *eke* so feble and so feynt,
With hote and colde my acces ys so meynt,
That now I shyver for defaute of hete,   230
And hote as glede now soaenly I suete.

XXXIV.

' Now hote as fire, now colde as asshes dede,
Now hote for colde, *now cold* for hete ageyn,
Now cold as ise, now as coles rede
For hete I bren; and thus betwexe tweyn
I possed am, and al forecast in peyn,
So that my *hete* pleynly as I fele
Of grevouse colde ys cause every dele.

XXXV.

'This ys the colde that of ynwarde high dysdeyn,
Colde of dyspite, and colde of cruel hate;   240
This is the colde that evere doth his besy peyn,
Ayenes trouthe to fight and to debate;
This ys the colde that wolde the fire abate
Of trewe menyng, alas, the harde while!
This ys the colde that wil me begile.

XXXVI.

'For evere the better that in trouthe I mente,
With al my myghte feythfully to serve,
With hert and alle to be dilygente,
The lesse thanke, alas! I can deserve:
Thus for my trouthe Daunger doth me sterve; 250
For oon that shulde my deth of mercie lette,
Hath made dispite new his swerde to whette

XXXVII.

'Ayens me, and his arowes to file,
To take vengeaunce of wilful cruelté;
And tonges false throgh her sleghtly wile,
Han gonne a werre that wel not stynted be;
And fals Envye, Wrathe, and Enemyté,
Have conspired ayens al ryght and lawe,
Of her malis, that Trouthe shal be slawe.

XXXVIII.

'And Malebouche gan first the tale telle,   260
The sclaundre Trouthe of indignacioun,
And Fals-report so loude ronge the belle,
That Mysbeleve and Fals-suspecioun
Have Trouthe brought to hys dampnacioun,
So that, alas! wrongfully he dyeth,
And Falsnes now his place occupieth,

XXXIX.

' And entred ys into Trouthes londe,
And hath therof the ful possessyoun.
O, ryghtful God ! that first the trouthe fonde,
How may thou suffre such oppressioun,   270
That Falshed shuld have jurysdixioun,
In Trouthes ryght, to sle him gilteles ?
In his fraunchise he may not lyve in pes.

XL.

' Falsly accused, and of his foon forjuged,
Without ansuere, while he was absent,
He damned was, and may not ben excused,
For Cruelté satte in jugement,
Of Hastynesse without avisement,
And bad Disdeyn do execute anoon
His jugement in presence of hys foon.   280

XLI.

' Atturney noon ne may admytted ben
To excuse Trouthe, ne a worde to spoke ;
To Feyth or Othe the juge list not sen,
There ys no geyn but he wil be *i*-wreke.
O, Lorde of trouthe ! to the I calle and clepe,
How may thou se thus in thy presence,
Withoute mercy, mordred Innocence ?

XLII.

' Now God that art of trouthe sovereyn,
And seest how I lye for trouthe bounde,
So sore knytte in loves firy cheyn,   290
Even at the deth, thro*gh* girt wyth mony a wounde,
That lykly are never for to sounde,
And for my trouth am damned to the dethe,
And noght abide, but drawe alonge the brethe :

XLIII.

'Consider and se in thyn eternal sight,
How that myn herte professed whilom was,
For to be trewe with al my fulle myght,
Oonly to oon the whiche now, alas!
Of volunté, withoute more trespas,
Myn accusurs hath taken unto grace,   300
And cherissheth hem my deth to purchace.

XLIV.

'What meneth this? what ys this wonder ure
Of purveyance, yf *that* I shal hit calle,
Of god of love, that fals hem so assure,
And trew, alas! doun of the whele be falle?
And yet in sothe this is tho worst of alle,
That Falshed wrongfully of Trouthe hath the name,
And Trouthe ayenwarde of Falshed bereth the blame.

XLV.

'This blynde chaunce, this stormy aventure,
In love hath most his experience,   310
For who that doth with trouthe most his cure,
Shal for his mede fynde most offence,
That serveth love with al his diligence :
For who can feyne under loulyhede,
Ne fayleth not to fynde grace and spede.

XLVI.

'For I loved oon ful longe sythe agoon,
With al my herte, body and fulle myght,
And to be ded my herte can not goon
From his heste, but holde that he hath hight ;
Thogh I be banysshed out of her syght,   320
And by her mouthe damned that I shal deye,
Unto my beheste yet I wil ever obeye.

XLVII.

'For evere sithe that the worlde began,
Who-so lyste loke and in storie rede,
He shal ay fynde that the trewe man
Was put abake, whereas the falshede
Yfurthered was : for Love taketh non hede
To sle the trewe, and hath of hem no charge,
Wher as the false goth frely at her large.

XLVIII.

'I take recorde of Palamides,   330
The trewe man, the noble worthy knyght,
That ever loved, and of hys peyne no relese ;
Notwithstondyng his manhode and his myght,
Love unto him dide ful grete unright,
For ay the bette he did in chevalrye,
The more he was *i*-hindred by envye.

XLIX.

'And aye the bette he dyd in every place,
Throgh his knyghthode and besy peyn*e*,
The ferther was he fro his ladys grace,
For to her mercie myght he never ateyn*e*,   340
And to his deth he coude hyt not refreyn*e*
For no daunger, but ay *obey* and serve,
As he best coude, pleynly til he sterve.

L.

'What was the fyne also of Ercules,
For al his conquest and his worthynesse,
That was of strengthe alone percles ?
For lyke as bokes of him list expresse,
He set *pileres*, throgh his highe prowesse,
Away at Cades, for to signifie,
That no man myght him passe in chevalric.   350

LI.

‘ The whiche pilers ben ferre byyonde Ynde
Beset of golde, for a remembraunce :
And for al that was he sete behynde,
With hem that Love list febly to avaunce ;
For *he* him set laste upon a daunce,
Ayens whom helpe may no*t* stryve,
For al his trouth*e* yet he lost his lyve.

LII.

‘ Phebus also for his persaunt lyght,
When that he went her in erthe lowe,
Unto the her*te* with *fresshe* Venus sight   360
Ywounded was, throgh Cupides bowe,
And yet his lady list him not to knowe ;
Thogh for her love his her*te* dide blede,
She let him go, and toke of him non hede.

LIII.

‘ What shal I say of yong*e* Piramus ?
Of trewe Tristram, for all his high*e* renoune ?
Of Achilles, or of Antony*us* ?
Of Arcite, or of him Palemoune ?
What was the ende of her passioune,
But after sorowe dethe, and then her grave ?   370
Lo, here the guerdon that *thes* lovers have !

LIV.

‘ But false Jasoun with his doublenesse,
That was untrewe at Colkos to Medé,
And Tereus, rote of unkyndenesse,
And with these two eke the fals Ené ;
Lo, thus the false, ay in oon degré,
Had in love her lust and al her wille,
And save falshed, ther was non other skille.

LV.

'Of Thebes eke the fals Arcite,
And Demophon eke for his slouthe,   380
They had her lust and al that myght*e* delyte,
For al her falshede and grete untrouthe.
Thus ever Love, alas, and that is routhe!
His fals*e* legys furthereth what he may,
And sleeth the trewe, ungoo*d*ly, day be day.

LVI.

'For trewe Adon *i*-slayn was with the bore
Amyde the forest in the grene shade,
For Venus love he felt al the sore;
But Vulcanus with her no mercy made,
The foule chorle had*de* many nyghtis glade,   390
Wher Mars, her *worthy* knyght, her *trewe* man,
To fynde mercy comfort noon he can.

LVII.

'Also the yonge fressh Ipomones,
So lusty fre as of his corage,
That for to serve with al his hert*e* ches
Athalant, so feire of her visage;
But Love alas quyte him so his wage
With cruel daunger pleynly at the last*e*,
That with the dethe guerdonlesse he past*e*.

LVIII.

'Lo, her the fyne of lovers servise!   400
Lo, how that Love can his servantis quyte!
Lo, how he can his feythful men dispise,
To sle the trewe men, and fals*e* to respite!
Lo, how he doth the swerde of sorowe byte
In hertis, suche as most his lust obey*e*,
To save the fals and do the trewe dey*e*!

LIX.

' For feythe nor othe, worde, ne assuraunce,
Trewe menyng, awayte, or besynesse.
Stil porte, ne feythful attendaunce,
Manhode ne myght, in armes worthinesse,   410
Pursute of wurshipe nor high prouesse,
In straunge londe rydinge ne travayle,
Ful lyte, or noght, in love dothe avayle.

LX.

' Peril of dethe, nother in se ne londe,
Hungre ne thrust, sorowe ne sekenesse,
Ne grete emprises for to take on honde,
Shedyng of blode, ne manful hardynesse,
Nor ofte woundynge at sawtes by distresse,
Nor in partyng of lyfe nor dethe also,
Al ys for noghte, Love taketh non hede therto. 420

LXI.

' But lesynges with her false flaterye,
Throgh her falshed, and with her doublenesse,
With tales new, and mony feyned lye,
By false-semblaunce, and contrefet humblesse,
Under colour depeynt with stedfastnesse,
With fraude covred under a pitouse face,
Accepte ben now rathest unto grace,

LXII.

' And can hemselfe now best magnifie
With feyned port and *fals* presumpsioun ;
They haunce her cause with false surquedrie, 430
Under menyng of double entencioun,
To thenken oon in her opinyoun,
And sey another, to set hemselve alofte,
And hynder trouthe, as hit ys seyn ful ofte.

LXIII.

‘ The whiche thing I bye now al to dere,
Thanked be Venus, and the god Cupide !
As hit is seen by myn oppressed chere,
And by his arowes that stiken in my syde,
That safe the dethe I nothing abide
Fro day to day, alas, the harde while !   440
Whan evere hys dart that hym list to fyle,

LXIV.

‘ My woful herte for to ryve atwo,
For faute of mercye, and lake of pité
Of her that causeth al my peyn and woo,
And list not ones of grace for to see
Unto my trouthe throgh her cruelté ;
And most of al *if that* I me compleyne,
Than hath she joy to laughen at my peyne.

LXV.

‘ And wilfully hath *she* my dethe sworne,
Al gilteles, and wote no cause why,   450
Safe for the trouthe that I have hade aforne
To her allone to serve feythfully.
O God of Love ! unto the I crie,
And to thy blende double deyté
Of this grete wrong I compleyne me,

LXVI.

‘ And unto thy stormy wilful variaunce,
Ymeynt with chaunge and gret unstablenesse,
Now up, now down, so rennyng is thy chance,
That the to trust may be no sikernesse ;
I wite hit nothinge but thi doublenesse,   460
And who that is an archer, and ys blende,
Marketh nothing, but sheteth *as he wend.*

LXVII.

' And for that he hath no discrecioun,
Withoute avise he let his arowe goo,
For lak of syght, and also of resoun,
In his shetyng hit happeth ofte soo,
To hurt his frende rathir then his foo ;
So doth this god with his sharpe flon,
The trewe sleeth, and leteth the false gon.

LXVIII.

' And of his woundyng this is the worst of alle, 470
Whan he hurteth he dothe so cruel wreche,
And maketh the seke for to crie and calle
Unto his foo for to ben his leche,
And hard hit is for a man to seche,
Upon the poynt of dethe in jepardie,
Unto his foo to fynde remedye.

LXIX.

' Thus fareth hit now even by me,
That to my foo that yaf my hert a wounde,
Mot axe grace, mercy, and pité,
And namely ther wher noon may be founde ;   480
For now my sore my leche wol confounde,
And god of kynde so hath set myn ure,
My lyves foo to have my wounde in cure.

LXX.

' Alas the while now that I was borne !
Or that I ever saugh the brighte sonne !
For now I se that ful longe aforne,
Or I was borne, my destanye was sponne
By Parcas sustren, to sle me if they conne,
For they my dethe shopen or my sherte,
Oonly for trouthe, I may hit not asterte.   490

LXXI.

'The myghty goddesse also of Nature,
That under God hath the governaunce
Of worldly thinges commytted to her cure,
Disposed hath, throgh her wyse purveaunce,
To yive my lady so moche suffisaunce,
Of alle vertues, and therewithal purvyde
To mordre trouthe, hath taken Daunger to guyde.

LXXII.

'For bounté, beauté, shappe, and semelyhed,
Prudence, witte, passyngly fairenesse,
Benigne port, glad chere, with loulyhed,   500
Of womanhede ryght plenteous largesse,
Nature in her fully did empresse,
Whan she her wroght, and altherlast Dysdeyne,
To hinder trouthe, she made her chambreleyne.

LXXIII.

'When Mystrust also, and Fals-suspecioun,
With Mysbeleve she made for to be
Chefe of counseyle, to this conclusioun,
For to exile Trouthe, and eke Pité,
Out of her court to make Mercie fle,
So that Dispite now holdeth forth her reyne,   510
Throgh hasty beleve of tales that men feyne.

LXXIV.

'And thus I am for my trouthe, alas!
Mordred and slayn with wordis sharp and kene,
Gilteles, God wote, of alle trespas,
And lye and blede upon this colde grene.
Now mercie, suete! mercye, my lyves quene!
And to youre grace of mercie yet I preye,
In youre servise that your man may deye.

LXXV.

'But and so be that I shal deye algate,
And that I shal non other mercye have,   520
Yet of my dethe let this be the date,
That by youre wille I was broght to my grave,
Er hastely, yf that *yow* list me save,
My sharpe woundes that ake so and blede,
Of mercie charme, and also of womanhede.

LXXVI.

'For other charme pleynly ys ther noon,
But only mercie, to helpe in this case;
For thogh my wounde blede evere in oon,
My lyve, my deth, stont in your grace,
And thogh my gilt*e* be nothing, alas!   530
I axe mercie in al my best entent*e*,
Redy to dye, yf that ye assent*e*.

LXXVII.

'For ther ayen*es* shal I never strive
In worde ne werke, pleynly I ne may,
For lever I have then to be alyve
To dye sothely, and hit be her to pay;
Ye, thogh hit be this ech*e* same day,
Or when that ever her lust*e* to devyse,
Sufficeth me to dye in your servise.

LXXVIII.

'And God, that knowest the thoght of every wyght
Ryght a*s* hit is, in every thing thou maist se,   541
Yet ere I dye, with al my ful*le* myght,
Louly I prey*e* to graunte unto me,
That ye, goodly, feir*e*, fressh, and fre,
Which sle me oonly for defaut of routhe,
Er then I die, may know*e* my trouthe.

LXXIX.

' For that in sothe sufficethe *unto* me,
If she hit know in every circumstaunce,
And after I am wel *a*payd that she
Yf that her lyst of deth to do vengeaunce   550
Unto me, that am under her legeaunce,
Hit sitte me not her doom to dysobey*e*;
But at her lust*e* wilfully to dey*e*.

LXXX.

' Without*e* gruching or rebellioun,
In wil or worde, holy I assent,
Or eny maner contradixioun,
Fully to be at her commaundement;
And yf I dye*n*, in my testament
My hert I send, and my spirit also,
What-so-ever she list with hem to do.   560

LXXXI.

' And alderlast *unto* her womanhede,
And to her mercy me I recommaunde,
That lye now here betwex*e* hope and drede,
Abyding pleynly what she list commaunde;
For utterly this nys no demaunde
Welcome to me while me lasteth brethe,
Ryght at her chose, wher hit be lyf or dethe.

LXXXII.

' In this mater more what myght I seyn,
Sith in her honde and in her wille ys alle,
Bothe lyf and dethe, my joy, and al my peyn;   570
And fynally my hest*e* holde I shal,
Til my spirit, be destanye fa*t*al,
When that her list*e* fro my body wende,
Have here my trouthe, and thus I make an ende.'

LXXXIII.

And with that worde he gan siken as sore,
Lyke as his herte ryve wolde atweyne,
And holde his pese, and spake a worde no more;
But for to se his woo and mortal peyne,
The teres gonne fro myn eyon reyne
Ful pitously, for verry inwarde routhe,   580
That I hym sawe so languysshing for his trouthe.

LXXXIV

And al this while my self I kepte close
Amonge the bowes, and my self gan hide,
Til at the last the woful man arose,
And to a logge wente ther besyde,
Wher al the May his custom was to abyde,
Sole to compleynen of his peynes kene,
Fro yer to yer, under the bowes grene.

LXXXV.

And for because that hit drowe to the nyght,
And that the sunne his arke diurnalle,   590
Ypassed was, so that his persaunt lyght,
His bryghte bemes and his stremes alle
Were in the wawes of the water falle,
Under the bordure of our ocean,
His chare of golde his course so swyftly ran

LXXXVI.

And while the twilyght and the rowes rede
Of Phebus lyght were deaurat a lite,
A penne I toke, and gan me faste spede,
The woful pleynt of thilke man to write
Worde be worde, as he dyd endyte;   600
Lyke as I herde, and coude hem tho reporte,
I have here set, your hertis to dysporte.

LXXXVII.

If oght be mys, leyth the wite on me,
For I am worthy for to bere the blame,
If eny thing *i*-mysreported be,
To make this ditie for to seme lame
Throgh myn unkunnyng, but for to seme the same,
Lyke as this man his compleynt did expresse,
I axe mercie and foryevenesse.

LXXXVIII.

And, as I wrote, me thoght I sawe aferre,   610
Fer in the west*e* lustely appere
Esperus, the goodly bryght*e* sterre,
So glad, so feire, so persaunt eke of chere,
I mene Venus with her bemys clere,
That hevy hertis oonly to releve
Is wont of custom for to shewe at eve.

LXXXIX.

And I as fast*e* fel doun on my kne,
And even thus to her I gan to preie :
· O lady Venus ! so feire upon to se,
Let not this man for his trouthe dey*e*,   620
For that joy thou haddest when thou ley*e*
With Mars thi knyght, when Vulcanus *yow* founde.
And with a cheyne unvisible yow bounde.

XC.

‘ Togedre bothe tweyne in the same while,
That al the court above celestial,
At youre shame gan laughe and smyle :
O, feire lady, wel willy founde at al !
Comfort to carefull, O goddesse immortal !
Be helpyng now, and do thy diligence,
To let the stremes of thin influence   630

XCI.

‘ Descende doune, in furtheryng of the trouthe,
Namely of hem that *be* in sorowe bounde;
Show now thy myght, and on her wo have routhe,
Er fal*se* Daunger sle hem and confounde:
And specialy let thy myght be founde
For to socoure, what-so that thou may,
The trewe man that in the erber lay.

XCII.

‘ And al*le* trewe further for his sake,
O glade sterre ! O lady Venus myn !
And cause his lady him to grace take;   640
Her hert of stele to mercy so enclyne,
Er that thy bemes go up to declyne,
And er that thou now go fro us adoune,
For that love thou haddest to Adoun.’

XCIII.

And when that she was goon unto her rest*e*,
I rose anon, and home to bed*de* went*e*,
For verry wery, me thoght hit for the best*e*,
Preying thus in al*le* my best entente,
That al*le* trewe, that be with Daunger shent,
With mercie may, in reles of her peyn,   650
Recured be, er May come eft ayeyn.

XCIV.

And for that I ne may noo lenger wake,
Farewel, ye lovers al*le* that be trewe !
Praying to God, and thus my leve I take,
That er the sunne to morowe be ryse newe,
And er he have ayen his rosen hewe,
That eche of yow may have such a grace,
His oune lady in armes to embrace.

XCV.

I mene thus, that in al honesté,
Withoute more ye may togedre speke   660
What so yow liste at goode liberté,
That eche may to other her herte breke,
On Jelosie oonly to be iwreke,
That hath so longe of malice and envie
I-werred trouthe with his tiranye.

LENVOYE.

XCVI.

Princes, pleseth hit your benignité
This litil dité to have in mynde!
Of womanhede also for to se,
Your trewe man may summe mercie fynde,
And Pité eke, that long hath *be* behynde,   670
Let *then* ayein be provoked to grace;
For by my trouthe hit is ayenes kynde,
Fals Daunger for to occupie his place.

XCVII.

Go litel quayre, go unto my lyves quene
And my verry hertis sovereigne,
And be ryght glad for she shal the sene;
Such is thi grace; but I alas in peyne
Am left behinde, and not to whom to pleyne;
For Mercie, Routhe, Grace, and eke Pité
Exiled be, that I may not ateyne,   680
Recure to fynde of *myn* adversité.

EXPLICIT.

THE COMPLAYNT OF MARS AND VENUS.

I.

LADETH, ye *foules*, of the morowe gray!
Loo, *Phebus* rysen amonge yon rowis
   rede!
And floures fresshe, honoure*th* ye this
   May,
For when the sunne uprist then wol *ye* sprede;
But ye lovers that lye in eny drede,
Fleeth lest wikked tonges yow espye!
Loo, yonde the sunne, the candel of jalosye!

II.

With teres blew, and with a wounded hert*e*
Taketh your leve, and, with seynt Johan to borowe,
Apeseth sumwhat of your sorowes smert*e*,   10
Tyme cometh *efte*, eese shal your sorowe;
'The glad*e* nyght ys worthe an hevy morowe,
Seynt Valentyne!' a foule thus herd I synge,
Upon your day, er the sunne gan up sprynge.

III.

Yet sange this foule, 'I rede yow al awake;
And ye that han not chosen in humble wyse,
Without*e* repentynge cheseth youre make,
Yet at this fest renoveleth your servyse:

And ye that han ful chosen as I devise,
Confermeth hyt perpetuely to dure,   20
And paciently taketh your aventure.'

IV.

And for the worshippe of this highe feste,
Yet wol I in my briddes wise synge,
The sentence of the compleynt, at the leste,
That woful Mars made atte departyng
Fro fressh Venus in a *fair* morwenynge,
Whan Phebus, with his firy torches rede,
Ransaked hath every lover in hys drede.

V.

Whilom the thrid*de* hevenes lord above,
As wel by hevenysh revolucioun,   30
As by desert hath wonne Venus his love,
And she hath take him in subjecioun,
And as a maistresse taught him his lessoun,
Commaundynge him that nevere in her service,
He ner so bolde no lover to dispise.

VI.

For she forbad him jelosye at alle,
And cruelté, and bost, and tyrannye;
She made *him* at her lust so humble and *th*ralle,
That when her deynede to cast on hym her ye,
He toke in pacience to lyve or dye;   40
And thus she brydeleth him, in her manere,
With nothing but with *scornyng* of her chere.

VII.

Who regneth now in blysse but Venus,
That hath thys worthy knyght in governaunce?

Who syngeth now but Mars that serveth thus
The faire Venus, causer of plesaunce ?
He bynt him to perpetuel obeisaunce,
And she bynt her to love him for evere,
But so be that his trespace hyt desevere.

VIII.

Thus be they knyt, and regnen as in heven,   50
Be lokyng moost ; til hyt fil on a tyde,
That by her bothe assent was set a steven,
That Mars shal entre as fast as he may glyde,
Into hir nexte paleys to abyde,
Walkyng hys cours til she had him atake,
And he preyede her to haste her for his sake.

IX.

Than seyde he thus, ' Myn hertis lady suete,
Ye knowe wel my myschefe in that place,
For sikerly til that I with yow mete,
My lyfe stant ther in aventure and grace,   60
But when I se the beauté of your face,
Ther ys no dred of deth may do me smerte,
For alle your lust is ese to myn herte.'

X.

She hath so grete compassioun on her knyght,
That dwelleth in solitude til she come,
For hyt stode so, that ylke tyme no wight,
Counseyled hym, ne seyde to hym welcome,
That nyghe her witte for sorowe was overcome ;
Wherfore she sped her as fast in her weye,
Almost in oon day as he dyd in tweye.   70

XI.

The grete joye that was betwex hem two,
When they be mette, ther may no tunge tel*le* ;
Ther is no more but unto bed thei go,
And thus in joy and blysse I let hem duel*le* :
This worthi Mars that is of knyghthode wel*le*.
The flour of feyrenesse lappeth in his armes,
And Venus kysseth Mars the god of armes.

XII.

Sojourned hath this Mars of which I rede
In chambre amyd the paleys prively,
A certeyn tyme, til him fel a drede,   80
Throgh Phebus, that was comen hastely
Within the paleys yates ful sturdely,
With torche in honde, of which the stremes bryght*e*
On Venus chambre *gan kythe ful grete* lyghte.

XIII.

The chambre, ther as ley this fresshe quene,
Depeynted was with white boles grete,
And by the lyght she knew that shone so shene,
That Phebus cam to bren hem with his hete ;
This cely Venus, nygh dreynt in teres wete,
Enbraceth Mars, and seyde :—' Alas, I dye !   90
The torch is come, that al this world wol wrie.'

XIV.

Up sterte Mars, hym luste not to slepe,
When that he his lady herde so compleyne ;
But, for his nature was not for to wepe,
Instide of teres, fro his eyen tweyne

Tho firy sparkes brosten out for peyne,
And hent his hauberke that ley hym besyde;
Flo wold he not, ne myght himselven hide.

xv.

He throw*eth* on him his helme of huge wyghte,
And girt him with his swerde; and in his honde
His myghty spere, as he was wont to fyght*e*,   101
He shaketh so, that almost it to-wonde;
Ful hevy was he to walken over londe;
He may not holde with Venus companye,
But bad her fleen lest Phebus her espye.

xvi.

O woful Mars! alas, what maist thou seyn,
That in the paleys of thy disturbaunce,
Art left byhynd in peril to be sleyn?
And yet therto ys double thy penaunce,
For she that hath thyn hert in governance,   110
Is passed halfe the stremes of thyn yen;
That thou ner swift, wel maist thou wepe and crien.

xvii.

Now fleeth Venus into Ciclini*u*s toure,
With voide cours, for fere of Phebus lyght.
Alas! and ther *ne* hath she no socoure,
For she ne founde ne saugh no maner wyght;
And eke as ther she had*de* but litel myght;
Wherfor her selven for to hyde and save,
Within the gate she *fledde* into a cave.

xviii.

Derke was this cave, and smokyng as the hel*le*, 120
Nat but two pases within the yate it stode;

A naturel day in derk I let her dwelle.
Now wol I speke of Mars furiouse and wode;
For sorow he wold have sene his herte blode,
Sith that he myght have done her no companye,
He ne *roghte* not a myte for to dye.

XIX.

So feble he wex for hete and for his wo,
That nygh he swelt, he myght unnethe endure;
He passeth but a sterre in dayes two;
But nertheles, for al his hevy armure, 120
He foloweth her that is his lyves cure;
For whos departyng he toke gretter ire,
Then for his *oune* brenning in the fire.

XX.

After he walketh softely a paas,
Compleynyng that hyt pité was to here.
He seyde, ' O lady bryghte Venus! alas,
That ever so wyde a compas ys my spere!
Alas! when shal I mete yow, *myn* herte dere?
Thys twelve dayes of Aprile I endure,
Throgh jelouse Phebus, this mysaventure.' 140

XXI.

Now God helpe sely Venus allone!
But as God wolde hyt happede for to be,
That while that Venus weping made her mone
Ciclinius ryding in his chevaché,
Fro Venus *Valanus* myghte his paleys se;
And Venus he salueth, and maketh chere,
And her receyveth as his frende ful dere.

XXII.

Mars dwelleth forth in h*is* adversyte,
Compleynyng ever *in oon* her departynge ;
And what his compleynt was remembreth me, 150
And therfore, in this lusty morwenynge,
As I best can, I wol hit seyn and synge,
And after that I wol my love take ;
And God yif every wyght joy of his make !

THE COMPLEYNT OF MARS.

XXIII.

The ordre of compleynt requireth skylfully,
That yf a wight shal pleyn*e* pitously,
Ther mot be cause wherfore that men pleyne.
Other men may deme he pleyneth folely,
And causeles.   Alas, that do not I !
Wherfor the grounde and cause of al my peyn*e*, 160
So as my troubled witte may hit atteyne,
I wol reherse ; not for to have redresse,
But to declare my grounde of hevynesse.

XXIV.

The first*e* tyme, alas, that I was wroght,
And for certeyn effectes hider broght,
Be him that lordeth ech intelligence,
I yaf my trewe servise and my thoght,
For evermore, how dere I have hit boght,
To her that is of so grete excellence,
That what wight that first sheweth his presence, 170
When she is wrothe and taketh of hym no cure,
He may not longe in joye of love endure.

XXV.

This is no feyned mater that I telle ;
My lady is the verrey sours and welle
Of beauté, lust, fredam, and gentilnesse,
Of riche aray, how dere men hit selle,
Of al disport in which men frendely duelle,
Of love and pley, and of benigne humblesse,
Of soune of instrumentes of al swetnesse,
And therto so wel fortuned and thewed,   180
That thorow the worlde her goodnesse is yshewed

XXVI.

What wonder ys then thogh that I beset*te*
My servise on suche one that may me knet*te*
To wele or wo, sith hit lythe in her myghte?
Therfore myn her*te* for-ever I to her hight*e*,
Ne tru*el*y for my dethe shal I not let*te*,
To ben her truest servaunt and her knyght.
I flater noght, that may wete every wyght;
For this day in her servise shal I dye,
But grace be, I se her never wyth ye.   190

XXVII.

To whom shal I plen*en* of my distresse?
Who may me helpe, who may my harme redresse?
Shal I compleyn unto my lady fre?
Nay, certes, for she hath such herynesse,
For fere and eke for wo, that as I gesse,
In lytil tyme hit wol her bane be;
But were she safe, hit wer no fors of me.
Alas, that ever lovers mote endure,
For love, so many a perilouse aventure !

XXVIII.

For tho*gh* so be that lovers be as trewe   200
As any metal that is forged newe,
In many a case hem tydeth ofte sorowe.
Som *ty*me hire ladies wil not on hem rewe ;
Somtyme, yf that jelosie hyt knewe,
They myghten lyghtly ley her hede to borowe ;
Somtyme envyous folke with tunges horowe
Departen hem, alas !   Whom may they plese ?
But he be fals, no lover hath his ese.

XXIX.

But what availeth suche a longe sermoun
Of aventures of love up and doune ?   210
I wol returne and speken of my peyne ;
The poynt is this of my distruccion,
My right*e* lady, my savacyoun,
Is in affray, and not to whom to pleyne.
O hert*e* suete !   O lady sovereyne !
For your disese I oght wel swou*n*e and swelt*e*,
Thogh I none other harme ne drede felt*e*.

XXX.

To what fyne made the God that sitte so hye,
Benethen love other companye,
And streyneth folke to love malgre her hede ? 220
And than her joy, for oght I can espye,
Ne lasteth not the twynkelyng of an eye.
And somme have never joy til they be dede.
What meneth this ? what is this mystihede ?
Wherto constreyneth he his folke so fast*e*,
Thing to desyre but hit shuld*e* last*e* ?

XXXI.

And thogh he made a lover love a thing,
And maketh hit seme stedfast and during,
Yet putteth he in hyt such mysaventure,
That rest nys ther in his yevinge. 230
And that is wonder that so juste a kynge
Doth such hardnesse to his creature.
Thus whether love breke or elles dure,
Algates he that hath with love to done,
Hath ofter wo than changed ys the mone.

XXXII.

Hit semeth he hath to lovers enemyté,
And lyke a fissher, as men al day may se,
Bateth hys angle-hoke with summe plesaunce,
Til mony a fissch ys wode to that he be
Sesed therwith; and then at erst hath he 240
Al his desire, and therwith al myschaunce,
And thogh the lyne breke he hath penaunce;
For with the hoke he wounded is·so sore,
That he his wages hathe for evermore.

XXXIII.

The broche of Thebes was of such a kynde,
So ful of rubies and of stones of Ynde,
That every wight that set on hit an ye,
He wend anon to worthe out of his mynde;
So sore the beauté wold his herte bynde,
Til he hit had, him thoght he muste dye; 250
And whan *that* it was his then shuld he drye
Such woo for drede ay while that he hit had*de*,
That welnygh for the fere he shulde mad*de*.

XXXIV.

And whan hit was fro his possessioun,
Than had he double wo and passioun,
That he so feir a tresore had*de* forgo ;
But yet this broche, as in conclusioun,
Was not the cause of his confusioun ;
But he that wroght hit enfortuned hit so,
That every wight that had hit shuld have wo ; 260
And therfore in the worcher was the vice,
And in the covetour that was so nyce.

XXXV.

So fareth hyt by lovers, and by me ;
For thogh my lady have so gret beauté,
That I was mad til I had*de* gete her grace,
She was not cause of myn adversité,
But he that wroghte her, as mot I the,
That put*te* suche beauté in her face,
That made me coveten and purchace
Myn oune dethe ; him wite I that I dye,   270
And myne *un*witte that ever I clombe so hye,

XXXVI.

But to yow hardy knyght*es* of renoun,
Syn that ye be of my devisioun,
Al be I not worthy to so grete a name,
Yet seyn these clerkes I am your patroun,
Therfore ye oght have somme compass*i*oun
Of my disese, and take hit not a-game ;
The pruddest of yow may be made ful tame.
Wherfore I prey yow, of your gentilesse,
That ye compleyn*e* for myn hevynesse.   280

XXXVII.

And ye, my ladyes, that ben true and stable,
Be wey of kynde ye oghten to be able
To have pité of folke that ben in peyn*e*,
Now have ye cause to clothe yow in sable;
Sith that youre emperise, the honurable,
Is desolat, wel ogh*t*e ye to pleyn*e*,
Now shuld your holy teres falle and reyne.
Alas! your honour and your emperise,
Negh ded for drede, ne can her not chevise.

XXXVIII.

Compleyneth eke ye lovers al in fere   290
For her that, with unfeyned humble chere,
Was evere redy to do yow socoure;
Comple*ineth* her that evere hath had yow der*e*;
Compleyneth beauté, fredom, and manere;
Compleyneth her that endeth your labour,
Compleyneth thilke ensample of al honour.
That never dide but *alwey* gentilesse;
Kytheth therfor in her summe kyndenesse.

THE COMPLEYNT OF VENUS.

XXXIX.

THERE nys so high comfort to my plesaunce,
Whan that I am in eny hevynesse,   300
As for to have leyser of remembraunce,
Upon the manhod and the worthynesse,
Upon the trouthe, and on the stedfastnesse,
Of him whos I am al whiles I may dure;
Ther ogh*t*e blame me no creature,
For every wight preiseth his gentilesse.

XL.

In him ys bounté, wysdom, and governaunce,
Wel more then eny mannes witte can gesse;
For grace hath wolde so ferforthe hym avaunce,
That of knyghthode he is parfite richesse;   310
Honour honoureth him for his noblesse;
Therto so well hath formed him Nature.
That I am his for ever, I him assure,
For every wight preysith his gentilesse.

XLI.

And not withstondyng al his suffisaunce,
His gentil hert ys of so grete humblesse
To me in worde, in werke, in contenaunce,
And me to serve is al his besynesse,
That I am set in verrey sikirnesse.
Thus oght I blesse wel myn aventure,   320
Sith that him list me serven and honoure,
For every wight preiseth his gentilesse.

XLII.

Now certis, Love, hit is right covenable,
That men ful dere bye the nobil thinge,
As wake, a-bed, and fasten at the table,
Wepinge to laugh and sing in compleynynge.
And doun to caste visage and lokynge,
Often to ehaunge visage and contenaunce,
Pley in slepyng, and dremen at the daunce,
Al the reverse of eny glad felynge.   330

XLIII.

Jelosie be hanged be a cable!
She wold al knowe throgh her espyinge.

Ther dothe no wyght nothing so resonable,
That al nys harme in her ymagenynge.
Thus dere abought is Love in *his* yevynge,
Which ofte he yifeth withoute ordynaunce,
As sorow ynogh, and litil of plesaunce,
Al the reverse of any glad felynge.

XLIV.

A lytel tyme his yift ys agreable,
But ful encomberouse is the usynge ;   340
For subtil Jelosie, the deceyvable,
Ful often tyme causeth desturbynge.
Thus be we ever in drede and suffrynge ;
In no certeyn we languisshen in penaunce,
And han ful often mony an harde *myschaunce,*
Al the reverse of any glad felynge.

XLV.

But certys, Love, I sey not in such wise,
That for tescape out of youre lace I men*te,*
For I so longe have be in your servise,
That for to let of wil I never assen*te.*   350
No fors ! *ye!* thogh Jelosye me turmen*te,*
Sufficeth me to se hym when I may ;
And therfore certys to myn endyng day,
To love hym best that shal I never repen*te.*

XLVI.

And certis, Love, whan I me wel avise,
Of eny estate that man may represen*te,*
Then have ye made me, thro*gh* your fraunchise,
Chese the best*e* that ever on erthe wen*te.*
Now love wel, hert, and loke thou never sten*te.*

And let the Jelousie put hit in assay,   360
That for no peyn, I wille not sey nay;
To love yow best, that shall I never repente.

XLVII.

Herte, to the hit ought ynough suffise,
That Love so highe a grace to yow sente,
To chese the worthiest in alle wise,
And most agreable unto myn entente.
Seche no ferther, neythir wey ne wente,
Sithe *I* have suffisaunce unto my pay,
Thus wol I ende this compleynt or this lay,
To love hym best *ne* shal I never repente.   370

LENVOY.

XLVIII.

Princes! resseyveth this compleynt in gre,
Unto your excelent benignité
Directe, aftir my litel suffisaunce;
For elde, that in my spirit dulleth me,
Hath of endyting al the subtilité
Welnyghe bereft out of my remembraunce:
And eke to me hit is a grete penaunce,
Syth ryme in Englissh hat*h* such skarseté,
To folowe worde by worde the curiosité   379
Of Graunson, floure of hem that maken in Fraunce.

EXPLICIT.

A GOODLY BALLADE OF CHAUCER.

MOTHER of norture, best beloved of al*le*,
And fresshest flour, to whom good thrift
God sende !
Your childe, if it lust you me so to cal*le*,
Al be I unable my selfe so to pretende,
To your discrecion I recommende
Myn herte and al, with every circumstance,
Al holy to be under your governaunce.

Moste desire I, and have and ever shal,
Thyng whiche might your hertes ease amende ;
Have me excused, my power is but smal ;   10
Nathelesse, of right, ye ough*te* to commende
My good*e* will*e*, which fayne wolde entende
To do you servyce ; for al my suffysaunce
Is holy to be under your governaunce.

Meulx un in herte which never shal appal*le*,
Aye fresshe and newe, and right glad to dispende
My tyme in your servyce, what so befal*le*,
Besechyng your excellence to defende
My symplenesse, if ignoraunce offende

In any wyse; sythe that myn affyaunce   20
Is holy to ben under your governaunce.

Daisy of lyght, very grounde of comforte,
The Sonnes doughter ye hight, as I rede;
For whan he westreth, farwel your disporte!
By your nature anon, right for pure drede
Of the rude night that with his boystous wede
Of derkenesse shadoweth our emyspere,
Than closen ye, my lives lady dere!

Dawnyng the Day to his kynde resorte,
And Phebus your father with his stremes rede   30
Adorneth the morowe, consumyng the sorte
Of misty cloudes that wolden overlede
Trewe humble hertes with her mistyhede,
Nere comforte a-dayes, whan eyen clere
Disclose and sprede my lyves lady dere,

Je vouldray—but greate God disposeth
And maketh casuel, by his provydence,
Suche thyng as mannes frele witte purposeth,
Al for the best, if that our conscience
Nat grutche it, but in humble pacience   40
It receyve : for God saythe, withoute fable,
A faythful herte ever is acceptable.

Cautels who so useth gladly, gloseth;
To eschewe suche it is right high prudence;
What ye sayd ones myn herte opposeth,
That my writyng japes in your absence
Pleased you moche better than my presence.
Yet can I more; ye be nat excusable,
A faythful herte ever is acceptable.

Quaketh my penne ; my spyrit supposeth   50
That in my writyng ye fynde wol some offence ;
Myn herte welkeneth thus sone ; anon it ryseth ;
Nowe hotte, nowe colde, and efte in fervence :
That mysse is, is caused of neglygence,
And not of malyce ; therfore bethe mercyable ;
A faythful herte ever is acceptable.

LENVOYE.

Forthe complaynt ! forthe lackyng eloquence !
Forthe lytle letter, of endytyng lame !
I have besought my ladyes sapyence
Of thy behalfe, to accept in game   60
Thyn inabylité ; do thou the same :
Abyde ! have more yet !—Je serve Jouesse.
Nowe forth I close the in holy Venus name !
The shal unclose my hertes governeresse.

A PRAISE OF WOMEN.

AL tho that lyste of women evyl to speke,
    And sayn of hem worse than they de-
        serve,
    I praye to God that her neckes to-breke,
Or on some evyl dethe mote tho janglers sterve ;
For every man were holden hem to serve,
And do hem worship, honour, and servyce,
In every maner that they best coude devyse.

For we oughte first to thinke on what manere
They bring us forth, and what payn they endure
First in our byrth, and syth fro yere to yere   10
How busely they done hir busy cure,
To kepe us fro every misaventure
In our youthe, whan we have no might
Our selfe to kepe, neither by day nor nyght.

Alas ! howe may we say on hem but wele,
Of whom we were fostred and ybore,
And ben al our sucoure, and ever trewe as stele,
And for our sake ful ofte they suffre sore ?
Withoute women were al our joye lore ;
Wherfore we ought alle women to obeye   20
In al goodnesse ; I can no more saye.

This is wel knowen, and hath ben or this,
That women ben cause of al*le* lightnesse,
Of knyghthode, norture, eschewyng al malis,
Encrease of worshyp, and of al*le* worthynesse ;
Therto curteys and meke, and ground of al good-
      nesse,
Glad and mery, and trewe in every wyse
That any gentyl herte can thynke or devyse.

And though any wold*e* trust*e* to your untruthe,
And to your fayre wordes wold aught assent*e*,   30
In goode fayth me thynketh it were gret ruthe,
That other women shold*e* for hir gylt be shent,
That never knew, ne wist*e* nought of hir entent,
Ne lyst*e* not to here the fayre words ye write,
Which ye you payne fro day to day tendyte.

But who may beware of your tales untrew*e*,
That ye so busyly paynt and endite ?
For ye wyl swere that ye never knewe.
Ne sawe the woman, neyther moche ne lyte,
Save onely her to whom ye had*de* delite,   40
As for to serve of al that ever ye sey*e*,
And for her love must ye nedes dey*e*.

Then wyl ye swere that ye knewe never before
What Love was, ne his dredful observaunce,
But nowe ye fele that he can wounde sore ;
Wherfore ye put*te* you into her governaunce,
Whom Love hath ordeyned you to serve and do
      plesaunce
With al your might your lytel lyves space,
Whiche endeth sone but if she do you grace.

And then to bedde wylle ye soone drawe,   50
And sone sicke ye wylle you than fayne,
And swere faste your lady hath you slawe.
And brought you sudeynly so high a payne
That fro your deth may no man you restrayne,
With a daungerous loke of her eyen two,
That to your dethe muste ye nedes go.

Thus wylle ye morne, thus wylle ye sighe sore,
As though your herte anon in two wolde breste,
And swere faste that ye may live no more,
' Myne owne lady! that might, if ye leste,   60
Bringe myn herte somdele into reste,
As if you lyst mercy on me to have ;'
Thus your untrouth wyl ever mercy crave.

Thus wol ye playne, thogh ye nothyng smerte,
These innocent creatures for to begyle,
And swere to hem, so wounded in your herte
For her love, that ye may lyve no whyle,
Scarsly so longe as one mighte go a mile,
So hyeth dethe to bringe you to an ende,
But if your soverayn lady lyst you to amende.   70

And if for routhe she comforte you in any wyse
For pyté of your false othes sore,
So that innocent weneth that it be as you devyse
And weneth your herte be as she may here,
Thus for to comfort and somwhat do you chere ;
Than wol these janglers deme of her ful ylle,
And sayne that ye have her fully at your wylle.

Lo, howe redy her tonges ben, and preste
To speke harme of women causelesse !

Alas! why might ye not as wel saye the beste, 80
As for to deme hem thus gyltelesse?
In your herte, ywis, there is no gentylnesse,
That of your owne gylt lyst thus women fame;
Now, by my trouth, me thynke ye be to blame.

For of women cometh this worldly wele,
Wherfore we oughte to worship hem evermore;
And thou it mishap one, we oughte for to hele,
For it is al through our false lore,
That day and night we payne us evermore
With many an othe these women to begyle 90
With false tales, and many a wicked wyle.

And if falshede shulde be reckened and tolde
In women, iwys ful trouthe were,
Not as in men, by a thousand fold;
Fro alle vices, iwys they stande clere,
In any thing that ever I coude of here,
But if entysing of these men it make,
That hem to flatteren connen never slake.

I wolde fayne wete wher ever ye coude here,
Withoute mennes tysing, what women dyd amis, 100
For ther ye may get hem ye lye fro yere to yere,
And many a gabbing ye make to hem, iwys;
For I could never here ne knowen ere this,
Where ever ye coude fynde in any place,
That ever women besoughte you of grace.

There ye you payne with al your fulle might,
With al your herte, and al your beysnesse,
To pleasen hem bothe by day and night,

Prayeng hem of her grace and gentylnesse,
To have pyté upon your greate distresse,   110
And that they wolde on your payne have routhe,
And slee you not, sens ye meane but trouthe.

Thus may ye see that they ben fautelesse,
And innocent to al*le* your werkes slie,
And al*le* your craftes that touche falsnesse,
They knowe hem not, ne may hem not espye ;
So sweare ye that ye mus*te* nedes die,
But if they wolde, of hir womanheed,
Upon you rewe, er that ye be deed.

And than your ' lady ' and your ' hertes quene '   120
Ye calle hem, and therewith ye sygh*e* sore,
And say, ' My lady, I trowe that it be sene
In what plite that I have lyved ful yore ;
But nowe I hope that ye wol no more
In these peynes suffre me for to dwel*le*,
For of al goodnesse, iwys, ye be the wel*le*.'

Lo, whiche a paynted processe can ye make,
These harmlesse creatures for to begyle !
And whan they slepe, ye payne you to wake,
And to bethinke you on many a wicked wyle ; 130
But ye shal se the day that ye shal curse the whyle
That ye so besyly dyde your entent
Hem to begyle, that falshede never ment*e*.

For this ye knowe wel, though I wolde lie,
In women is al trouthe and stedfastnesse ;
For in good faythe I never of hem sye
But moche worshyp, bounté, and gentylnesse,

Right comyng, fayre, and ful of mekenesse,
Good and glad, and lowly, I you ensure,
Is this goodly angelyke creature.   140

And if it happe a man be in disease,
She dothe her busynesse and her ful*le* peyne
With al her might, him to comforte and please
If fro his disease she might*e* him restreyne ;
In word ne dede, iwys, she wol not fayne,
But with al her might she dothe her besynesse
To bringe him out of his hevynesse.

Lo, what gentyllesse these women have,
If we coude knowe it for our rudenesse !
How besy they be us to kepe and save,   150
Both in heale, and also in sicknesse !
And alway right sory for our distresse,
In every maner; thus shewe thy routhe,
That in hem is al goodnesse and trouthe.

And syth we fynde in hem gentylnesse and trouth,
Worshyp, bounté, and kyndenesse evermore,
Let never this gentylesse through your slouth
In hir kynde trouthe be aught forlore
That in woman is, and hath *y*ben ful yore,
For in reverence of the hevens Quene,   160
We ought*e* to worshyp al*le* women that bene.

For of al*le* creatures that ever were get and borne,
This wote ye wel, a woman was the best*e* ;
By her was recovered the blysse that we had*de* lorne,
And thruogh the woman shal we come to rest*e*,
And ben ysaved, if that our selfe leste ;

Wherfore, me thynketh, if that we had*de* grace,
We oughten honour women in every place.

Therfore I rede that, to our lyves ende,
Fro this tyme forth, while that we have space, 170
That we have trespaced, pursue to amende,
Prayeng our Lady, wel of al*le* grace,
To bringe us unto that blysful place,
There as she and al*le* goode women shal be infere
In heven above, amonge the angels clere.

EXPLICIT.

MINOR POEMS.

THE COMPLEYNTE OF THE DETHE
OF PITÉ.

ITÉ, that I have sought so yore agoo
With herte soore, and ful of besy
    peyne,
That in this worlde was never wight
    so woo
Withoute the dethe; and yf I shal not feyne,
My purpose was *of* Pitee *for* to pleyne,
And eke upon the crueltee and tirannye
Of Love, that for my trouthe doth me dye.

And when that I be lengthe of certeyne yeres
Had, evere in oon, soughte a tyme to speke,
To Pitee ran I, al bespreynte with teres,   10
To prayen hir on Crueltè me wreke;
But er I myghte with any worde out breke,
Or tellen any of my peynes smerte,
I fonde hir dede and buried in an herte.

And doune I fel when *that* I saugh the herse
Dede as stone while that the swogh laste;

But up I roose with coloure wel dyverse,
And pitously on hir myn eyen I caste,
And ner the corps I came to pressen faste,
And for the soule I shope me for to preye; 20
I was but lorne, ther was no more to seye.

Thus am I slayne sith that Pité is dede ;
Allas, the day that ever hyt shulde falle !
What maner man dar now hold up his hede ?
To whom shal now any sorwful herte calle ?
Now Cruelté hath caste to slee us alle
In ydel hope *we lyve* redelesse of peyne ;
Sith she is dede, to whom shulde we compleyne ?

But yet encreseth me this wonder newe,
That no wight woot that she is dede but I, 30
So mony men as in her tyme hir knewe ;
And yit *she* dyede not so sodeynly ;
For I have sought hir ever ful besely,
Sith I hadde firste witte or *mannes* mynde ;
But she was dede er that I koude hir fynde.

Aboute hir herse there stoden lustely
Withouten any woo, as thoughte me,
Bounté, parfyte wel ar*a*ied and richely,
And fressh Beauté, Lust, and Jolyté,
Assured-maner, Youthe, and Honesté, 40
Wisdome, Estaat, Drede, and Governance
Confedred bothe by honde and alliance.

A compleynt had I writen in myn honde,
To have put to Pittee, as a bille,
But when I al this companye ther fonde,
That rather wolde al my cause spille

Then do me helpe, I helde my *compleynt* stille ;
For to that folke, withoute*n* ony fayle,
Withoute Pitee ther ne may no bille availe.

Then leve we alle vertues, save oonly Pité,   50
Kepynge the corps as ye have herde me seyn,
Confedered by bonde and by Cruelté,
And ben assented when I shal be sleyn.
And I have put my complaynt up ageyn,
For to my foes my bille I dar not shewe,
Theffect of which seith thus in wordes fewe.

THE COMPLEYNT IN THE BILLE—

' Humblest of herte, higheste of reverence,
Benygne flour, coroune of vertues alle !
Sheweth unto youre rialle excellence
Youre servaunt, yf I durst*e* me so calle,   60
His mortal harme, in which he is *i*-falle,
And noght al oonly for his evel fare,
But for your renoun, as *I* shal declare.

' Hit stondeth thus :—your contrary Crueltee
Allyed is ayenst your regaltye
Under colour of womanly beauté,
(For men shulde not know hir tirannye)
With Bountee, Gentilesse, and Curtesye.
And hath depryved yow nowe of your place,
That is hygh beauté, appartenent to your grace. 70

' For kyndely, by youre herytage *and* ryght
Ye be annexed ever unto Bounté,
And verrely ye oughte do youre myght

To helpe Trouthe in his adversyté ;
Ye be also the corowne of beauté ;
And certes, yf ye wanten in these tweyn
The worlde is lore, ther is no more to seyn.

' Eke what availeth maner or gentilesse
Withoute yow, benygne creature ?
Shal Cruelté be *now* youre governeresse ?   80
Allas, what herte may hyt longe endure ?
Wherfore but ye the rather taken cure
To breke that perilouse allyaunce,
Ye sleen hem that ben of your obeisaunce.

' And furtherover, if ye suffre this,
Youre renoun is fordoon *then* in a throwe,
Ther shal no man wete welle what pité is.
Allas, that ever your renoun is falle so lowe !
Ye be also fro youre heritage ythrowe
By Cruelté, that occupieth youre place,   90
And we despeyred that seken to youre grace.

' Have merey on me, thow hevenes quene,
That yow have sought so tendirly and yore,
Let somme streme of youre light on me be sene,
That love and drede yow ever lenger more ;
For sothely for to seyne, I bere so sore,
And though I bee not kunnynge for to pleyne,
For Goddis love have merey on my peyne.

' My peyne is this, that what so I desire,
That have I not, ne nothing lyke therto ;   100
And ever setteth Desire myn hert on fyre
Eke on that other syde, where-so I goo.

That have I redy, unsoghte, every where ;
What maner thinge that may encrese my woo,
Me lakketh but my deth, and than my bere.

' What nedeth to shewe parcel of my peyne,
Syth every woo, that herte may bethynke,
I suffre; and yet I dar not to yow pleyne,
For wel I wote, *al*though I wake or wynke,
Ye rekke not where I flete or synke.   110
Yit natheles my trouthe I shal sustene
Unto my deth, and that shal wel be sene.

· This is to seyne, I wol be youres ever ;
Though ye me slee by Crueltee, your foo,
Algate my spirite shal never dissever
Fro youre servise, for eny peyne or woo.
Now Pité that I have sought so yore agoo !
Thus for your deth I may wel wepe and pleyne
With herte sore, al ful of besy peyne.

EXPLICIT.

BALLADE DE VILAGE SAUNS PEYNTURE.

THIS wrechched worldes transmutacion,
As wele and woo, now poverte, and
    now riche honour
Withouten ordre or wise discrecion,
Governed ys by Fortunes erroure ;
But natheles the lakke of hir favour

Ne may not doo me synge, though I dye,
J'ay tout perdue, mon temps et mon laboure,
For fynally Fortune I diffye.

Yet ys me lefte the sight of my resoun,
To knowen frend fro foo in thy meroure,   10
So moche hath yet thy turnyng up and doun
Ytaught me to knowen in an houre ;
But truely noo fors of thy reddoure
To him that over himself hath the maistrye,
My suffisaunce shal be my socoure,
For fynaly Fortune I dyffye.

O Socrates, thou stedfast champion,
She myght*e* never be thy turmentoure,
Thow never dreddest hir oppression,
Ne in hir chere fonde thou noo savoure ;   20
Thow knew*e* wel the deceyt of hir coloure,
And that hir moost*e* worship is to lye ;
I knowe hir eke a fals dissymuloure,
For fynaly Fortune I diffye.

LA RESPONS DU FORTUNE AU PLEINTIF.

Noo man is wrechched but himself yt wene,
And he that hath himselfe hath suffisaunce.
Why seysthow than I am to the so kene,
That havest thy self out of my governaunce ?
Sey thus :—' Graunt mercy of thyn habundaunce
That thow havest lent or this ; ' thou shalt not strive. 30
What wooste thou yet how I thee wol avaunce ?
And eke thou havest thy best*e* frend alyve.

I have the taught divisioun betwene
Frend of effect, and frend of countenaunce.

The nedeth not the galle of noon hiene,
That cureth eyen derke fro *her* penaunce
Now seesthow cleer that were in ignoraunce.
Yet halte thin ankre, and yet thow maist arrive
There bounté berith the keye of my substaunce,
And eke thow hast thy beste frend alyve.   40

How many have I refused to sustene,
Sith I the fostred have in thy plesaunce !
Wolthow than maken a statute on thy quene,
That I shal ben aye at thin ordinaunce ?
Thou borne art in my regne of variaunce,
Aboute the whele with other maisthow drive ;
My loor ys bet, than wikke is thy grevaunce,
And eke thow havest thy beste frend alyve.

LE PLEINTIF ENCOUNTRE FORTUNE.

Thy loore I dampne ! hit is adversité !
My frend maisthow nat reve, blynde goddesse ! 50
That I thy frende knowe, I thanke yt the ;
Take hem ageyn ! let hem goo lye a-presse !
The negardes in kepinge hir richesse,
Pronostik ys thow wolt hire toure assayle ;
Wikke appetite cometh aye before sekenesse,
In general this rule may nat fayle.

FORTUNE ENCOUNTRE LE PLEINTIF.

Thou pynchest at my mutabilité,
For I the lent a drope of my rychesse ;
And now me likith to withdrawe me,
Whi shuldest thow my royaltee oppresse ? 60

The see may ebbe and flowe more and lesse;
The welkene hath myght to shine, reynne, and hayle;
Ryght so mote I kythe my brotelnesse,
In general this rule may nat fayle.

Loo, thexcucion of the Magesté
That alle purveyth of hys ryghtwisnesse,
That same thing Fortune clepen ye,
Ye blynde beestes ful of lewdenesse!
The hevene hath proprety of sikernesse;
This worlde hath ever restlesse travayle;   70
The laste day ys ende of myne interesse,
In general this rule may nat fayle.

LENVOYE DU FORTUNE.

Princes! I pray yow of your gentilesse
Lat not thys man on me thus crie and pleyne,
And I shal quyte yow this besynesse.
And but yow liste releve him of his peyne,
Prayeth ye his beeste frende of his noblesse,
That to some beter estate he may atteyne.

BALLADE SENT TO KING RICHARD.

SOMETYME the worlde was so stedfast
          and stable,
     That mannes worde was holde obliga-
          cioun;
And now hyt is so fals and disceyvable,

That worde and dede, as in conclusyoun,
Ys lyke noothyng; for turned up-so-doun
Is alle this worlde, for mede and wilfulnesse,
That alle is loste for lakke of stedfastnesse.

What maketh this worlde to be so variable
But luste, that folke han in dissensioun?
For amonges us nowe a man is holde unhable,   10
But yf he kan, by somme collusyoun,
Do his neghbour wronge or oppressioun.
What causeth this but wilfulle wrecchednesse,
That alle ys loste for lakke of stedfastnesse?

Trouthe is put doun, resoun is holden fable;
Vertu hathe now noo dominacioun;
Pitee exiled, noo man ys merciable;
Thurgh covytyse is blente discrecioun;
The worlde hath made permutacioun
Fro ryght to wrong, fro trouthe to fikelenesse,   20
That alle ys lost for lakke of stedfastnesse.

LENVOYE.

O Prince desire to be honourable;
Cherysshe thy folke, and hate extorsioun;
Suffre nothing that may be reprovable
To thyn estaate, doon in thy regioun;
Shew forth the swerde of castigacioun;
Drede God, do law, love trouthe and worthinesse,
And wedde thy folke ayeyne to stedfastnesse.

EXPLICIT.

THE COMPLEYNTE OF CHAUCER TO HIS PURSE.

T O yow my purse and to noon other wight
Complayn I, for ye be my lady dere!
I am so sory now that ye been lyght,
For, certes, but-yf ye make me hevy chere,
Me were as leef be layde upon my bere,
For whiche unto your mercy thus I crye,
Beeth hevy ageyne, or elles mote I dye!

Now voucheth sauf this day, or hyt be nyghte,
That I of yow the blissful soune may here,
Or see your colour lyke the sunne bryghte,   10
That of yelownesse hadde never pere.
Ye be my lyfe! ye be myn hertys stere!
Quene of comfort and goode companye!
Beth hevy ayeyne, or elles moote I dye!

Now, purse! that ben to me my lyves lyght,
And saveour as doun in this worlde here,
Oute of this toune helpe me thurgh your myght,
Syn that ye wole nat bene my tresorere;
For I am shave as nye as is a frere.
But I pray unto your courtesye,   20
Bethe hevy ayeyn, or elles moote I dye!

L'ENVOY DE CHAUCER.

O conquerour of Brutes Albyoun,
Whiche that by lygne and free eleccioun,
Been verray Kynge, this song to yow I sende,
And ye that mowen alle myn harme amende,
Have mynde upon my supplicacioun.

GOOD COUNSEIL OF CHAUCER.

FLE fro the pres, and duelle with soth-
              fastnesse;
      Suffice the thy good though hit be smale;
      For horde hath hate, and clymbyng
              tikelnesse,
Pres hath envye, and wele is blent over alle.
Savour no more then the behove shalle;
Do wel thy self that other folke canst rede,
And trouthe the shal delyver, hit ys no drede.

Peyne the not eche croked to redresse
In trust of hire that turneth as a balle,
Grete rest stant in lytil besynesse;   10
Bewar also to spurne ayein an nalle,
Stryve not as doth a croke with a walle;
Daunte thy selfe that dauntest otheres dede,
And trouthe the shal delyver, hit is no drede.

That the ys sent receyve in buxumnesse,
The wrasteling of this world asketh a falle;
Her is no home, her is but wyldyrnesse.
Forth pilgrime! forth best out of thy stalle!
Loke up on hye, and thonke God of alle;
Weyve thy lust, and let thy goste the lede,   20
And trouthe shal the delyver, hit is no drede.

PROSPERITY.

RIGHT as povert causith sobirnesse,
    And febilnesse enforcith continence,
    Right so prosperité and grete riches
    The moder is of vice and negligence;
And powre also causeth insolence,
·And honour oftsise changith gude thewis;
Thare is no more perilouse pestilence
Than hie astate gevin unto schrewis.

A BALLADE.

THE firste fadir and fynder of gentilnesse,
    What man desirith gentil for to be,
    Moste folowe his trace, and alle his wittes
        dresse,
Vertu to shew, and vicis *for* to flee;
For unto vertu longith dignitee,
And nought the revers, savely dare I deme,
Al were he mitre, corone or diademe.

This firste stoke was ful of rightwisnesse,
Trewe of his worde, soboure, pitous and free,
Cleene of his gooste and lovid besynesse,   10
Ageynste the vice of slowthe in honeste;
And but his heire love vertu as did he,
He nis not gentille thouhe him riche seme,
Al were he mytre, corone or diademe.

Vyce may welle bee heyre to olde richesse,
But there may no man, as ye may welle see,

Byquethe his sone his vertuous noblesse;
That is approperid into noo degree,
But to the firste Fadir in Magestee,
Which maye His heires deeme hem that Him queme,
Al were he mytre, corone or dyademe.

EXPLICIT.

L'ENVOY DE CHAUCER A SCOGAN.

TO-BROKEN been the statutes hye in
     hevene,
That creat weren eternaly to dure,
Syth that I see the bryght*e* goddis sevene
Mowe wepe and wayle, and passioun endure,
As may in erthe a mortale creature:
Allas! fro whennes may thys thinge procede?
Of whiche errour I deye almost for drede.

By worde eterne whilome was yshape,
That fro the fyfte sercle in no maner*e*,
Ne myght a drope of teeres doun eschape;   10
But now so wepith Venus in hir spere,
That with hir teeres she wol drenche us here.
Allas! Scogan this is for thyn offence!
Thou causest this deluge of pestilence.

Havesthow not seyd in blaspheme of this goddis,
Thurgh pride, or thrugh thy grete rekelnesse,·
Swich thing as in the lawe of love forbode is,
That for thy lady sawgh nat thy distresse,

Therfore thow yave hir up at Mighelmesse?
Allas, Scogan! of olde folke ne yonge, 20
Was never erst Scogan blamed for his tonge.

Thow drowe in skorne Cupide eke to recorde
Of thilke rebel worde that thow hast spoken,
For which he wol no lenger be thy lorde;
And, Scogan, thow*gh his* bowe be nat broken,
He wol nat with his arwes been ywroken
On the ne me, ne noon of youre figure;
We shul of him have neyther hurte nor cure,

Now certes, frend, I dreed of thyn unhappe,
Leste for thy gilte the wreche of love procede 30
On alle hem that ben hoor and rounde of shappe,
That ben so lykly folke in love to spede,
Than shal we for oure laboure have noo mede;
But wel I wot thow wolt answere and saye,
' Loo, tholde Grisel lyste to ryme and playe!

Nay, Scogan, say not soo, for I mexcuse,
God helpe me so, in no ryme dowteles:
Ne thynke I never of slepe to wake my muse,
That rusteth in my shethe stille in pees;
While I was yonge I put her forth in prees; 40
But alle shal passe that men prose or ryme,
Take every man hys turne as for his tyme.

Scogan, that knelest at the stremes hede
Of grace, of alle honour, and of worthynesse!
In thende of which streme I am dul as dede,
Forgete in solytarie wildernesse;
Yet, Scogan, thenke on Tullius kyndenesse;
Mynde thy frend there it may fructyfye,
Farewel, and loke thow never eft love dyffye.

EXPLICIT.

L'ENVOY DE CHAUCER A BUKTON.

Y maister, Buktoun, whan of Crist our
      kyng,
  Was axed, what ys trouthe or sothe-
      fastnesse?
He nat a worde answerde to that axinge,
As who saith, noo man is al trew, I gesse;
And therfore, though I highte to expresse
The sorwe and woo that is in mariage,
I dar not writen of hit no wikkednesse,
Leste I my-self falle eft in swich dotage.

I wol nat seyn how that hyt is the cheyne
Of Sathanas, on which he gnaweth evere;   10
But I dar seyn, were he oute of his peyne,
As by his wille he wolde be bounde nevere.
But thilke doted foole that ofte hath levere
Ycheyned be than out of prison crepe
God lete him never fro his woo dissevere,
Ne no man him bewayle though he wepe!

But yet lest thow do worse, take a wyfe;
Bet ys to wedde than brenne in worse wise,
But thow shalt have sorwe on thy flessh, thy lyfe,
And ben thy wyfes thral, as seyn these wise.   20
And yf that hooly writte may nat suffyse,
Experience shal the teche, so may happe,
That the were lever to be take in Frise,
Than eft falle of weddynge in the trappe.

This lytel written proverbes or figure
I sende yow, take kepe of hyt I rede:

Unwise is he that kan noo wele endure.
If thow be siker, put the nat in drede.
The wyfe of Bathe I pray yow that ye rede
Of this matere that we have on honde.   30
God graunte yow your lyfe frely to lede
In fredom, for ful harde is to be bonde.

EXPLICIT.

ÆTAS PRIMA.

I.

 BLISFUL lyfe a peseable and a swete
Leddyn the peplis in the former age;
Thei held them paied with the frutes
           that they ete,
Wich that the feldes gafe them by usage,
Thei ne were for-pamprid with owtrage.
Vnknowen was the qwerne and eke the melle;
Thei etyn mast, hawys, and suche pownage,
And dronken watyr of the colde welle.

II.

Yit was the ground not woundyd with the plowgh,
But corne upsprange onsowe of mannys hand,   10
The which thei knoddyd and ete not half i-now;
No man yit knew the forous of hys land;
No man yit fier owt of the flynt fand;
Vncarvyn and vngrobbyd lay the vyne;
No man in the morter yit spices grand.
To clarré ne to sause of galantine.

III.

No madder wellyd or woode no lister,
No knew the flese was of hys former hewe;
Ne flesche ne wyst offence of egge or spere;   19
Ne coyne ne knew man whiche was fals or trewe;
No shyppe yit karfe the wawys grene and blewe;
Ne marchand yit ne fet owtlandische ware;
No batayllys trumpys for the warre folk ne knew
Ne towrys hight and wallys rownd and sqware.

IV.

What shuld it haf avaylyd to warrey?
Ther lay no profite, ther was no richesse;
But cursyd was the tyme, I dar well say,
That men dyd first hyr swety besinesse,
To grobbe up metall lurkyng in derknesse,
And in the ryuers first gemmys sowghte;   30
Alas! than sprang up all owre cursidnesse,
Of couetyse that first owre sorow browghte.

V.

Theys tirantes put hem gladly not in prese,
No place of wildnesse ne no busshys for to wynne.
There povert is, as sayth Dyogenes,
There as vitall eke is so skars and thynne,
That nowt but mast or applys is ther-in;
But ther as bagges ben and fatte vitayle
There wylle they gone and spare for no synne
With all hyr ost the cité for to asayle.   40

VI.

Yit were no palys chambris, ne no hallys
In cavys and wodes soft and swete;
Sleptyn thys blessyd folk withowte wallys,
On grasse or levys in parfite joy and quiete;

No downe of fedrys ne no blechyd schete
Was kyde to hem but in surté they slept*e* ;
Hyr herte were alle oone without gallys,
Everyche of hem to odyr hys fayth kept*e*.

VII.

Vnforgyd was the hauberke and the plate ;
The lambisshe pepyl, voyd of alle vice,   50
Hadden noo fantasye to debate,
But oche of hem wold oder well cheriche
No pride, none envy, none avarice,
No lord, no taylage by no tyrannye,
Humblesse, and pease, good fayth the emprise.

VIII.

Yit was *not* Jupiter the likerous,
That first was fadyr of delicacye
Come in thys world, ne Nembroth desirous
To raygne had*de* not made hys towrys hyg*he*.
Alas! alas! now may men wepe and crye.   60
For in owre days is not but covetyse,
Doublenesse, treson, and envye,
Poysonne, manslawtyr, mordre in sondri wyse.

FINIT ETAS PRIMA CHAUCER.

LEAULTE VAULT RICHESSE.

WARLDLY joy is onely fantasy,
    Of quhich nane erdly wicht can be
        content ;
    Quho most has wit leste suld in it affy,
Quho traistes it most sall him repent.

Quhat valis all this richesse and this rent,
Sen no man wate quho sall his tresour haue?
Presume noght gevin that God has done but lent,
Within schort tyme the quhiche he thinkes to crave.

PROVERBES OF CHAUCER.

I.

WHAT shul these clothes thus manyfolde,
Loo, this hoote somers day?
After greet hete cometh colde;
No man caste his pilch away.
Of al this worlde the large compace
It wil not in myn armes tweyne;
Whoo-so mochel wol embrace,
Litel thereof he shal distreyne.

II.

The worlde so wide, thaire so remuable,
The sely man so litel of stature;   10
The grove and grounde, and clothinge so mutable,
The fire so hoote and subtil of nature,
The water never in oon—what creature
That made is of these foure thus flyttynge,
May stedfast be, as here, in his lyvinge?

III.

The more I goo the ferther I am behinde,
The ferther behinde the ner my wayes ende;
The more I seche the worse can I fynde;
The lighter leve, the lother for to wende;
The bet Y serve, the more al out of mynde;   20
Is thys fortune not I, or infortune;
Though I go lowse, tyed am I with a lune.

EXPLICIT.

ROUNDEL.

I.

1.

YOURE two eyn will sle me sodenly,
I may the beauté of them not sustene,
So wendeth it thorow-out my herte kene.

2,

And but your words will helen hastely
My hertis wound, while that it is grene,
Youre two eyn will sle me sodenly.

3.

Upon my trouth I sey yow feithfully,
That ye ben of my liffe and deth the quene,
For with my deth the trouth shal be *i*-sene.

Youre two, &c. 10

II.

1.

So hath youre beauty fro your herte chased
Pitee, that me navaileth not to pleyn*e*;
For daunger halt your mercy in his cheyne.

2.

Giltless my deth thus have ye purchased;
I sey yow soth, me nedeth not to fayn*e*;
So hath your beauté fro your herte chased, &c.

3.

Alas, that nature hath in yow compassed
So grete beauté, that no man may atteyn*e*
To mercy, though he stewe for the peyn*e*.

So hath youre beauté, &c. 20

III.

1.

Syn I fro love escaped am so fat,
I nere thinke to ben in his prison lene;
Syn I am fre, I counte him not a bene.

2.

He may answere, and seye this and that,
I do no fors, I speak ryght as I mene;
Syn I fro love escaped am so fat.

3.

Love hath my i-strike out of his sclat,
And he is strike out of my bokes clene
For ever mo, ther is non other mene.
Syn I fro love escaped, &c.

VIRELAI.

LONE walkyng,
In thought pleynyng,
And sore syghyng,
Al desolate,

Me remembryng
Of my lyvyng,
My deth wyshyng
Bothe erly and late.

Infortunate
Is soo my fate
That, wote ye whate?
Oute of mesure

My lyfe I hate:
Thus desperate,
In suche pore estate,
      Do I endure.

Of other cure
Am I nat sure;
Thus to endure
      Ys hard certayn;   20

Suche ys my ure,
I yow ensure;
What creature
      May have more payn?

My trouth so pleyn
Ys take in veyn,
And gret disdeyn
      In remembraunce;

Yet I full feyne
Wolde me compleyne,   30
Me to absteyne
      From thys penaunce.

But in substaunce,
Noon allegeaunce
Of my grevaunce
      Can I nat fynde;

Ryght so my chaunce,
With displesaunce,
Doth me avaunce;
      And thus an ende.   40

CHAUCER'S PROPHECY.

WAN prestis faylin in her sawes,
And Lordis turnin Goddis lawes
Ageynis ry*ght*;
And lecherie is holdin as privy solas,
And robberie as fre purchas,
Bewar than of ille!
Than schall the Lond of Albion
Turnin to confusion,
As sumtyme it befelle.

*Ora pro Anglia Sancta Maria, quod Thomas
Cantuarie.*

Sweete Jhesu heven-king
Fayr and beste of alle thyng
Thou bring us owt of this morning
To come to the at owre ending.

CHAUCER'S WORDS UNTO HIS OWN

SCRIVENER.

DAM Scrivener, if ever it thee befall*e*,
Boece or Troilus for to write new*e*,
Under thy long*e* lockes maist thou have
the scall*e*,
But after my making thou write more trew*e*!
So oft a day I mote thy werke renew*e*,
It to correct and eke to rubbe and scrape:
And åll is thorow thy necligence and rape.

INCIPIT ORATIO GALFRIDI CHAUCER.

ORISOUNE TO THE HOLY VIRGIN.

MODER of God, and virgyne undefouled,
   O blisfull*e* quene, our quenys emperice!
   Preye thou for me that am in syn ymouled,
   To God thy sone, the punyschar of vice,
That of his merci, thogh that I be nyce
And negligent in keping of his lawe,
His hie mercy my soule unto him drawe.

' Thou moder of mercy, way of indulgence,
That of alle mercy art superlatyve!
Savour of saulis be thy benevolence!   10
O humble lady, maide, moder, and wyfe!
Causar of pes, styntar of wo and stryfe!
My prayere to thy sone that thou present,
Syn of my gilt hooly I me repent.

' Benynge confort of us wrecches alle-weye
Be at myn ending quhen that I schall deye.
O well of pitee, unto the I calle,
Fulfillit of swetnesse, helpe me to weye
Agane the fende, that with his handis tweye
And alle his mycht wille pluk at the balance   20
To wey us doune, kepe us from his mischance.

' And for thou art ensample of chastité,
And of alle virgynes, worschip, and honour,
Above all women blessed mote thou be!
Now speke, now preye, unto oure Salviour,

That he me send suych grace and favour
That alle the hete and brynnyng lecherye
He sloke in me, blissit maden Marye!

' Most blissit lady, clere licht of day!
Temple of oure lord, and voice of alle gudenes! 30
That by thi prayer wipist clene away
The filth of oure soulis wikkitnesse!
Put furth thi hand; help me in my distresse,
And fro temptacioun, lady, deliver me
Of wikkit thocht, for thi benignitee.

' So that the wille fulfillid be of thi sone,
And that of the Holy Goste he me illumyne,
Preye thou for us, as ever hath been thy wone,
Al suich emprise *hath* sekirly been thyne;
For suich an advocate may no man devyne,   40
As thou, lady, oure greves to redres;
In thi refute is all oure sekirnesse.

' Thou schapen art by Goddis ordynaunce,
To preye for us, flour of humilitee!
Quherefore of thyne office have remembraunce,
Lest that the fende, throu his subtilitee,
That in awayte lyith for to cacche me,
Me never ourcum with his trecherye;
Unto my soule-hele, lady, thou me gye.

' Thou art the way of our redemcioun,   50
For Crist of the dedeynyt not for to take
Bothe flesche and blood, to this entencioun,
Upon a croce to deyen for oure sake;
His preciouse deth maide the fendis quake,
And cristyn folk for to rejoisen ever;
Help, from his mercy that we noght dissever!

' Remember eke upon the sorow and peyne,
That thou sufferit in to his passioun,
Quhan watir and blood out of thyne eyen tweyne,
For sorow of him, ran by thy chekes doune ;   60
And syn thou knowist *weil* the enchesoune
Of his deying was for to save mankynd ;
Thou moder of mercy, have that in thy mynd.

' Wele aughten we the worschip and honour,
Palace of Crist, flour of virginitee!
Seing that upon the was laid the cure,
To bere the Lord of hevin, and erth, and see,
And of all thinges that formyt ever myght be ;
Of hevynnis king thou was predestynate,
To hele oure saulis of thy sik hie estate.   70

' Thy maidnis wambe, in quhich that oure Lord lay ;
Thy pappis quhite, that gave him souk also
Unto our saving, blissit be thou ay !
The birth of Crist oure thraldome put us fro ;
Joy and honour be now and ever mo
To him and the, that unto liberté
Fro thraldomme have us brocht ; blissit be ye !

' By the, lady, ymaked is the pes
Bitwix angelis and man, it is no dout ;
Blissit be God, that suich a moder chees !   80
Thy passing bountee spredith all about :
Though that our hertis sterne be and stout,
Thou *canst* to Crist for us be suich a mene,
That all oure gilt forgevin be us clene.

' Paradise yettis all opin be throu the,
And brokyn been the yettis eke of helle ;
By the the world restorit is, pardee ;

Of al vertu thou art the spring and welle ;
By the all gudenes, schortly for to telle,
In hevin and erth by thyne ordynaunce   90
Parformyt is oure saulis sustenaunce.

' Now, sen thou art of suich autorité,
Thou pitouse lady and virgyne wemlesse,
Preye thy dere sone my gilt forgeve it me,
Of thy request I knowe wele doutelesse :
Than spare noght to put the forth in presse,
To preye for us, Cristis moder so dere !
For thy prayere he will benignely here.

' Apostle and frend famuliar to Crist,
And virgyne, ychose of him, sanct Johne !   100
Shynyng apostle and evaungelist,
And best beloved amongis thamme echone !
With our lady, I praye the, thou be one,
That unto Crist schall for us alle preye ;
Do this for us, Cristes derlyng, I seye !

' Mary and Johne, O hevynnis gemmys tweyne !
O lightis two, shynyng in the presence
Of oure Lord God, now dooth your lusty peyne,
To wesche away oure cloud full of offence,
So that we myght maken resistence   110
Agane the fende and make him to bewaille,
That your prayere may us so miche availle.

' Ye been the two, I knawe verily,
In quhiche the fadir God gan edifye,
By his Sone onely-gottyn, specialy
To him a hous ; quharfor to you I crye
Beeth lechis of oure synfull maladye,

Preyeth to God, Lord of misericord,
Our olde giltis that he noght recorde.

'Be ye oure help and oure protectioune,
Sen for mercy of your virginitee,
The previlege of his dilectioune
In yow confermyt God upon the tree
Hanging; and unto one of you, said he
Ryght in this wys, as I reherse can,
'Behold and se, lo, here thy sone, womman!'

'And to that othir, 'Here is thy moder lo!
Than preye I yow for the greteful swetnesse
Of the holy love that God betuix yow two
With his mouth maid, and of his hie noblesse
Commaundit hath yow, throu his blissitnesse,
As moder and sone to helpe us in oure nede
And for our synnes make oure hertes blede.

· Unto yow tweyne now I my soule commende,
Mary and Johnne, for my salvacioune,
Helpith me that I my lyf may mende,
Helpeth, now that the habitacioune
Of the Holy Goste, oure recreacioune,
Be in my herte now and evermore;
And of my saule wesche away the sore.

'EXPLICIT ORATIO GALFRIDI CHAUCER.'

THE END.

CHISWICK PRESS:—PRINTED BY WHITTINGHAM AND WILK
TOOKS COURT, CHANCERY LANE.